C000253671

deadly
MATCH

USA TODAY BEST SELLING AUTHORS
K.A KNIGHT
IVY FOX

Deadly Match (Deadly Love Book Two).

This is a work of fiction. Any resemblance to places, events or real people are entirely coincidental.

Copyright © 2022 K.A. Knight & Ivy Fox, all rights reserved.

No part of this book may be reproduced in any form or by any electronic or mechanical means, including information storage and retrieval systems, without written permission from the author, except for the use of brief quotations in a book review.

Written by K.A. Knight & Ivy Fox
Edited By Jess from Elemental Editing and Proofreading.
Proofreading by Norma's Nook.
Formatted by The Nutty Formatter.
Cover by Opulent Designs.

Deadly Match

He was my demon when I was a child.

A hellish force protecting me from the evil that hid in the dark and preyed on the weak.

But I'm not that innocent girl anymore, and he's no longer my savior.

He's filled with so much cruelty and madness, my survival instincts tell me I should run the other way, but how can I when my madness matches his own?

When his darkness sings to mine?

What happens when two lost souls are just meant to be?

When their ugly scars fit so perfectly together?

Some matches, like my sister's, are created through love...

Other matches are just plain *deadly*.

Prologue

ZOEY

I pull my knees tighter to my chest and press my face into them to muffle my sobs, not wanting to wake anyone. The cold, tiled bathroom floor chills the soles of my feet, and the nightdress Layla handed down to me, covered in holes, barely reaches my knees. The tile at my back has me shivering as I close my eyes against the sting of tears, my body shaking with the force of my pain.

Since Layla is heavily knocked out on her pain meds, and it's the only time I can get away from her and the other girls, I snuck out of our shared room. The eight other girls are sleeping in their cots, like I should be, but I can't. Instead, I'm huddled in the shared bathroom in the foster home we were dumped in when Layla was released from the hospital.

She almost died.

I almost lost her too…

Gage.

Mom.

I did lose them. I won't ever tell Layla that I remember it all—the sounds of the gunshots, the feel of their blood on my hands, and the echoes of my own screams in my ears. I lost everyone I love apart from

Layla. The only reason she is still here is because of the blue-eyed angel who stopped to save us.

Even thinking of him now has me crying harder, wishing he were here to protect us and save us from this life.

It's stupid to cry. I'm alive, and so is Layla. We are safe, even if this place gives me the creeps, but I miss them. I miss them so badly. I wish I hadn't gotten angry with Gage and yelled. I wish I could chase him around or sneak into his room to read with him at night.

Mom wasn't the best mother, but I loved her, and on those rare, good days, she would bake for us. I miss the smell of her cookies and the sound of her laugh when I would steal one. Now, there is just a black hole where they were, and it hurts so much.

I miss home. I don't like it here.

I just want to go home.

Sometimes at night, I swear I hear screams, and none of them are mine.

I haven't told Layla this. She would run away with me and protect me at any cost, but she needs to heal so I won't lose her too. Instead, I try to ignore it and everything and everyone.

I hear footsteps, and I curl around myself—a habit I know Layla hates. It always made her eyes flash with anger before she stepped in front of me and took the blow. Maybe if I'm small enough, they will go away and leave me alone, but I still hear them next to me.

I feel their heat as they slide down the wall beside me. I don't look. I can't. I'm worried I will be punished for crying or being out of bed at this hour, but then a soft, slightly bigger than my own hand covers mine on my shaking knee.

Something about it makes me cry harder.

No words are spoken, and when the sun rises, he walks me back to my bed and tucks me in. At the door to my room, he looks back at me once. He's just a shadow in the dark, a boy, a face I can't make out, but it sticks with me.

That was the first night my protector came to me, promising he would never leave my side.

He came every night after that to hold me as I cried.

Today was a bad day. The other girls were picking on me again, and I feel so alone. Layla is still on her pain meds, and every night, like a ritual, I find myself crying in the bathroom for everything I lost. This time, however, when the arm slides around me, I lift my head and see him for the first time.

He has startling, bright gray eyes the color of the storms we used to get back home, serious twisted lips, and a slightly rounded face with curly black hair flopping over his forehead. He's older than me, a teenager, and judging by the pained look in his eyes, he's hurting just as badly as I am. That's when I notice the blood staining his shirt.

"Are you okay?" I whisper, voice cracking.

He blinks, and a slow smile curls his lips. "Shouldn't I be asking you that, little doe?"

"Doe?" I repeat in confusion.

"You have big green eyes, and you remind me of a doe I saw once," he explains and starts to pull away, but I move closer, burying my head in his chest.

"My name is Zoey," I tell him when the tears stop. His hand is curled into my hair, holding me close. He doesn't say anything, so I lift my head. "This is where you tell me your name." I sniffle and wipe my face.

He searches my eyes as if he's looking for something. "Gray. My name is Gray." He shoots me the most blinding smile I've ever seen. "So, Zoey, want to hear a joke?"

GRAY

I look forward to nighttime. That's when I get to see her.

No matter what has happened that day, and no matter what injuries I carry, I drag myself to the bathroom to see my little doe.

I hate her tears.

She cries every night. I don't know why, and I'm too scared to ask, because what if it's something I can't fix? What if I'm too late? What if the reason she is crying is the same reason I'm hunched tonight with my arm hanging strangely.

I should go to the doctor, as ordered, but I can't miss this and let her think I'm not coming. I know she's been let down a lot, and I won't be another person who disappoints her, so even though I'm in pain and exhausted, I stumble into the bathroom.

But tonight is different.

She's not curled in her usual spot with tears flowing from her bright green eyes. No, tonight she's whimpering and scampering back on the tiled floor to get away from *him*—the man standing before her with his back to me.

I freeze in place. I know him. I know every man who enters this place, and this one is a cruel bastard. He doesn't hear me, too focused on his fresh meat. He chuckles and grabs his belt, starting to unfasten it. "Oh, you will be so sweet," he croons, his voice thick with sickening desire.

Something inside of me cracks like a fissure splitting open, and darkness spills out.

When Zoey whimpers again, her big green eyes flash up to me, begging me to save her.

That fissure splits open further, exploding inside of me.

The darkness spreads through me, filled with fury I hold back. I always have, because the depth of it scares me, but now as all the pain, hopelessness, and bitterness builds within me, I fling myself at his back with a roar.

He won't get her. He won't hurt her and steal her innocence the way he has others.

Not my Zoey.

I will always protect her.

He turns at the noise and stumbles back a step. His brown eyes widen when he spots me, but the shock soon fades to a familiar anger as he bats me away like a fly. I hate how skinny I am, how weak. I'm unable to fight back or defend. I hit the sink with a sickening thud and slide down to the floor, and I feel blood flowing down my head and back, but I'm used to pain.

He turns back to Zoey. "Now, where were we?"

No. Not her.

Lifting up onto shaking hands, I look around for something, anything, and my eyes land on a bit of broken porcelain from the sink from where I must have hit it. Clutching it in a shaky, weak grip, I stumble to my feet, breathing heavily.

"No." I don't know if I say it out loud as I move forward. "You will not touch her!" I realize I'm screaming when he turns, and without thinking about my next action, I give into the darkness inside me.

One they created.

Leaping like a madman, I slash at him with the shard, cutting into my own hand. He tries to block me, but I'm quick, and he howls as he falls back, a huge gash splitting open the right side of his face. Roaring again, I slice at him, but he blocks me with his arm and kicks out.

"Stop it, you brat!" he yells.

The noise draws them—the guards, as we call them—but I don't stop, not even as they try to grab me. I'm determined to protect her, to stop him. Their arms drag me back as I kick and scream, still slashing the piece of sink.

When they wrangle it from my hand and slam me to the floor, pressing my face to the bloodied tile, I turn to meet her eyes again. They are wide but unafraid as she watches me. My name is on her lips as she reaches for me.

She's safe. I'll make sure of it.

As I'm dragged away, I watch the man stumble out of the bathroom, almost running from me.

My arms are held above and behind me, but I kick my legs in frustration, wanting to get back to her as they pull me away. I know whatever will happen next will be bad, but I'd do it again.

I'd do anything to keep her safe.

She's the first innocent thing I've seen walk into this place, and she might be the last innocent thing I'll ever see.

Zoey is mine to protect.

I was right, I did pay for it, but they didn't touch Zoey. I asked, and now they never can. I stand at the window to my cell, the bars marking it as such. They call it solitary, but we all know it's as close to a cell as they can get here. My hands wrap around the bars, still covered in my and the man's blood. The position pulls on the flesh wounds on my back, but I absorb that pain and use it.

I watch her climb into a car with her sister. When the door shuts, she scoots to the window and presses her hand to the glass, searching the house before they land on me. Her big green eyes stay on mine, even as they pull away.

I stay here, watching the window as if I'm waiting for her to come back.

I know what's coming next will be worse than any horrors I have faced before, but it doesn't matter because she's safe.

A rare smile curls my lips.

A hand lands on my shoulder. "It's time for your next visit, Gray."

CHAPTER 1

Gray

Eleven years later…

It's been a year and a half since I last saw Zoey in person. At first, I didn't believe it was her standing in the too normal backyard belonging to Alaric, the man meant to train me, and his wife, Layla—the same sister of the little girl I have thought about every day of my life.

I tried to stop obsessing over her, and for a while, I managed it. I threw myself into my life. I graduated school, and at eighteen, I enlisted. I spent years in the Army, giving them my life over and over. I needed that rush of adrenaline to feel anything.

I am Gray Hart, but they called me heartless over there, and how could they not?

I gave mine away to a green-eyed doe when I was a kid.

It didn't matter, though, because I was really fucking good at my job. Maybe it's because I was born into bloodshed and death and I lived in it for so long that I became used to killing. Regardless, nothing could have prepared me for what happened over there.

After all, I am legally dead. KIA, or so they say.

I thought I knew pain as a child, but I was wrong. It was nothing compared to what they did to me when I was captured. It's a time of my life I like to forget, just like everything before now, before this version of myself. All I know is that it led me here, back to America. I escaped their clutches, and after stumbling onto a base, when they realized who I was, I was airlifted away to another undisclosed location and made into this.

A killer for hire.

It's a government program that is run by private, rich businessmen recruiting the best killers from every walk of life. I was still scarred and burnt from torture when they welcomed me into their ranks. After all, I couldn't be a Marine anymore.

But this? This I can do.

I can hunt, track, and kill.

Thanks to them, and Alaric, who signed me off into the full role just two months after training me, I am now a full-fledged member. For just over a year, I have been completing as many contracts as I can, barely sleeping or eating.

I have no friends, no family, no hobbies, and no days off.

All I do is kill.

I have no weaknesses apart from her, and that is something no one will ever know, not even her. I am too messed up to be in her life.

Alaric warned me away, but he didn't have to. I won't put Zoey through that. The girl deserves a chance at a good life, one without death and pain, so I'll stay away. I will be the monster they all made me into and nothing else.

I will keep this world safe for her.

Covered in sweat from my workout, I make my way into my kitchen, grab the only mug I own, and make myself coffee before settling in front of my laptop to accept my next contract. I finished my last one at 2AM, and I'm already itching to kill, needing that release.

Sometimes I think if I didn't have it, I might truly go off the deep end.

While the laptop loads, I sip my coffee, not even noticing the burn as I swallow. My scarred knuckles of my other hand rap on the marble island impatiently.

The house is mine, I bought it with my savings—the ones I could access, since being dead makes things like banking hard—but it's just that, a house, one that's empty and cold.

It's a place to lay my head, one I've fortified so that I can sleep without being on guard.

The laptop finally loads, and I bring up the system that allows us to communicate privately and anonymously about contracts. The one I finished last night is marked as completed, and the money was transferred immediately after I finished it, but there is one already waiting. After all, they know better than to leave me to my own devices.

That's when things go bad, like last time.

Clicking on the file, I open the dossier on the target. They always hold the parameters, such as torture or public execution. This one is to be private, and they want a hunt, not just a kill. They have a picture of the target, but no name. They don't need it.

I know that face.

It's one that throws me back to being a scared fifteen-year-old. We called him Sir back then, because he ran the foster home I grew up in. If I'm a demon, then he's the devil. He stole kids' souls and sold them. My hands curl into fists as the familiar darkness roars inside of me. It's clear he's finally pissed someone off, and I find my lips curling in a cruel smile filled with vengeance.

It never crossed my mind to go after all of them, but now that it's there, I can't get it out. It might have started with him, but it won't end there. Not now.

I quickly type a message.

Me: Will accept, have conditions.

I wait as they type back.

Contact: What conditions?

Me: After the job is complete, I want free rein to go after his accomplices.

There is a moment of hesitation as they debate what I mean and if they can let me off my leash for that. It will happen either way, and they know that, because once I have my mind set on something, there is no getting it out.

Contact: Mission conditions accepted only once current target is dead.

Me: Accepted.

I log off and drain the mug of the last remnants of coffee, purpose filling my steps as I head upstairs to shower and prepare for the hunt. Oh yes, he'll be dead, and anyone who ever helped him will be too.

It's time to avenge the scared kid they killed back then.

It's time to protect Zoey in the only way I know how.

I feel Layla's gaze on me as I continue to read Gage and Sophie their bedtime story. No matter how much they try to fight off sleep, they are slowly losing the battle with each soft word I utter. So much so, they don't even realize their mom is leaning against their bedroom doorframe, watching them succumb to their slumber. I continue on and flip two more pages until I'm sure they are both fast asleep, their deep, soft breaths a telltale sign that they are going to be out for the night.

"Don't just stand there and stare. How about a little help here?" I whisper to my sister with a smile, stretching out my hand so she can pull me out of the bed I'm sharing with her kids.

Anytime I come over, the little rug rats stick to me like glue, and bedtime is no different.

Gage always leaves his bed in favor of snuggling up against me on Sophie's bed, wanting to be as close to the action as possible. My little man never leaves my side when I come over, as if he knows his name-sake used to jump in my bed back in the day when Layla read to us.

"Here, let me," my sister whispers quietly enough not to disrupt her children's dreams. Ever so gently, she picks Gage up from the bed and slowly places him in his, tucking him in and kissing his forehead. I carefully get out of Sophie's bed so Layla can repeat the nightly ritual with her daughter.

When Layla's done making sure her kids are safe and snuggled in their beds, she tilts her head over to me, her silent order for me to follow her out of the room and into the hallway.

"They are getting so big," I murmur as she closes their door halfway, and I take one last glance at them.

"They are." She smiles proudly, happiness shining from her eyes and pride written in every line of her features. I'm so happy for her and the family she has created for herself. No one deserves happiness more than my sister.

"Pretty soon they won't want me to read to them anymore," I complain wistfully, glancing back at the door and debating sneaking back in.

"Or they will take a page out of your handbook and make you read to them well into their teens." She giggles softly as she walks downstairs with me behind her, reminding me how I had Alaric read me bedtime stories until I was thirteen.

I snort. "Doubtful. I only did that to mess with your husband."

She arches a suspicious eyebrow, calling me on my bullshit.

"Fine. Maybe I liked it too," I concede with a shrug. "Still, pretty soon your kids won't want to hang out with me," I mumble, passing the living room and heading over to the kitchen in search of something to drink. A beer or whiskey would be my choice to take the edge off, but I'm in my sister's house, which means water or soda is all I'm afforded here.

Alaric would shit a brick if he saw his underage kid drinking hard liquor.

And for all intents and purposes, I'm his just as much as Gage and Sophie are.

"Give them a few more years, and they won't want anything to do with me," I add, my melancholy rearing its ugly head.

"That's nonsense. Both Gage and Sophie love you too much," she protests, sitting on her favorite stool on the kitchen island and picking up her glass of red wine. "Where is all this coming from, Zoey? You're not usually this insecure."

She's right. I'm not. But lately, I feel like I'm drifting, like I'm lost at sea with no safe port in sight. If I say any of this to Layla, though, she will only worry, and Layla has worried about me enough to last a lifetime.

I refuse to give her any more reasons to keep her up at night. I'm beyond happy she has found her forever, and they have never given me any reason to doubt what we have, but watching them raise their kids makes me wonder if, before long, I will even fit in it.

"It's nothing." I shake my head with a fake smile. "I guess I'm just a little bit nostalgic tonight. Sometimes I miss living here."

"Well, the door is always open for you. You can always come live with us instead of the dorms. I know Alaric would sleep a whole lot better if he had all his kids sleeping under his roof."

Yeah, that's not happening. Living at the dorms finally gave me some sort of freedom. As much as I love Alaric to death, his constant overprotectiveness can be a bit stifling. If my adopted father had his way, he would have kept me under house arrest and only let me out when I was forty. Maybe not even then.

Layla loves that side of him. His possessive streak does it for her, but that's because she's his wife. If she were his kid, she wouldn't find it so amusing.

When he found out I had my first kiss, he tracked the kid down and threatened to kill him if he touched me again. I was twelve. That poor boy couldn't even look at me again without pissing his pants.

"Speaking of which, where is Alaric tonight?" I change the subject quickly, not wanting the worry in her eyes to bloom any further.

Layla runs the pad of her finger over the rim of her wine glass, not making any eye contact with me. To say my sister is the worst liar on planet Earth is an understatement, so before the words have left her mouth, I already know they are her diluted way of telling me the truth.

"He was called into work tonight. He should be home soon."

"Work?" I raise my eyebrows. "For a guy who's retired, his previous job sure keeps him busy."

"You know how it is. His employer views him as indispensable and was sad to let him go, so Alaric promised to train someone to take his place, and until that person has shown he can pick up the slack, they want Alaric to keep an eye on him. After those loose strands are tied up, then I'm sure he can enjoy his retirement in peace," she explains vaguely, her words hurried.

"Right," I mumble, turning my back to her so I can grab a bottle of water from the fridge and prevent myself from calling my sister out on that whopper of a lie.

I would have to be living under a rock not to know what my sister means when she says Alaric still has unfinished business to attend to. As much as they tried to hide it from me, I know exactly what Alaric does for a living.

Or at least, I did.

Not only do I still have the memory of him blowing my prick of a father's brains out, but I also have other lingering memories too. Like how Alaric would jump out of his seat and fly out the front door at all hours of the night anytime his burner phone rang. Or how when it was my turn to do the laundry, I would always find specks of blood on his clothes. Not to mention whenever we threw a party at our house, his friends and so-called coworkers were less than the unsavory kind.

They all had this air about them, like they had seen their fair share of death. It's like the grim reaper kissed their forehead, leaving his permanent mark, and some, more than others, can't seem to shake that imprint.

That's what death does to a person. It clings to you like an oversized coat, swallowing you whole until the fucked-up fabric chokes the very life out of you.

I would know. Death's black hand has paid me plenty of visits in the past too. I was marked on the day I helplessly watched my mom and brother die before my very eyes.

But death's grip didn't stop there.

Like a promise that I would meet the same fate, my health started to decline. It was subtle at first, but like a cancer, it grew until I was sure that death's heavy hand would pull me to the other side where I would join my brother and mother earlier than I ever intended.

Just as I was losing all hope, my sister's vengeful angel severed death's ice-cold fingers, coming to my rescue for a second time and giving Layla the means to help me get better.

Even after Alaric made sure I got my operation and I was given a clean bill of health, death never let me out of its hold. Its nails dug deeper into my soul and spoiled everything from within, like rot that I can't scrape off no matter how much I try.

"Zoey?" my sister calls, bringing me out of my reverie. "Are you okay?"

"Why wouldn't I be?" I reply, noticing that I have been staring off into space instead of grabbing my water like I intended. I snap open the bottle and take a sip of the cool water, wishing it could wash away all these solemn thoughts.

My sister stares at me long and hard, making cold sweat run down my back.

"Stop looking at me like that. I told you I was fine," I snap, sounding meaner than I intended.

She takes a minute longer to stare at me, each second making my heart jackhammer in my chest. I've tried to hide my darkness from Layla as much as possible. She's happy now. She found her happily ever after and has a beautiful home and family to prove it. I don't want to be the thing that tarnishes that for her. My sister has suffered enough in her life, and she doesn't need me to drag her down to my own personal hell.

"Layla," I start but shut my mouth when she holds up her hand.

"I was serious when I said you could move back home. If life at college is too hard for you, then we can also put a pin in it for a while."

My shoulders instantly relax when I realize how far off she is.

Of course my sister would think that my inner turmoil is caused by a heavy schedule back at school. I mean, why wouldn't she? That would be the normal conclusion to leap to.

There is no way would she ever think that her baby sister has been in a deadly match with death since she was eight. That I dream of darkness and thrive in its shadows. That death's grip feels like an old lover's embrace to me now, protectively keeping me warm at night and reminding me that it will never let me go.

No.

Layla would find a plausible real-world problem to point a finger at. She would never suspect that I feel like I'm death's paramour.

I put on a smile and walk over to her, hugging her from behind as I place my chin on her shoulder. "You have to stop worrying about me, Layla. I can handle a little schoolwork."

She places her hands on mine and gives it a little squeeze. "I'll never stop worrying about you, Zoey. You're my baby sister."

"Well, your baby sister is all grown up now. I've got this, so don't worry, okay?"

"Are you sure?" she asks, concerned.

No. No, I'm not. I'm drowning, Layla.

Those aren't the words I tell her. Instead, my smile only widens. "Worry about the little ones upstairs. I'm good. I promise," I lie, and when I feel her body relax, guilt starts clawing away at my throat. "Speaking of school, I should head back to the dorms. I don't want to be out past curfew."

"Alaric will be sad that he missed you, but I don't want you to be late. I'll make sure he's here for next Sunday's dinner," she replies softly.

"You do that." I smile, kissing her cheek before I walk into the living room to grab my backpack.

After I have my things, Layla walks me to the door and waves me off. Since I know she won't budge until I've left, I start my car and slowly drive away from her street. Once I'm a few blocks away, I find a dark parking space and grab my bag. I take out a shimmering black halter top, my black leather miniskirt, and high-heeled boots to match, and then proceed to take off my flowery summer dress that I wore over to my sister's place. Layla wouldn't mind my clothing choice so much if I ever showed up at the house dressed in my usual gear, but Alaric would lose his shit if he saw me showing off so much skin.

To him, I'm still his little girl, and it's just easier for me to let him hold onto that image, but I haven't been a little girl in quite some time now. Maybe I never really was, not when the only time I truly feel alive is when death is close by.

Tonight, I fully intend to walk the tightrope between light and shadows, not really caring which side I end up landing on.

Let the dark have at it. It feels better there anyway.

Men.

They are simple creatures fueled by the most absurd things.

Be it a pair of long legs or bursting cleavage, nine out of ten times, men will act the fool because of a woman's gifts. Sometimes I find it entertaining to see how far men will go to share a total stranger's bed just because she coos sweet nothings in their ears or bats her eyelashes at them.

Women aren't as easily tempted.

They won't fall all over themselves just because a good-looking guy flashes his winning smile at her. She needs a lot more stimulation than that to hold her interest.

Right now, nothing seems to captivate mine.

I came into this dive bar tonight looking for something or someone to take the edge off, but unfortunately, nothing here has managed to come close to what I need. Especially not the two morons who are going at it on my behalf, making total jackasses of themselves. I mean, I may have a hand in their petty argument. I have to amuse myself somehow.

"She said she was going to dance with me next, asshole," the blond one blurts, his face so red with fury it looks like he's about to pop.

"That isn't happening. The girl told me she was going to have a drink with me next," the ginger one shouts, his spit landing on the other man's beet-red face.

"You want a drink? Here's one for you," the blond retorts, picking up my glass of whiskey from the nearby table and pouring it on the ginger's head.

"You fucker!" the ginger yells, landing a punch in his nemesis's jaw.

Predictably, they both start swinging left and right, so focused on their fight that they don't even realize I've walked to the other side of the bar to grab another glass of whiskey since one of them decided to use mine to prove a point.

"Hit me with another, Jack," I shout over the ruckus, slapping the bar to get the bartender's attention.

Even though those two fools are still at it, no one in here seems to care. That's why I love places like this.

You can give into your demons, and no one will lift a finger to help you, not when they came here trying to unleash their own dark side. No matter how many years I've lived in my sister's home on the other side of this city, Hell's Kitchen always feels like home to me. It's where the sewer rats come out to play, and no one looks down on you for where you came from or the past you've had. We all have scars here, badges of honors we proudly put on display to show the world they can't fuck with us.

"Any one of those dipshits yours?" the barkeep asks after he hands me my whiskey.

"Does it look like I'm taken?" I retort before emptying my glass in one full swig.

"Not right now," he muses, pouring me another. "But keep drinking like that, and I'm sure you'll end up being someone's later tonight."

"Or they'll be mine," I mutter before winking at him and raising my voice so he can hear. "Well, here's hoping that *someone* walks through the door. It's slim pickings from what I can see."

The bartender licks his lips and leans against the bar, his gaze on my chest before he meets my eyes.

"Tell you what. If Prince Charming doesn't come in tonight, I can take you home with me."

I smirk at his lame pickup line and take stock of the man before me. His broad shoulders and muscular arms say that he would have no problem lifting me up and pocketing me away as easily as he would a pair of car keys—not that it would be too hard for him to do. At barely over five feet, I'm tiny compared to most women, let alone most of the men here.

But size only matters to a man.

I may be small, but I pack a punch.

Still, the barkeep's light eyes and soft smile tell me he likes his women sweet, and that's just not me.

I point my finger at him, making sure my breasts hike over the bar so he can have a better look as he leans in.

"More pouring and less talking. I don't fuck the help," I whisper seductively.

His smile immediately turns to a scowl, and he mutters, "Bitch," under his breath as he pulls away. I've been called worse.

Not wanting to look at the scorned bartender's face all night, I walk over to the jukebox with my whiskey and pick out a song I can dance to.

"You fucker!" someone behind me shouts out, making me look over my shoulder.

I roll my eyes when I see that the two guys I left brawling at the pool table are still going at it.

It isn't their fault really.

They are slaves to their own impulses. A fact I knew all too well when I agreed to dance with one and grab a drink with the other. I thought it would make me feel better to see two strangers fight for my attention, but all it did was add to the gaping hole of emptiness in my chest.

Nothing.

That's what I feel most of the time.

Absolutely nothing.

I take a sip of my drink and turn once more to the jukebox, my eyes trailing over each song, and then I realize that none of them really call out to me.

"Fuck," I growl, kicking the damn thing and adding it to the long list of disappointments tonight.

I walk over to a hidden booth and slide in, sulking at what appears to be another wasted night. These are the times when I actually envy my sister. Layla has never asked for much, and yet she has it all.

The devoted husband.

The two cute as hell kids.

The big house in the swanky part of the city.

She has all the love and security she could have ever dreamed of, and sometimes I find myself wishing I were more like her in that way. That my happiness could be so easily achieved.

But the white picket fence life was never for me.

I crave something else. I just wish I knew what.

These are the thoughts that tumble through my mind as a cold hand starts running down my spine, causing goosebumps to erupt all over my skin. I look up from my glass and scour the bar, wondering what could have possibly brought on the sensation. The one that is only brought on by darkness and death.

That's when I see him walk through the door.

My eyes never leave him as he strides into the bar with a purpose no one who comes to places like this should have. In a black hoodie, with the hood pulled up and covering his head, it's impossible for me to see his face, but the way his large body agilely glides through the crowd, like a ghost that no one sees, has me hypnotized. When he stops at one of the pillars in the large bar and leans against it, my breathing quickens. What could have possibly brought such a creature here in the first place? It's like he sucks in all the light around him, becoming a shadow, much like the one I feel like I am sometimes.

Yes, places like this are known for hosting all sorts, but this man is different.

He's not a hustler looking for a score or one of the many lowlifes that you normally find in Hell's Kitchen. The way he carries himself tells me that much.

But he's something akin to the darkness that dwells inside me.

I can taste it on the tip of my tongue, even though he's a good ten feet away from me.

My heart pounds in my chest so loudly that it causes all the other noises surrounding me to lessen to a faint hum of my heartbeat.

Thump.

Thump.

Thump.

With each beat, I observe him, taking in every small movement. My breathing stops as his full, pouty lips lift just a fraction of an inch at the corners in a threatening smile when he sees whatever he's been looking for. Another cold shiver runs down my back, knowing full well that when a man like this one smiles, it's for all the wrong reasons.

Just like the ghost he is, his fluid moves are too quick for me to track as he effortlessly treads through the large crowd of people, vanishing from my view in a matter of seconds.

"Shit," I blurt, lifting from my seat in pursuit of the only thing that has been remotely exciting for me all night.

Or for a long time, in all honesty.

I try to follow his path, hating that there are so many people in here tonight. I'm about to give up on my search when my eyes land on an exit sign at the far back of the bar, its door not fully shut. Without a minute to lose, I rush toward it, wondering if the ghost I saw evaporated like white smoke in the night air. I leave the door open behind me and slither into the dark alley, holding my breath so I don't spook him if he's out here. On featherlight feet, I slowly walk toward two large trash containers and stop when my eyes finally land on who I've been looking for.

Whispering something in another man's ear while holding a blade at his throat, my ghost doesn't even register he has a captive audience in me. I stay hidden behind one of the containers as I watch the man whose back is against the brick wall spill all his secrets to his tormentor. Unfortunately, I'm unable to hear what they are saying, but the vision before me leaves little doubt.

This man will die tonight.

He knows it.

My ghost knows it.

And I know it.

The only question is if it will be a quick death or a slow, tortuous one.

By the way the man is offering up all his secrets on a silver platter, I'm assuming he hopes mercy will be his benefactor. When both men grow silent, my ragged heartbeat picks up speed.

There are no more secrets to tell.

No more lies or negotiating pleas to utter.

As if I've summoned the knife to deal its worst just with my thoughts, my ghost slices the man's throat. Blood gushes every which way, leaving another mark on his soul. I stand in a daze as the bleeding corpse slides down the wall and lands at the assassin's feet. The same feet that start to kick the dead man's face in, as if cutting his neck in one fell swoop deprived him of the satisfaction he craved. I stand there frozen, watching this vengeful force kick bone, flesh, and teeth into a messy pulp until the man's face is completely unrecognizable. Not even his own mother would be able to say this was her son if she laid eyes on him now. Adrenaline courses through my veins as I watch his murderer lower to his haunches and begin to slice off each of the dead man's fingers as easily as one would cut through butter and then slip them into a plastic bag.

Casually.

Practiced.

The only thing that pulls me away from my hypnotic state is when the man I have been diligently in awe of since he stepped foot inside this bar stands up to his full height and pulls down his hoodie, wiping away the splatters of blood that are currently streaking down his face.

Something akin to glee fills me when I finally see his face, recognizing his haunting silver gaze.

Most people would run right now.

Most people would call the cops or scream for help as loud as their vocal cords would allow them.

But that's not what I do.

Instead, I leave my hiding spot and walk toward the man who still has blood on his hands from his fresh kill. My light footsteps must ring as loud as a thunderstorm, since it's all it takes for him to turn around and face me, his hand already fisting his blade. His stormy eyes flash as I approach.

"Hi, Gray." I smile silkily. "Looks like you might need some help with that."

CHAPTER 4
Gray

I stare at the woman before me.

I say woman because that's what she is, especially right now. Her painted lips are kicked up in a smile, and her eyes shine as they lock on me confidently. Her blonde hair is curled away from her beautiful, sharp face, and her curves are on full display in a fuck me outfit. I bet she has all the boys drooling after her, and I find myself snarling at the thought, wanting to kill them at the same time I want to rip those clothes off her and bend her over right in this dirty alley and give her what she so clearly wants.

Instead, I step back, eyeing her warily. I try to hide the body, but it's no use, and her eyebrow arches as if she's amused.

"What the fuck are you doing here, Zoey?" I snarl.

She shrugs her shoulders elegantly and circles me like a predator, but Zoey has never been one of those. She's always been prey, and right now, she's looking far too good and tempting for a bastard like me to sink his teeth into.

Too young.

Too sweet.

I remind myself of all the reasons I stay away and only let my fantasies take hold of me late at night. But the Zoey I know lives in

27

sweet summer dresses, with a face clear of makeup and a smile as sweet as pie. Where the hell did this Zoey come from? Is she playing dress-up?

Or is this the real her?

"So you remember my name," she purrs, her voice low and sensual, making sure that the timbre of her voice wraps around my cock and hardens it while simultaneously sending my heart into overdrive.

The only person who has ever had any effect on my cold heart and apparently still does is always her. Even if the cause of my rapid heart-beat is painstakingly different from the innocent way she used to play with it, I'm not sure if this version is any easier for me to handle.

Fuck that.

It's much worse.

"Do not play games with me, little girl." I turn to her and back her into the wall. She grins at me the entire time, her chin tilted up in defiance. She isn't the least bit scared despite the fact I'm covered in blood and holding a knife with a body lying behind me—one I need to get rid of quickly or get the hell out of here.

Yet I find myself leaning into Zoey and inhaling some sultry perfume she's wearing. I place my arm above her head to trap her in place. "Answer me, now," I demand. "What the fuck are you doing here?"

"Me? Oh, I was just passing by." She flutters her lashes at me innocently. "After all, I'm just a little girl." The fake pout she gives me shouldn't be as fucking sexy as it is, nor should it have me imagining tanning her ass red for her sass, but fuck does it ever.

"Go home, Zoey, now, and if I catch you on this side of town again, I'll—"

"What? You'll what?" She cocks her head to the side and runs her gaze over me, her tongue touching her lips in a way that has my cock jerking. "Kill me? We both know you won't, Gray." The way she drags out my name shouldn't have me fantasizing about all the ways I could have her screaming it, but to my dismay, it does, and I hate myself for it.

It's what makes me step back and withdraw, reminding myself who she is… and who I am.

A killer.

"Go home."

"All by myself this late at night? There might be bad people around," she teases.

"There are, and you are staring right at him. Last warning, Zoey. Leave," I snap.

Pushing from the wall, she moves toward me, only stopping when her chest presses against mine, and she rubs her tight little nipples against me. It's torture not to reach out and touch her, but if I cross that line, I will never go back, and I promised myself I would keep away from her.

I refuse to stain her life with what lives inside of me.

She's Alaric's daughter. She's a civilian. She's innocent.

I repeat those reasons in my head, but it doesn't help.

"Or what, Gray? What will you do? I'm not good at behaving." The grin she gives me has me seeing red, and before I know what I'm doing, my hand is wrapped around her arm as I drag her down the alley with me. She laughs breathlessly, stumbling in her heels but keeping up.

"Ooh, kinky. I figured you liked it rough."

I ignore her teasing and grit my teeth to hold back my anger and need for her.

She has no idea who she's playing with.

And why would she?

As far as she's concerned, she believes I'm one of Alaric's business acquaintances and nothing more. The man whose job I was meant to fill.

She thinks I've only come into her life now, but that couldn't be further from the truth. Even though a part of me is saddened that I was so easily forgotten, it's a blessing in disguise that she has no recollection of me, because this way she also has no idea that I've spent every day of my life thinking of her, or that every scumbag I kill is for her, to keep her safe. Yet here she is, tempting fate, dressed like a whore instead of the bright-eyed girl I met and swore to protect all those years ago.

At the mouth of the alley, I clean the knife and put it away. The police won't bother testing the crime scene since they'll think it's just another junkie murder or turf war gone bad, especially in this part of town. My black Jag idles at the end of the alley, and I shove her in the passenger seat before sliding into the driver's. Unable to see her in the dim light, I bark, "Buckle up."

She does as she's told, thank God, and without waiting for another response, I gun it, throwing her back in her seat. When I hit the main road, I finally slow down, not wanting to get a ticket or be pulled over, but it doesn't stop my hands from curling into the steering wheel and clawing at it.

I am angry at her, at the world, and at myself.

I can feel her gaze, and I finally give in and look over before swearing and jerking my eyes forward, knowing it was a mistake. Her legs are parted temptingly, showing off her shapely thighs I'd love to mark up, and her skirt is riding up, flashing red panties. Her tits almost fall from her shirt.

When did she get so fucking grown up?

"What's the matter, Gray? Cat got your tongue?" she purrs, leaning over and placing her hand on my arm. I glare at it until she removes it, slumping in her seat with a sigh. Yet the place she touched burns, lighting me up in a way I've never felt, and I fucking hate it as much as I crave it.

She doesn't know how close I am to pulling over, bending her over the hood of my car, and taking that sweet, young cunt. And she just keeps teasing, walking the line.

Maybe she's not as innocent as I thought.

"Even though I hate repeating myself, I'm going to ask you one last time. What the fuck were you doing there, Zoey?"

"Having fun," she answers with a nonchalant shrug. "But from what I saw earlier, not as much fun as you were having. Isn't that right, Gray?"

I don't answer that loaded question. It's filled with mines, and I'm too close to exploding as it is.

I refuse to talk to her for the rest of the trip so I can get my bearings around her, but unfortunately for me, I don't need her bratty mouth to torment me when her perfume manages to do the job easily enough. Her scent fills my car's interior, and I know I'll have to burn the fucker to get it out. It's a comforting thought, thinking I could blow shit up just to erase all vestiges of her, but in the end, I know I won't do anything of the sort. I'll keep this car and drive it everywhere I go just to torture myself with it.

When we pull up outside her place, I turn the engine off. I don't look at her or speak a word, hoping she'll get the hint and just get out of my car, leaving me to deal with my hard as hell dick and twisted thoughts alone.

She chuckles as she stares at her dorm. "You know where I live?"

Fuck if I'll admit I drive by it every single fucking night, or the fact that I broke into her room and slept in her bed after a particularly hard day, just needing to smell her on my skin. Or that I stole her panties and jerk off into them every single day.

I'm a sick bastard.

"Get out," I say slowly, without looking at her.

"No. Not until you tell me how you know where I live. Should I be worried?"

When I glance over at her, she looks anything but concerned. She looks intrigued.

That look alone could get her killed.

"Go back to your perfect fucking life, little Zoey, and behave," I warn her.

"Stop treating me like I'm a child," she hisses, her eyes flashing in anger, and I want to feel her claws in my back as she yells at me.

Shit, this is getting out of hand. "You are a kid," I deadpan.

She flinches at my cold words, which makes me glad that something finally got through her thick head, but instead of crying or running like I expect, she leans closer to me. "No, I'm fucking not,

31

Gray. Maybe I should show you." Without waiting for a response, she slams her lips onto mine, shocking me to my very core.

Her lips are soft and supple, and when her tongue darts out and licks mine, tasting of strawberries and whiskey, my desire explodes through me in a roar. Before I can do anything in return, she pulls back, watching me smugly like she knows exactly what she did to me.

"Not a kid now, am I, Gray?" She slides from the car, slamming the door and storming off.

Oh no she fucking doesn't.

I'm about to go after her to prove just exactly why she shouldn't play with me before I get control of myself. I count back from ten, keeping my eyes on her retreating back the entire time. When the door of the dorm shuts behind her, I slump back, breathing heavily. I fist my hands to stop myself from chasing her down.

And I would.

Before I do something stupid, I rev the engine and peel away, racing away from her and my sick needs. When I reach the intersection, however, I can't move, I can't go forward, and with a snarl, I turn around and park my car at the back of the lot of her dorm. Submerged in the darkness, I watch as the lights come on in her room. The curtains are pulled completely open, not that she seems to care. She's framed in the light, running her hands through her hair before she reaches down.

I should look away. I should leave.

I do neither of those things. Instead, I watch as she strips from her little skirt, leaving her in a tiny lace thong and that ridiculous excuse for a top. My hand drifts down without my permission, cupping and gripping my cock through my jeans as she bends over, showing her supple, perky ass and perfect legs.

What I wouldn't do to be between them, tasting her pussy. She wouldn't be so cocky then. Licking my lips, I still taste her, and I can't resist. I unzip my jeans and palm my cock, stroking myself as I watch her.

Sick, sick, sick.

It repeats in my head, but I don't care. Zoey has always been mine, and I have always been hers; she just doesn't know it.

And she never will. If she knew the power she had over me… Groaning, I stroke my cock, watching her move around her room. I would destroy the world for her. She's the only person in this entire, fucked-up world that would never have to fear me, and she doesn't even know it.

I'm just about to pull my cock fully out when she turns and grabs her phone. Frowning, I watch as she smiles at whatever the person on the line said. The call must last all but a couple of minutes before she's rushing around her room to where I can't see her. When the light goes out, I quickly zip up my pants, knowing full well that Zoey didn't shut them off to go to bed. My eyes narrow when I see her sneak out of the front door again in nothing but that stupid shimmering top and leather skirt.

"Where the fuck you do you think you're going, little doe?" I whisper to myself.

Heart hammering, I kill the engine and pocket the keys. I get out and stalk after her, sticking to the dark. The slam of her heels on the pavement as she makes her way through the dorm buildings and side-walks covers the sound of me behind her. She's completely oblivious, and that pisses me off.

At the end of the road, she turns, and I duck behind a tree, watching as she checks the road before hurrying across. Getting more pissed with each step she takes, I speed up after her, watching as she slips inside the sports center at her university. The track is laid out behind her, and when I see who's waiting under the bleachers, I want to pull my gun.

It's some stupid fucking idiot jock who's grinning at her lustfully, and when she gets close, she goes on her toes and kisses him like he's her boyfriend.

Kisses him like she kissed me.

Swallowing hard, I try to beat back my anger, even as he grabs her hair, turns her, and pins her to a pole. His hand sneaks under her skirt as she moans. The sound cuts through the night, and I'm moving before I know it.

She's mine, and he dared to touch her.

He's dead.

Ripping him away from her, I throw him to the ground, putting my back to her. He goes to speak but pales when he sees his death written in my eyes. "Hey, man, look—"

"Do not speak," I snarl, smashing my foot into his face. I break his nose, but the blood and his scream only please me a little. I want to cut his fucking hand off for touching her. In fact... I pull my knife when she slides before me, pressing her hand against my chest.

I freeze, and darkness engulfs me as I stare into those bright eyes. I don't see anger, disgust, or even fear.

"Don't," she whispers. "He's not worth it."

I stare into her eyes. "He has two seconds to go before he's dead," I tell her, and it's the only warning he'll have.

"Go, now!" she snaps at the boy without looking at me. He takes off running, the pussy. He doesn't even check if she's okay, just leaves her here with an angry, deranged man. The fucking moron. I go to chase him, but her other hand touches my chest, bringing my attention back to her.

"What the fuck do you think you were doing?" I snarl.

Sighing, she steps back, retreating from me, but I won't let her. Not now, not ever.

"Answer me now, Zoey. What the fuck do you think you were doing?"

CHAPTER 5

Zoey

"Having fun?" I repeat the same words I uttered when he asked why I was at the bar. My hands are propped on my hips while I try really hard not to sound or look as pleased as I am that he followed me. It should scare me, but it doesn't. He obviously waited, watched, and stalked me here to my midnight booty call. All it does, however, is make me fucking wet. I want to test him and see how far he's willing to go. When I saw him storming toward us, his gray eyes flashing with lightning like an avenging demon coming to steal my soul, I had never felt so alive. Watching him hurt that boy whose name I've already forgotten had me so turned on it's embarrassing, my thighs slick.

He was willing to kill him for touching me. In fact, he would have; I saw it in his eyes—death.

The same death I've lived with.

The same darkness no one else seems to understand but Gray.

He's clearly as crazy as I am.

When he just stares at me, I turn and start to walk away, but he doesn't let me. He moves fast, grabbing me and slamming me back into the same pole the frat boy did. The difference here is that Gray can't decide if he wants me or wants to kill me.

His leg slams between my thighs, and his jeans rub against my aching pussy, making me gasp. His eyes flare at the sound.

"You should be scared of me, little doe." His voice is low and deadly, and I see a promise in his eyes, but it's the nickname that leaves me reeling. It's as if something clicks inside of me, but I don't know what.

"Why would I be?" I reply breathlessly, shamelessly grinding against his leg as he watches me. I'm wet as hell and needy. When I got that text from a jock I hook up with every now and again, I took the chance, still turned on from my run-in with Gray, but I never expected this, nor the desire I see in his eyes as he watches me mercilessly.

"Why don't I scare you? You know what I am, so say it, Zoey," he demands, gripping my chin. The pinch of pain makes me moan, and his eyes darken at the sound. "Say it," he grits out.

"A killer," I reply, my voice hoarse and filled with lust. "Death. But here's the truth, Gray. I've known death my entire life, so it doesn't scare me anymore. In fact, it's pretty much a fucking comfort for me," I purr, rocking my hips. My clit rubs against his jeans as pleasure spirals through me. "So stop trying to push me away."

I don't know what I said or did, but just as suddenly as he grabbed me, he pulls away, his eyes narrowed. "Let's go." He jerks his head but doesn't grab me, as if he's afraid to touch me again.

I start to walk, and he leads me back to my dorm. I expect him to leave me at the door, but instead he follows me up the stairs to my room.

My heart slams and anticipation spirals through me, but once we step inside my room, he moves to my bed and pulls back the covers. "In," he demands.

Frowning, I slide between the sheets fully dressed, and he flips them back over me, tucking me in before moving to the door.

"Stay and behave."

Sitting up, I watch as he hesitates before pulling it open. His eyes meet mine, and for a moment, I feel a sense of familiarity. A memory of a little boy who did the same thing claws at my mind before it floats away.

"Aren't you at least going to finish me off?" I tease, unable to help myself. He doesn't respond, so I swallow, my voice sounding small in the dark. "This isn't over."

"Yes it is, little doe."

Without another word, he leaves, the door shutting and locking behind him. My heart is still racing, and I feel a desire so strong it's a physical ache, so I push the covers away and flop back, my skin over-heated from his touch.

With his eyes still flashing in my mind, his voice in my ear, and the knowledge he's out there watching me, I slide my hand down my body, moaning as I cup my dripping pussy. I slide my fingers through my wetness before circling my clit. I don't tease; I'm too needy for that. Instead, I rub my clit quickly before sliding my other hand down and thrusting two fingers inside myself. I pretend they are his and that it's his harsh, brutal touch on me, demanding my release. My back arches, and I roll my hips as I reach for my release, fucking myself on my fingers, wishing it were his cock slamming inside me.

With that image in my mind, I tumble over the edge, my pussy clenching on my fingers as my thighs jerk and shake.

His name is on my lips when I come.

As I come back down from the high, I realize two things. One, I want him more than I've ever wanted anybody in my life. Two, he's exactly what I've been looking for. He makes me feel alive, despite the fact he's determined to stay away from me.

But I always get what I want.

He just doesn't know it yet.

Game on, Gray.

When I get home, I slam the door behind me so forcibly it threatens to come off its hinges, the loud racket perfectly mimicking my fury.

I'm pissed.

I'm beyond pissed.

I'm fucking inconsolable.

And it's all because I let a little girl like Zoey get to me.

Fuck.

She always did have a knack for getting under my skin, but it's so fucking different now. Before, she was able to coax out the best version of myself, the one who was her guardian and protector... someone who was good.

Now, however, I feel like I'll break if she so much as looks my way. Worst of all, though, is that she causes this need inside me to taint her with all of my ugliness and unleash all my damage on her, uncaring that it will end up ruining her.

I yearn to force her to face my demons since she seems to want to.

Fuck!

White-hot anger consumes me as I walk toward my living room and pour myself a hard drink. I down the amber liquor in one full swig, letting it burn my throat as it goes down. Unfortunately, it does little to soothe away the guilt I feel. Disgust and hatred battle for first place in my long list of fucked-up feelings, but it's shame that wins out in the end.

I fucking hate myself for letting Zoey get to me the way she did. She has no idea of the effect she has on me. None whatsoever. How could she? I'm nothing but a stranger to her, some guy her adoptive dad works with. That's all I am to her. She has no recollection of me, and while there was a sliver of sorrow that I was so easily forgotten, there was also an overwhelming sense of relief that she completely erased all memories of that time in her life.

My gratitude for that small mercy was quickly overshadowed, however, by her overt advances. A girl her age should want nothing to do with the likes of me, yet she tested my boundaries tonight, seeing just how far she could push me. It's safe to say that when it comes to Zoey, there is a fine line that should never be crossed.

But the look in her eyes, the one that told me that all I had to do was crook my finger and she would willingly step over that line and fling herself into my abyss, eyes wide open with a fucking smile on her face, was too fucking seductive for words.

Too fucking tempting to resist.

My cock instantly hardens at the image, not that it seems to be anything but when it comes to her.

I shake my head and do my best to push all thoughts of Zoey out of my mind, grabbing the whiskey bottle and taking it with me over to the couch. I sit down and pick up the remote to turn on the TV. I don't really care that it lands on some vapid reality show, just needing the mindless chatter to drown out the loud noise in my head. Taking a large swig of alcohol straight out of the bottle, I wipe the remnants off my lips with my sleeve.

Some blonde appears on the screen, and my mind travels to memories of Zoey once again. She looked different tonight, nothing like the girl I first met. It's not a stretch, really, since Zoey was only seven when she came into my life.

Innocent.

Pure.

Untouched and untainted.

I, on the other hand, was already broken by the time she came along, but I remember when I saw her, I didn't want to be. I wanted to be something else, something opposite to what *that* house made me.

Someone good. Someone worthy.

I can still remember every second of our first encounter, how fragile and scared she was as she sat on the cold bathroom floor all scrunched up as she tried to make herself even smaller than she already was. But then she looked up at me, and my heart stopped. Her gaze told me so much, reflecting the horrors my own soul knew. She had suffered terrors beyond anyone's comprehension, and she was barely hanging in there, trying her best to be strong, but all it would take was one more brush with evil for her to lose herself for good.

Right there and then, I vowed I wouldn't let that shit happen.

I would protect her.

I would keep her safe and whole, even if that meant I would take the brunt of the savagery that happened in that house.

I was already damaged goods anyway, and I'd make sure Zoey wouldn't suffer the same fate.

That was then, though, and this is now. Zoey is no longer the lost little girl I protected back in foster care, and she sure as shit isn't the same girl I met at Alaric's party last year.

She changed, and I missed it.

How the fuck did I miss it?

Especially since I thought I was keeping good tabs on her all these years.

The minute I was freed from my hell and I enlisted in the Army, I made it my mission to track down the little girl I saved when I was just a kid myself. I needed to know that all my sacrifices hadn't been made in vain and that I was able to do one good thing in my pathetic excuse of a life. That's what she was to me, the only light in a dark, fucked-up life, and I wanted to keep her that way. Luckily, the Army had plenty of unsavory friends, and as I worked my way up the ladder, I met one of said friends who possessed the skills to track down anyone who didn't want to be, which meant finding the whereabouts of a civilian was a piece of cake for him. I can still recall how Hale—the vain, cocky fuck—walked into my tent one afternoon, looking like a million bucks while everyone else had Afghani sand in their ass crack, and said the words I'd been dying to hear for years.

"I found your girl."

After that, I paid whatever ransom Hale asked of me just so he could send me photographs of Zoey, each one a testimony of the good life she was leading. She was only twelve when I found her living with her sister and new husband in a big house and posh neighborhood. My girl was living the American dream, going to a private school and taking all the right steps to ensure an even brighter future.

She remained pure.

She remained untouched.

It was enough for me to go about my days knowing that somewhere out there, she was living her best life, and all the horrors of the past never consumed her as they did me. Amongst all the bloodshed of the war I was fighting in, my life finally had some meaning to it, knowing that I played a big part in Zoey's happily ever after.

But then I did something stupid.

I fucking died.

And with death comes a whole other set of problems.

It never crossed my mind that those problems would bring me right to Zoey's doorstep. When the agency rescued me from enemy lines and offered a ghost like me another shot at life, I took it, never thinking it would mean my life would once again be entangled with hers.

I could either blame serendipity or karma for playing such a cruel joke on me, but when the agency paired me with Alaric, of all people, to become his protégé, I didn't know if I should laugh or weep. This was the man who Hale had informed me had been raising my Zoey as his own for years, the man who had taken my spot in protecting her, and now here I was, being trained to be an even better killer just so I could fill the empty seat he would leave in the agency once he retired. The role reversal between us felt all types of wrong to me, yet I did my part by learning all the tricks of the trade that he taught me, always on pins and needles as I waited for her name to slip out of his lips.

Since I arrived stateside, I resisted the urge to seek Zoey out, not wanting to risk her having traumatic flashbacks of her childhood, but then Alaric made the mistake of inviting me to a birthday party at his house, and for the life of me, I couldn't stay away a second longer. I knew his goal for such an invite was for us to bond or some shit, but all his good intentions went out the window the minute I locked eyes with his baby girl and saw Zoey for the first time in a decade. She was no longer the scrawny little kid I found on the bathroom floor and became obsessed with protecting. She was fully grown and something out of a fucking wet dream. My brotherly affection for her switched to something dark and sinister that very day. Like a light switch turned on, it shed light on a desire I had no business feeling toward her.

It was for the best that Alaric kicked me out of his home that day and made sure to keep me away from his family after. He wouldn't take too kindly to me ravishing his daughter right there and then in his own backyard.

My cock hardens again at the image of Zoey in that flowy skirt and how easy it would have been for me to slam her up against the wall, hike it up to her waist, pull her panties down, and pound that tight pussy of hers until her juices ran down her thighs. That day at the party, I would have sworn that she had never felt a cock fill her to the hilt before, and I'd have gladly volunteered to be the one to stretch that virgin pussy until it memorized the length and girth of my shaft.

I didn't put up much of a fight with him that day since, deep down, I knew Alaric was right. A good girl like her should be kept away from me. She deserved to be with someone her own age, someone who would shower her with sweetness, flowers, and rainbows—shit that good girls like.

But the Zoey I met tonight was different.

That girl doesn't do sweetness, flowers, and rainbows.

She does shadows and death.

Like me.

A loud groan springs out of my throat as my hand clenches around the whiskey bottle. I take another gulp and still feel unsatisfied, knowing I need a far better release than this shit. Pissed at myself for not having better control of these urges, I fling the bottle across the room, the glass shattering into a million pieces just as my sanity is about to. With my eyes closed, I recall how she looked when she came out of the bar and found me in the back alley with a dead body at my feet. Zoey didn't so much as flinch, stepping closer to me in that fucking leather skirt and black halter top that showcased her long neck and naked shoulders. I could easily see her puckered nipples in that fucking thing, showing she was turned on that I had just extinguished the light in that fucker's eyes. The way she licked her lips before smiling at me, her green eyes shining brightly at what she encountered, had been fucking intoxicating. Then when I got her into the car, I swear I could even smell her arousal every time I breathed in. All I had to do was put my hand between her thighs, and I knew I'd find her wet and wanting.

Fuck, did I want to taste that sweetness as she screamed my name. I wanted to ruin her and make her forget anyone other than me until she was as obsessed as I am.

With her scent still lingering on my skin, I slouch back into the couch, widen my legs, pull down my zipper, and release my aching cock. I spit into my palm before I grab the base of my dick and start fucking my own hand with images of the Zoey I met tonight playing through my mind. She looked at me like she wanted nothing more than to have my cock thrust into that wet mouth of hers, like she wanted to fuck me raw right there in that alley with a lifeless body lying dead in the corner.

When I left her untouched in her dorm room, staring at me in complete agony, it took inhumane effort on my part not to fling myself on top of her, kick her legs open, and let myself get lost in her pussy. My tongue licks over my front teeth, wishing I had let myself just have a little taste of her. Just a small taste to keep me sane. But it would have been a lie. One lick, and I'd be done for. I'd eat her out until she screamed for me to fuck her, and fuck her I would. I'd pound into her so hard she'd leave her silhouette on the mattress. Right after she came on my tongue, I would have grabbed her by those lovely golden locks of hers and made her suck me off, brutishly and savagely. I'd have made her mascara run down her pretty cheeks, making her a mess as she choked on my length, deprived of air and sanity. I'd ruin her, ruin all of her. She'd be a fuck doll in my hands and thank me for it in the end, begging for more.

And fuck, I would have given it to her.

My balls swell at the fantasy, making my hand quicken its speed on my cock and tighten its grip even more. I'm no longer in my living room but back at that dorm in her room that's filled with her prized possessions.

"Please. Please, Gray."

"For you, little doe. Always for you," I reply on a groan. *"Only ever for you."*

Just as I imagine thrusting inside of her, spurts of cum fly every which way on my hand, landing on my stomach and soaking through my shirt. My breathing is hard as I come back to reality, and when I open my eyelids and see what I've done, I slam my head repeatedly against the couch, shame rearing its ugly head once again.

This isn't how we're supposed to be.

This was never the deal.

What started off as a need to keep the little girl of my youth safe has morphed into something I'm not emotionally equipped to handle.

A ghost craves nothing.

A ghost desires nothing.

A ghost loves nothing.

Not wanting to prolong my self-deprecation longer than I need to, I pull myself up and walk toward my bedroom, not looking at the pictures Hale was able to obtain for me of Zoey over the years hung on my wall, especially now that I know all of them are a lie. None of them have captured the real Zoey. They are just a sham she puts out into the world, a fabrication she's invented to make others feel safe.

Zoey isn't safe.

She's danger personified, and she'll end me if given half the chance.

I rush to take off my clothes and step into my shower to wash away the guilt of what I just did. Unfortunately for me, my impure thoughts never waver, and I end up jacking off two more times in the shower, the cold spray of water doing nothing to cool my lust for the one girl I should never want to touch with my bloodstained hands.

When I hear a notification on my phone, I finally step out of the shower and head back into my bedroom to find my phone in my jeans pocket. A low growl escapes me when I see that the tracking app I installed in Zoey's phone when she wasn't looking tells me she is no longer safe and sound, tucked away in her bed back at her dorm. The little heathen is on the move again, no doubt trying to hook up with that jackass I found her with earlier tonight, hoping that man is enough to scratch the itch I left.

He's not, and he never will be.

Like me, she needs to get off, and while I found some release in my fantasies, Zoey isn't as easily satisfied. She needs the real deal. She needs to lick the sweat off her lover's skin and feel her back arch as he fills her to the brim. Fantasies won't cut it when the real thing is so much better.

My nostrils flare as I grip my phone in my hand, almost crushing it into a pulp with the thought of someone else making her come tonight. Pure hatred of this nameless asshole has me quickly getting dressed, determined to put a stop to their encounter.

Just as I pull a clean T-shirt over my head, I stop and rethink my actions. I fall onto my bed and just stare at the white ceiling, counting my rapid heartbeats until they even out.

I can't go after Zoey.

If I do, I know what will happen.

I'll end up scaring off whatever fucker she's with, and then I'll succumb to her will and give her what she truly wants—me. And if I do that, then all bets are off.

Ghost or not, there wouldn't be a person on God's green Earth who could tear me away from her ever again. I let that happen too many times already.

As if this night hasn't fucked with my head enough, memories of other men who wanted to take her from me crawl into the forefront of my mind, and I'm suddenly fifteen again, trapped in the house of horrors.

Shit.

I'm late.

I'm so fucking late.

Like a fool, I let myself fall asleep after dinner, and now I'm late.

Zoey must be losing her mind, wondering where I am.

Unlike her older sister, she doesn't sleep much. I don't think she's slept more than a few hours a night since the day she arrived here, and I learned the hard way that nothing good happens in this group home after midnight.

That's when the devils come out to play.

Not wanting her to share in that lesson, I rush upstairs to the third floor where all the girls sleep. When I finally reach the girls' floor and stumble into the narrow corridor, my stomach churns, finding little Zoey dressed in only a large, tattered T-shirt as she shifts from side to side, unable to pass with Roland standing in her way.

"Come here. Don't be shy, girl. I won't hurt you," Roland coos at Zoey, flashing her all his predatory teeth.

Not wanting the sick fuck to lay a hand on her little golden head, I rush to her side and push her behind me.

"Leave her alone," I growl with all the courage I can muster.

Roland straightens his spine, his menacing smile widening on his lips.

"Now, now, Gray. You can't keep her all to yourself. We have a visitor who is dying to meet her. This one likes them small, and your girl here is just his type."

"Fuck you. He can't have her," I seethe through gritted teeth, stepping closer to him while making sure Zoey is out of his reach. "I swear I'll scream bloody murder if you so much as touch her."

Roland's gaze bounces from me to Zoey, and he frowns when he sees I'm not bullshitting him. Not everyone in this house is aware of the twisted games the night shift gets into, and me waking everyone up is something Roland would rather avoid. I'm not sure who's on call tonight, but I'm hoping at least one of them isn't on the old man's bankroll. If they all are, then I'm shit out of luck. The fine hair on the nape of my neck stands on end as I watch him debate if calling my bluff is worth it.

When his tense shoulders relax before my very eyes, I know I fucked up.

"I just remembered something." He smiles sinisterly. "Our visitor tonight has varied tastes. There's something that appeals to him better than breaking in pretty little fillies. He likes taming wild stallions so much more. Take one guess as to whom I'm talking about."

My blood chills, knowing exactly whom he's referring to—the general. He's the only one I've ever met who treats his victims like live-stock, using prods and hot irons to leave his mark on their flesh. I swallow dryly, the cold fingers of unrepressed fear choking me from within.

"So what do you say, Gray? It's not your night today, but I'm sure he'll make an exception for you."

Roland's eerie smile of victory only makes my skin crawl further.

He knows he's won.

Without looking at her, I grab Zoey's tiny hand in mine and bypass Roland in the hall.

"Go back to your room, Zoey. I can't stay with you tonight."

"No." She shakes her little head, pulling my hand so I step farther away from the man who is going to hand deliver me to that fucking psychopath. "Come with me."

I crouch so we are eye level with each other and hold both of her hands in mine. I want to fight, to scream, to take her and run away, but I can do none of those things, and for a moment, I just drink in her innocence and hope. I'll need it to get through what's next.

"It's okay, little doe. I've got this."

"But Gray," she starts to protest but stops when I pull her hands up to my lips to kiss her fingers.

"Go to your room, Zoey. Do that for me, okay?"

Reluctantly, she nods and starts walking away. My gaze never leaves her. I need to make sure she reaches her destination before I *have to go back to mine. When she arrives at her bedroom door at the end of the hall, she looks back at me. My forehead furrows, though, when I realize she's not looking at me at all, but at the man who is now standing too close for comfort behind me.*

"If you hurt him, my guardian angel will kill you just like he killed my daddy. I'll make sure of it."

She gives him her meanest glare and walks into her room, locking it behind her just like I taught her to.

"Stupid bitch," the monster behind me scoffs, but I tune him out, overcome with relief now that she's safe and out of his grasp.

It's only when I feel Roland's fingers dig into my shoulders that I remember this nightmare isn't done yet.

Not for me at least.

"Come on, Gray. It's playtime."

Cold sweat drips down my neck as I swiftly pull myself out of bed, pick up my phone and car keys, and rush out of the door, intent on finding Zoey wherever she is. Living with Alaric must have given her a false sense of security if she thinks she can just go out at this ungodly hour and come back unscathed.

But I know the truth.

Monsters rule the night.

If she keeps tempting the devil, sooner or later, he'll come for her.

W ith my hands on the steering wheel, I glance over at my phone on the console and smile. Maybe I should have a word with Alaric and tell him he's dropping the ball where Gray's tutoring is concerned. I mean, did Gray really think he could put a tracking device on my phone and I wouldn't notice? Does he think I'm that naïve?

I shake my head and chuckle.

"Ah, Gray, you have to be a lot smarter than that to pull a fast one on me."

Although there could be another explanation as to why he would assume I'd be clueless to his sly ways. Maybe he doesn't know that Alaric came clean with Layla and me years ago about what he did for a living. Now that I think about it, that does sound more than likely. Most of the hitmen my father thought were safe enough to bring home to meet us didn't have families, and only a seldom few of those who did shared the truth about their day job to their loved ones. I guess not everyone is as open-minded and accepting as Layla and I. Then again, not everyone has had the same horrific childhood experiences we did, which allowed us to understand that some evils are justified.

"Come on, Gray!" I slap my steering wheel. "I saw you kill a dude tonight, and I didn't even flinch. Hello! If that doesn't give you an inkling that I'm in the loop, then I don't know what will."

I let out another giggle and turn up the volume on my radio so I can sing along to the tune. The streets open up for me, and I take advantage of it as I press the pedal to the metal.

God, I love New York at this hour.

Sure, I should be asleep back in the dorm, especially since I have classes in the morning, but I've always been a night owl. Plus, after Gray left me all hot and bothered, there was no way I could fall asleep. I was too wired, too on edge, and I needed something—*someone*. As luck would have it, when I picked up my phone to mindlessly scroll through my social feed and saw that it had been tampered with, I knew exactly which *someone* would scratch my itch perfectly. First, though, I need to have a little fun with him. It serves him right for leaving me high and dry.

Now it's his turn.

After I drive aimlessly around for a half hour, giving Gray enough time to track me, I change lanes and go to the last place he'll want me to be.

Without him knowing, Gray showed me his cards tonight.

Like my dad, he can't curb that protective streak inside him, and for whatever reason, he feels extremely protective of me. While my sister found Alaric's need to keep her safe endearing, I think it's a very convenient quality to exploit. If his overprotectiveness means I get to see him again, then by God, I'm using it.

Maybe that makes me a bad person, but I've met plenty of people who did a whole lot worse to get what they wanted, and all I want is to spend time with the one man who intrigues me like no other.

"Stay away from Gray, Zoey. I don't want him anywhere near you." I hear my father's voice in my head as if my conscience decided to make an appearance just as I'm about to put my plan in motion.

My smile drops from my face as I think about how Alaric would react if he knew what I was planning.

Crap.

He would have a coronary if he even so much as found out what

I've been up to since I left home for college. After he gets out of the hospital, he would lock me up in my room and only let me leave when I turn forty. Maybe not even then.

I sigh audibly.

Don't get me wrong, I love my dad. I'd kill and die for him. But sometimes I get the feeling that he doesn't want me to grow up, and as hard as I have tried to give him the memo that I'm eighteen and a grown-ass woman, it always falls on deaf ears. I even make sure I always drop by the house in my 'nice girl' clothes so I don't give him any more ammo to use against me. I mean, he knows me well enough to recognize that isn't me, but I know it gives him comfort, and what sacrifices wouldn't I make to keep my family happy?

I just wish it were that easy for me to find an ounce of happiness for myself.

Who am I kidding?

I'd settle for just being content.

That's not me either though. Somewhere along the line, my head got so messed up that I only get a rush when I'm doing stupid shit— things that would scare the bejesus out of my family.

Like what I'm about to do right now.

I turn off the ignition to my car and stare at all the Harleys parked in front of the biker bar.

"You better show up, Gray, or otherwise this might be more than I can chew," I mumble under my breath before smoothing my hair and adjusting the girls so they look like they are seconds away from spilling over my tank top.

Not wanting to lose my nerve, I get out of the car and make a beeline toward the most notorious biker bar in all of Hell's Kitchen, known for being the Red Devil MC's preferred hangout spot. Just as I'm a few feet away from the front door, I feel someone grab my arm and pull me back.

My skin breaks out in goosebumps when Gray's arm snakes around my waist and holds me to his chest.

"What the fuck are you doing?" he growls in my ear, making my heart pitter-patter in glee.

"I was about to grab something to eat. What about you?" I sass.

"You were about to get gang raped every which way; that's what you were about to do," he spits.

Fear starts creeping up my throat, but when Gray tightens his hold on me, it disappears into thin air.

"That's a bit judgmental of you, don't you think? Where is it written that a woman will automatically get assaulted if she walks into a bar filled with motorcycle enthusiasts?"

"Those" —he points a menacing finger at three scary-ass bikers leaving the bar— "are not bikers. They are criminals. They are evil men who use sweet-looking little things like you in very bad ways."

I turn around and press my open palms to his chest. "Do I look sweet to you?" I bat my lashes at him.

He grinds his teeth and groans, his grip starting to leave a mark on my hips. "You look like trouble," he admits through gritted teeth.

I can't help but preen at his description of me.

"What kind of trouble?" I purr.

"The kind that will get any fucker who looks at you killed."

My mouth dries immediately at the threat in his words.

He means it.

If he had been a minute late and I ventured inside, he'd have killed every last one of them. He wouldn't even feel guilty about it. But then again, I don't think Gray is capable of feeling anything. Aside from his overzealous need to keep me safe, he hasn't shown that he is equipped to feel much of anything else. It leaves me to question if his protective-ness is solely due to loyalty to my father or something else. Until tonight, we haven't had much of an opportunity to get to know each other, so there wasn't any reason for there to be any justifiable feelings between us, but there is something here.

Interest.

Curiosity.

Lust.

Something.

And I'm completely invested in learning what that something is.

"You made your point," I reply nonchalantly while brazenly rolling my body against his. "But I'm still hungry. In fact, I'm famished. And if I can't go in there, then I guess you'll just have to take me someplace else. Maybe your place?"

My insinuation couldn't be any clearer if I slapped him with it, but Gray doesn't bite the line I'm feeding him.

Instead, he drops his hands, my body instantly screaming in protest, and takes a full step away from me.

"If you want to eat then I know just the place. Get into your car and follow me," he orders.

My shoulders slump in defeat, but I follow his orders.

I guess I should look on the bright side.

He came for me, so that must mean something.

Right?

With that positive thought doing backflips in my head, I skip over to my car and wait for him to get into his. When he flashes his lights, I turn on the engine and follow him out of the bar's parking lot.

I guess it *was* pretty reckless of me to come here alone so late at night, but I was desperate. If I had gone anywhere else where Gray thought I could handle myself, he would have left me to my own devices—or at least I think he would. I wonder if he'd have come for me no matter where I ended up tonight. I mean, he did stalk me back at school.

I pin that theory to test out another day and focus on driving so I don't lose him. Unsurprisingly, he drives us as far away from Hell's Kitchen as possible. Although when we enter the Upper East side, I scoff at how little this man really knows about me. The Upper East side was never my scene. It's too fake for me. Too rich and shallow. When I think of this side of the city, the first thing that comes to mind are those Wall Street types who think they rule the world while they are, in fact, slowly killing it, and don't even get me started on the Botox socialites they love to have hanging on their arms, hoping some paparazzi will take a picture to post on page six.

The only Manhattan girl I can stand to be around for more than a minute is my best friend, Cara. She was the first girl I met at St. Augustine, and we have been stuck together at the hip ever since. It's a good thing, too, since my girl has no street smarts or survival skills to speak of. If I hadn't been there to look after her, most of the stuck-up hyenas at that school would have made a meal out of Cara. She might look like she just stepped straight out of a fairy tale, born and bred to act like a goddamn princess with a capital P, but in all the ten years I've known her, no Prince Charming ever came knocking at her door to keep the dragons at bay. All the other girls were passing out their hoochies like they were punching cards at Seven Eleven, while Cara kept hers under lock and key, making her a pariah at our school.

Not that she cared much.

With her nose always inside a book, my best friend always gives me the impression that she's perfectly content living solely in her imagination rather than venturing out into the real world and experiencing such things.

I guess she's right on her reasoning.

The male leads in the books she reads are always so gallant and noble. Even the villains, at times, are swoon worthy enough to make you want to root for them.

Out here in the real world though?

Not so much.

I've seen men at their worst, and speaking from personal experience, villains always deserve what's coming to them. If I had it my way, Cara would never be put in a position where she would have to face such men. Not on my watch.

Hmm.

Maybe I'm more like my father than I thought.

The minute Cara and I met, I knew she needed me to watch out for her.

She's like a frail piece of beautiful crystal. Someone could come right on up to her and make a crack, shattering her innocence to smithereens. She's too damn good for that to happen. People like Cara, who don't have a mean bone in their body, are few and far between—a precious commodity this city is running low on. Someone needs to champion and stand guard over these pure souls, otherwise the world will swallow them whole, and all that will be left is rot and despair.

And what a fucking shithole that would be.

Hence why Cara is the only person I truly trust aside from my family. The unlikely bond between Hell's Kitchen hood rat and The Upper East side virgin princess has only grown stronger over the years, and to this day, she's the best friend a girl like me could ever have.

Having said that, it doesn't mean I don't keep a few secrets from her.

For example, I have no intention of telling her what I've been up to all night. Cara would shit a brick if she knew I was trying to seduce a man who's older than me. And if she knew it was Gray, the guy she knows my dad told me to stay clear of, I would bet my left titty that she would run to Layla and Alaric and sing like a canary, thinking she was doing me a favor.

Nope.

Nuh-uh.

Not going to let anyone ruin my fun until I have some worth spoiling.

My mind is still on Cara when I realize that Gray has already parked his car in front of what looks to be a long silver trailer of sorts, very reminiscent of the fifties. It's cute and so out of place that I immediately love it. I quickly unclasp my seat belt and jump out of the car, excited that he brought me to a laid-back diner instead of a swanky bar.

When he opens the door and waits for me to pass, my lady bits clap at his attempt at being a gentleman. One look at Gray and you know he doesn't have that in him, so for him to purposely try his hand at being chivalrous for me merits a reward. I stop right beside him, his arm still occupied with holding the door out for me, and go to the tips of my toes so I'm tall enough to act like I'm going to kiss his cheek. Of course I make sure that my calculations are off and kiss the edge of his lips instead.

"Thank you," I whisper as the soles of my feet fall back on solid ground.

"Get inside," he growls menacingly, but I'm not scared, not when his other hand went straight to the small of my back after such a kiss. I don't say anything and just let him gently guide me to our booth, his hand burning through my clothes. He could guide me to hell and back as long as he kept his hand right where it is, and I wouldn't say a peep otherwise.

All too soon, we get to our table, where Gray prefers to sit opposite me in the booth where his hands won't be tempted to roam all over my body like I want them to.

A bubbly waitress in a vintage red polka-dot dress and Doris Day hairdo takes our order of burgers, fries, and vanilla milkshakes, and in less than ten minutes flat, she brings all that goodness to our table. With my stomach growling at the sight of such deliciousness, I dig in with gusto, not bothering to wait for Gray.

"I thought it was a lie," Gray mutters, his food still untouched as he watches me devour mine.

"What was?" I ask absentmindedly, eyeing his fries. "Are you going to eat those?"

He shakes his head and pushes his plate of fries toward me, and then surprises me further when I see his upper lip lift somewhat, almost resembling a smile.

"Hell must have frozen over, because I think you might have just smiled at me," I tease, waving a fry in his face before cutting it in half with my teeth.

His lips thin, and he looks like his expressionless self again, but it's too late. The damage is done.

He smiled.

At me.

Gotcha, Gray.

Not wanting to celebrate my victory yet, I lower my gaze from his and seductively place a straw in the center of my lips before looking up at him.

"What did you think I was lying about?" I ask him, making my voice sound like smooth silk, before wrapping my lips around the white straw and beginning to suck. I try not to grin when I see his hands clutch the table's edge.

"When you said you were hungry back in Hell's Kitchen. I thought you were lying."

"I don't lie," I state evenly, to which he arches a brow, calling me on my shit. "Omitting some truths isn't the same thing as lying."

"It is to me," he retorts.

"Well, if you had Alaric as your dad, you'd be inclined to think differently."

"A lie is a lie, even by omission," he deadpans.

"Does that mean you would rather I tell my father the truth?" I taunt. "I wonder how that would go. If you want, I can tell him how you're here with me, having a grand old time at four o'clock in the morning on a school night. Would that make you think better of me?"

When he cracks his knuckles, I know I got him yet again.

Neither one of us is ready for the outside world to know about us. Even if there is no us.

Yet.

"That's what I thought," I retort triumphantly. "And like I said, I don't lie. I was hungry. In fact," I goad, wiping my mouth with a napkin and placing it on my empty plate, "I'm still famished."

Before he pushes his food across the table for me, I place my hand on his wrist and shake my head.

"Not for food, Gray. You know exactly what I want."

The words have barely left my lips when Gray pushes himself over the table and grabs hold of my chin so brutishly, I feel it in my clit. My heart pounds in my chest, and I think this is when he's going to kiss me, when I suddenly feel his thumb caress the corner of my mouth, wiping ketchup off it before releasing me from his grip to suck it clean.

I become transfixed, watching his tongue taste me on his skin, imagining all the places I'd like him to use that wicked tongue next.

"That mouth of yours will get you in a world of trouble one day," he says after he's made sure I've left a puddle on the leather seat.

"So I'm told," I choke out, rubbing my thighs together.

We lock our gazes for what feels like an eternity, wanting to see who will break first.

"Stay here. I'll be right back," he orders, breaking our staring contest just so he can stand up from his seat to walk over to the cashier to pay our bill. I close my eyes and lean my head into the leather cushion, trying to get my head screwed on straight.

Here I am, trying to be the dominant one and seduce this man into fucking me, but all it takes is one touch from him to tilt my world on its axis, leaving me a complete hot mess who is ready to do whatever he orders me to.

What the fuck is wrong with me?

I glance over at the cashier once more and see Gray walk toward the men's room instead of returning to our table. Needing to correct the powershift between us, I stand up and march over to him.

"Just what do you think you're doing?" he asks once he hears me lock the bathroom door behind me.

"This." I push him with all my might, surprising him enough for his stance to falter, and I succeed in pushing his back flush against the wall. Not wanting to give him an opening to stop me, I fall to my knees and unzip his pants, smiling when I find him already hard.

"Don't," he chokes out just as my fingers hook on his boxers.

My challenging gaze rises up to his. Gray is standing on a ledge and mere inches away from stepping off it. His teeth grind together, his eyes are bright with desire, and his hands grip the sink on either side of him.

"Stop me," I taunt, arching my eyebrow. After all, I don't take what isn't freely given.

But Gray doesn't stop me.

He doesn't stop me when I pull his boxers down and release the angriest-looking cock I've ever seen. It's huge and in desperate need of fucking something hard and relentlessly.

He doesn't stop me when I lick the beads of precum over his mushroom head with a moan, his salty taste exploding on my tongue.

And he sure as hell doesn't stop me when I wrap my lips around his length and suck as much of him as I can into my mouth.

His head slams against the wall, his hands balled up into two large fists at his sides. Although he refuses to touch me as I lick him from base to crown, my heady gaze never leaves his. Aside from the way his cock is responding to my advances, his half-mast eyes are the only parts of himself Gray allows to be active participants. The way they shine like silver bullets ready to slice me open, ready to leave a gaping hole in my heart just so he can fuck it as good as my mouth is fucking him, is all the incentive I need to do my worst.

I firm my lips around him, making sure my wet mouth is as tight as my pussy so he can see what he's missing out on. I hollow my cheeks and suck him to oblivion while leaving my hands free to grab his ass and push him mercilessly deeper down my throat. The back of my throat clenches with his size, coaxing out my gag reflex. The inexperience of sucking a cock this big frazzles me for a split second, making me close my eyes just so I can concentrate on my breathing. The fraction of hesitation on my part must grate on Gray's nerves, because before I know it, his fingers are in my hair, and suddenly I'm no longer in command of my actions—he is.

Tears start forming at the corners of my eyes as he fucks my mouth like it wants to replace all the air in my lungs. He suffocates me with each thrust, and yet all I do is welcome his vicious assault. My scalp is on fire with him pulling at the strands of my hair, guiding my mouth to the very base of his cock. Tears now fall freely down my cheeks as his cock takes his pound of flesh. His gaze feels like lightning on my skin as Gray keeps fucking my mouth like there is no tomorrow. My panties are soaked with the display of such dominance, and all I need is to flick my clit a few times to have me coming.

This isn't just a blow job.

This is war.

One that I know he'll win.

The only warning I get that he's at his wit's end is when I hear him let out a toe-curling growl. Hot cum spurts down my throat, and Gray doesn't let up until I swallow every last drop. After he's released his grip on me, I use the flat of my tongue to clean his cock, worshiping it for a job well done.

Gray picks me up with just his thumb gently pressed under my chin, ordering me back to my feet. My heart beats a mile a minute, thinking he's finally going to kiss me, but instead, all he does is stare at me with the blankest expression, one that I can't decipher no matter how much I want to.

"You're nothing like I expected," he mutters dryly, his reprimanding words feeling like a slap to the face.

I stand there, mouth agape, that those were the words he decided to utter when I know for a fact that I just rocked his world. But it was so much more than that. It was electrifying. Like our connection could burn down cities. He had to feel it. He just had to.

Right?

I'm still standing there speechless when Gray decides that playtime is over by pulling away from the wall and walking over to the door to make his quick getaway.

Not wanting this infuriating man to have the last word, I call out his name. Like I predicted, he stops, but his hand remains on the doorknob, his back turned to me.

"That's it? That's all you have to say to me?"

When he refuses to even so much as look at me, my short temper shifts to full-blown fury.

"Fuck you, Gray. Fuck you."

He turns his head a little bit over his shoulder, enough so I can see the silver moonlight in his eyes.

"Not today, little doe, but soon." My throat clogs as his smoldering gaze trails over my body until it fixes on my swollen lips—the same lips that can still taste him. "Really fucking soon."

CHAPTER 8

Gray

I left her in that diner last night, or so she thought. I watched her storm out, and then I followed her home and stayed until sunrise to make sure she didn't sneak out again.

She didn't, but that didn't stop the tempest from brewing inside me, nor the memory of her mouth wrapped around my cock replaying in my mind. She was so fucking dirty, those beautiful eyes ripping my defenses to shreds as she gave me more pleasure than I've ever had in my entire life. If she knew all the incredibly horrible things they did to me, she would feel sick to her stomach at the idea of putting my cock in her mouth.

I should have stopped her, but I couldn't, and fuck if her desperation for my pleasure wasn't such a turn-on.

I couldn't stop even if I tried.

Even now, as I shower, my cock hardens at the memory, the vile fucking thing desperate for her. It's completely hers now, just like every inch of me, soul and heart.

Or whatever is left of them.

I tried to be good, to stay away from her and let her have a better life, but I couldn't walk away from her now even if I tried. She's mine, she just doesn't know it yet.

She has been since she was a kid.

I'm so tired of fighting it. I made her a promise in that diner, whether she knew it or not. Before I die, I will have her, and she will regret begging me for it. She will hate me and fear me just like everyone else, yet I won't be able to stop this even if I want to.

Not now that I've had a taste.

Snarling, I slam my fist into the shower wall and watch the tile crack. Blood blooms across my cut knuckles, and I feel nothing, but the sight satisfies the beast inside me, so I do it again and again before washing the blood off and getting out.

After all, I have a job today, so I can't afford to spend the day tearing my house to pieces simply because the one person in the world I should never have is determined to rip all my darkness away, but she'll soon realize the only thing that is underneath is more darkness.

Whatever was left of a living, feeling man after the group home was killed all those years ago when I died.

I truly am the ghost they call me, only coming to life around her.

And I will drag her into the grave with me.

The job is too easy. It's a tracking one, but the idiot is so unaware, he uses his credit cards for everything, even when trying to lie low. I play with him for a few hours, stalking him and letting him feel me watching, and he starts to panic before locking himself in some shady hotel room. Paying off the reception staff, I wait for night, and when he's asleep, I unlock the door and wake him with my knife pressed to his throat.

He awakens quickly then, opening his mouth to scream. "I wouldn't do that," I warn, my voice quiet and deadly. I know he sees my silhouette over him and feels my sharp blade against his throat as he swallows.

I don't know what he's done, and I don't care. This has nothing to do with my personal mission. It's just another day at the office, but that doesn't mean I won't enjoy it. I need the escape killing provides to forget about Zoey, so I block him out as he begs for his life, wondering what she would think of me if she could see me now.

Annoyed that all thoughts come back to her, I slit his throat, giving him a quick death instead of the prolonged one I had planned, and watch the blood spurt on the pillowcases as he dies slowly, choking on his own blood. Even as he gasps his last breath, I still feel nothing. Cleaning my blade and any vestiges of my presence from the room, I leave the hotel, intending to race back to my house to blow off some steam. I thought the job would help keep my mind occupied, but it didn't. I can't forget her. She's firmly invading my brain, intent on becoming a permanent fixture inside it, and it's pissing me off.

Just as my feet touch the sidewalk, I freeze. Standing smugly just around the corner and leaning casually back against my car, is the reason for my madness. My obsession grins at me, her eyes wicked as she looks me over. She licks her lips, and I remember her on her knees and the feel of her wet, hot mouth greedily gripping my length as she sucked it.

"What are you doing here?" I snap before I prowl up to her, not stopping until we are nearly pressed together. Her head tilts back, and she appears totally unafraid despite what she knows I can do. That lack of fear is addictive in itself. Regardless of my plans, one thing is certain—I never want those stormy eyes of hers to fill with terror like everyone else's does.

Yet I know they will.

It's unavoidable.

"I stalked *you.*" She grins. "Turnabout is fair play, don't you think? Though I have to say I'm disappointed you didn't notice sooner. Slipping, are we?" she purrs, sliding her hand up my chest as she speaks. I step back to avoid her touch, burning where she did. I'm itching to grab her and bend her over the car so I can fuck some sense into her, since it's becoming fucking apparent nothing else will.

Instead, I curl my hands into fists, anger filling me at the fact that I didn't notice she was tailing me like she was so quick to point out. That's never happened before. No one has ever gotten the drop on me, not since the group home. I learned real fast that to survive in that house, I needed to watch my own back, yet this little girl did, and she clearly loves rubbing it in.

My eyes narrow as I glare at her and walk around the car, trying to escape her. "Go home."

"Nope." She pops the P like a brat as she leans into my car, grinning at me. "Not until I get what I came for."

My cock instantly hardens. "And what could a little girl like you want?" I challenge.

Her gaze falls to the bulge in my pants, making my whole body stiffen. She licks her lips, her heated stare telling me she can still taste me on them. Her gaze is slow to move away from my aching cock and back to my eyes.

"I can think of a couple of things," she taunts, "but I'm here on business. I want in."

I scoff as I lean my arms on the car and glare at her. Doesn't she know that even now she isn't safe with me? I could hop over this car and be on her before she could even move. She doesn't really know how much danger she is in right now.

"No," is my reply to her outrageous offer.

"I can help," she protests.

"No, you can't."

"Yes, I can," she fires back.

"No. Now get in before I lose my patience," I order.

Thankfully, she climbs into my car willingly, and I snarl as I reach over and buckle her up, ignoring the heat of her breasts pressing against my arm as she leans into me. Gunning it, I drive as fast as I can back to her dorm and idle outside, gripping the wheel hard and not even looking at her.

"Inside, now," I snarl, my words clipped. I'm on the verge of losing it, feeling suffocated by her scent, and my cock is so hard it hurts.

She sighs, and I think she's about to relent, but I should know better.

Zoey always gets the last word.

Leaning into me, she licks the shell of my ear, making me jerk as she giggles. The sound is too bright to be in my presence. "Have fun thinking about my mouth while you jerk off tonight. I know I'll be thinking about your cock while I fuck myself." With that, she slides from the car, and just like she wanted, I watch her go.

Her ass sways enticingly, and I barely resist following her inside. *Barely.*

Hanging by a thread, I speed away as fast as I can before I forget everything else and make her mine in every way possible. She doesn't know what she's asking, because once I have her, there's no going back. Every single inch of her is mine. There won't be a place left untouched, and she will be nothing but mine. Her every action will be controlled, and her life will be restricted because I'm a bastard who needs all her attention.

All her time and safety.

Can't she see I'm trying to save her from the devil inside me?

My girl is no angel though. No. She'd love nothing more than to be right there burning alongside me, daring me to leap into the flames with her.

Shaking my head, I force all thoughts of her away, and when I get home, I down half a bottle of Jack and open my laptop, decisively working through the notes I was making on the bastards who made me this way. If it wasn't for them, then maybe Zoey wouldn't be in danger every time she was with me.

Starting from the bottom up, I leave the cells tracking as I go to bed, but even when I sleep, there is no reprieve, no peace.

There never is.

"Tell me, boy." The guttural grunt makes my eyes close in both disgust and terror. If I don't, the punishment will be much worse than it is now. "Now," he orders, his voice sharp.

"I like it, thank you," I say, my tone flat and dead despite the burning emotions inside me. Usually, I ride away when this happens, escaping to my own head and dreaming of a better life, of what it will be like when I'm free of this place, but with him, I can't.

They call him Master. I never see his face, only feel his hands, his body, and hear his voice—a voice that haunts me. Unlike the general, he isn't cruel. No, he's almost... kind. He wants my pleasure, and I hate it. I can handle the pain, I can handle my body being tortured and used, but this?

I hate it more than anything else.

I hate his touch. I hate how it makes me react.

I hate it so much tears splash down my cheeks without thought as he works me, sliding his fist down my length and ordering me to tell him how much I want this.

How much I like this.

When he's done, the door slamming sometime later, I crawl to the toilet and throw up over and over again before scrubbing my body in the cold sink. I dash my tears away and wash away things I can't even begin to think about. Hanging my head into the sink, I let my scarred shoulders bend under the pressure.

The only reason I don't give up is because of her.

Zoey needs me.

Before, I would not give them the pleasure of seeing me break, but now the only reason I exist, the only reason I fight, is because of her.

The door opens again, and the night shift guard, Toma, grins at me. "You have another visitor."

"No, you promised!" I yell.

"I lied." He laughs, and I almost scream when the general steps into the room and grins smugly at me. The door slams shut behind him, taking my only haven, my only escape with it, and there is nothing I can do about it.

"Are you ready to scream for me, boy?" He grins, unbuckling his belt.

For a moment, I imagine taking it and strangling him, imagine going on a killing spree and murdering every single person who ever touched me or allowed me to be touched. I know if I ever make it out of here, that's exactly what I'll do.

I'll make them all pay.

Even if it's the last thing I do.

I'm exhausted the next day. I scrub myself for hours in the shower, but I don't feel clean no matter how hard I try. I never do. Instead, I go to the gym for hours, punishing my body, and when I head home, I feel relaxed enough to focus on work.

I even stopped myself from tracking Zoey.

When I get home, I plan to find my first man and take him down, but when I get there, I instantly know something is wrong. My system is disarmed, and I never even got an alert. Snarling, I pull my gun. Whatever idiot picked this home will regret it. I silently slip inside but stop when I see the intruder.

Zoey is sitting at the kitchen table with her feet propped up and a cup of tea in front of her. She's wearing one of my shirts, her bare legs making me snarl, but it's what she has in her hands that really has me on edge—the folder for my current job.

She grins up at me wickedly, making my heart slam. "I'm going to help you whether you want me to or not."

I stare, wondering how far in that folder she got and if it triggered her memory. I fucking hope not. I don't want her to remember me, because I'm not her hero like she always thought. I'm her demon, her devil, dragging her to hell, but her eyes are clear, and there's a dare written in them as she watches me, not recognition.

I relax slightly, putting my gun away as I glare at her. "No, you are not. Now get out before I call Alaric."

"You won't." She shrugs as she stands, my shirt hanging to mid-thigh. She looks so good in it my brain shorts-circuits until she moves before me, her tight nipples pressing against the shirt.

"Are you naked under there?" I ask, my voice hoarse.

"Would you like to find out?" she purrs, reaching down to lift the shirt, so I stumble away, pressing my back to the table to contain myself as she chuckles. She picks up the folder again and bends over the table, giving me a tantalizing view of her peachy bare ass.

Fuck!

"Like I said, I'm going to help you." She looks over her shoulder at me, her eyes sparkling. "You can't get close to these people, you look too old, but me? I can."

CHAPTER 9

Zoey

H e grabs the folder from me and turns away, refusing to look at me. "You don't know what you're talking about," he finally responds.

"Yes I do. It's a pedophile ring run out of foster care, right? It's pretty obvious, and you're going to kill them. There's only one catch. There is no way you can get close to these assholes. No offense, but you look to be exactly what you are, a killer. But me?" I flutter my lashes as he glances back at me and purposely pout my lips. "I'll be able to infiltrate that bitch no problem. I can be young and innocent. Would you like to see?" I can't resist flirting with him, loving his clenched jaw and flashing eyes.

"Get out." Each word is snarled. "And take my shirt off."

"Your shirt? Are you sure?" I ask, frowning.

"Now," he orders, his chest heaving in anger as he glares at me.

I shrug, playing dumb. "Okay." I reach for the hem and rip it over my head, hearing him swear as I drop it to the floor and stand naked before him. I want to tell him how it was almost too easy to get in here, how I lay in his bed and touched myself and stole his clothes just to

For a moment, we just stare at each other, his eyes momentarily refusing to drop to my body before he gives in. They slam shut as he scrubs at his face, grabbing the shirt on the floor and throwing it at me. "Put it on and get out." To my amusement, he practically runs away from his kitchen.

I just stare after him, grinning. I put the shirt on because it's warm and comfy, but I don't leave. I follow him upstairs to the sound of running water. I stop when I reach the bathroom in the middle of the hallway and let myself in.

"Need a hand with that?" I tease. His cock is hard as hell, bobbing under the spray. He ignores me and it, scrubbing at his body. I take my time drinking him all in, perving on him because, fuck, he's magnificent.

He's all hard lines and muscle. There isn't an inch of fat on him. He has an incredible deep six pack and V pointing at his huge cock. His thighs are the size of my body, cut with muscle, and his ass is round enough that I want to bite it. His shoulders are thick, and my fingers curl, wanting to grip them as he pounds into me.

Gray is a fucking masterpiece, scars and all—and he has a lot.

I guess I should expect it considering his line of work, but it doesn't stop me from wondering how he got each and every one. I wonder who Gray was before he became a hitman, not that it really matters since all I care about is who he is now and how I feel when I'm around him—free.

The need I have for adrenaline is addictive. He pushes my limits and makes me want more. He forces me to be myself—no facade, no games—and I fucking love it.

I feel alive around him.

My eyes trace as many of his scars as I can. They crisscross his back, almost looking like whip marks, deep and furrowed. There are smaller random scars dotted across his back, his chest, and even his thighs. There are more big ones, one practically on his pec near his heart, that look like bullet wounds.

He has tattoos intersecting some. The ink doesn't hide them, but highlights them, like he refuses to be ashamed of them, and I love that.

"Finished?" he snarls. "Got your fill and feel disgusted now?"

For a moment, I just stare at him before sense comes back to me. I pull his T-shirt over my head once more and climb into the shower with him, seeing the weakness in him that he would never show anyone else. Pressing my head to his back, I trace the scars. He's stiff against me before he shivers as I run my lips along them, kissing their raised edges. "You are magnificent, scars and all. They show what you survived. Too many people are untouched by this world, and they don't know what it means to face death, but these? They show you do." I kiss along his back, and his hands hit the wall, his body trembling, so I continue to kiss over his scars. I slide my hands to his chest, holding him to me, sensing this isn't a side he's comfortable with or used to showing anyone.

"Just like me. We've looked death in the eye, and we wear its scars." I pull back, and he turns, looking confused, so I turn and lift my hair, showing him the wicked scar at the base of my skull. I'm nervous and scared, but then his thick, scarred fingers run across the wound so delicately, my eyes close.

"How?" His voice is hoarse.

"I had a brain tumor. It almost killed me. I came so close, I can still almost taste the other side. I used to go to bed every night wondering if I would wake up in the morning, and every time I got sick, I wondered if it would be my last." I turn and meet his eyes. "You see now, Gray? You might be death personified, but that doesn't scare me. I told you that death and I are old friends. It feels like home to me, and I can't go back. I can't be the perfect little girl they all want me to be. How can I when I know exactly what the darkness feels like? When I feel more at home fighting to survive and living every moment like it's my last than I do in the sunlight?"

My hands hit his chest as I press myself against him. He blocks the spray, the water dripping across his face, and for a moment, he looks younger than he is. All that fury and coldness is stripped away until it's just Gray and me, our scars laid bare to each other.

"That's why I need to help. That's why I have to. I don't fear dying; I fear never being truly alive. I-I only feel alive around you."

"Little doe." He groans and reaches for me, gripping my hips as we just stare at each other. The warm water bathes us both as we fight an internal battle.

"Fuck it," he mutters.

I see him actually let go of whatever was holding him back and give into this feeling between us. I almost scream hallelujah. He lifts me with ease, and I wrap my legs around his waist as he slams his lips to mine. He kisses me hard and fast, biting my bottom lip until I gasp and clutch his shoulders to pull him closer.

Refusing to let him go, like he might fade away if I do, I drink down his desperation and the pained ecstasy that is Gray's brand of pleasure as he slams me into the shower wall. He pins me there as he sucks on my lip. "You drive me fucking crazy," he growls, biting my lip until it bleeds. I moan at the pain and roll my hips again, grinding against his hard cock.

"What are you going to do about it?" I taunt as I stare into his cold eyes.

"Show you exactly why you shouldn't play with fire," he retorts, kissing me hard once more before pulling me away from the wall. His gaze rises to the silver shower bar above us.

"Hold on and do not let go," he demands. "If you do, I'll stop touching you and never touch you again."

He means it, I see it in his eyes, so I grip the bar as he lifts me into the air, wraps my legs around his head, and buries his head between my thighs.

He's giving me exactly what I want.

Him.

This.

Us.

The first touch of his lips against my pussy has me crying out and clenching my thighs around his head hard enough to hurt, but he never complains. He grips my ass and tugs me closer. This is supposed to be a punishment to deter me, but fuck if it doesn't make me want more.

I want all of him. I want to feel his scars against my body and experience the brutal edge of violence that is Gray.

His lips seal on my clit and suck. The sudden shock of pleasure makes me scream. I use the bar to lift myself and roll against his face, riding it, fucking it, needing more. He doesn't tease, no; Gray goes straight for the kill.

He attacks my cunt like it's the enemy.

One hand leaves my ass, and then he slams two fingers into me, forcing me to accept them as he spreads them inside and starts to fuck me with them. All the while, his tongue lashes my clit before dipping inside alongside his expert fingers.

He fucks me hard with them, thrusting them like he would his cock. I cry out as I roll my hips, and pleasure explodes through me from the onslaught.

"Oh fuck!" I yell, dropping my head forward to meet his devilish eyes as he eats me.

He smirks against my clit, and it shouldn't be as hot as it is, nor should I come as hard as I do when he drags his teeth across my clit at the same time he curls his fingers inside me and strokes a spot that makes me scream.

My release slams through me so suddenly, I jolt and almost let go of the bar. My thighs lock up as my pussy clenches on his invading fingers. I ride the waves, and when they abate, I sag. He pulls his fingers free of my clinging cunt and kisses my clit before unwrapping my legs. I let go of the bar and drop to my feet, staring at him with a heaving chest.

I have never come that fast or that hard.

Watching me, he wraps his slick hand around his cock and strokes it before stopping. "Now I'll smell like your need all day." He turns away.

He actually turns away.

I stare at him as he gets out and ties a towel low on his hips. "What, one measly orgasm? You're not even going to fuck me?" I huff.

He looks back at me, his eyebrow raised. "Next time you'll behave, and then you'll come so many times you won't be able to walk."

"Promises." I throw my wet hair over my shoulder and storm after him. "If you won't take care of me, I will." I lean back into the sink, sliding my fingers between my thighs and pushing them inside my wet pussy as he watches.

"Zoey," he warns.

I moan loudly, rocking my hips to ride them, and his nostrils flare as he watches my fingers thrust in and out of my cunt. I widen my legs so he can see better.

With a curse, he grabs my hands and spins me, locking them behind my back as he bends me over the sink, the cold porcelain making me gasp. "You want to be filled, little doe?" he snarls.

"Yes," I demand, pushing back.

I expect his cock or his fingers, but what I don't expect is for him to grab the knife he must have stripped off when he got in the shower. As I watch, he flips it midair before pressing the hilt to my pussy.

This is so messed up, yet I couldn't stop myself if I tried. Not when he hoists my arms higher so it hurts and I'm off balance before wedging his leg between mine, keeping them wide for his assault. Running the hilt over my pussy, he coats it in my cream and leans down to bite my neck as he slams the hilt inside me.

I cry out, shifting forward from the force. It borders on too much, too painful, but he doesn't care as he pulls it out and slams it back inside of me like a cock. He fucks me with it as he releases my neck and watches me. I feel his eyes on my pussy, which is stretched around his weapon.

It makes me crazy, the cold sink a stark contrast against my over-heated skin. The ribbed handle hits a spot inside me that has me writhing in ecstasy.

"You like that, little doe? I think you love it. Look at your greedy cunt swallowing it down, desperate for my cock. You're willing to fuck anything to get me, isn't that right? Look how wet you are. Does it turn you on knowing that I killed someone with this knife a few hours ago and now it's impaled in your bratty little cunt?"

I whimper, unable to speak as he slams it into me in punishment.

"Answer me, Zoey."

"Yes! Yes, I like it. Fuck, it feels amazing." He won't shame me. I know he's trying to disgust me, to turn me away, but the joke's on him. I've never been so turned on, and I'm already on the verge of coming. "Jesus, I've never been so turned on." I push back, impaling myself on it as he stills. "Knowing you're watching, knowing you'll have to hold this knife after and think of me like this, wet and fucking it, every time you do?" I throw my hair over my shoulder, moaning loudly when he twists it inside me. Cruel, perfect man.

"You little brat."

"You love it," I taunt, but my words end on a cry when he slaps my clit.

"I fucking hate that I do," he snarls, speeding up his thrusts as I writhe and fight his grip. The pain of his hold and the pleasure of the object inside me makes me crazed. "But I can't stop. I need to see you come, and the next time I kill someone with it, I'll be so hard I'll have no choice but to fuck my own fist while I remember you like this."

He slaps my clit again, and I cry out his name.

"This was supposed to be a punishment. You were supposed to scream and run away, but look at you. You fucking loving it, you dirty little bitch. I bet if I pulled this knife out and slammed it into your ass while I fucked your dripping cunt with my cock, you'd come so hard you'd pass out."

"Oh fuck!" I shout. "Please, shit, please do that!"

Cursing my name, he slaps my clit in rapid succession, and it sends me over the edge once more. I scream as I come on his knife, clenching around the handle. My body trembles from the strength of my release, and my legs almost give out, but his hand keeps me upright.

He slowly thrusts the handle in and out, fucking me through it before pulling it free, and I can't help but whimper at the loss. He throws it in the sink next to me, making me jump.

Tightening his hold on my wrists, he leans into me as he lifts me to meet his cruel gaze in the mirror. "Now get dressed. I have work to do that doesn't involve your greedy cunt." He shoves me away and leaves me there.

My legs are jelly, and my pussy is sore, but I wear a smirk on my lips.

He thinks what he did will push me away, but if anything, I'm even more addicted to him now.

He's fucking perfect, and I always get what I want.

CHAPTER 10

Zoey

"I'm not sure I can do this," Cara mumbles nervously beside me, wringing her hands together as we walk up the street to my sister's place.

"You can and you will," I order a little too sternly, judging by the way she immediately flinches.

Shit.

I turn to face her and cover her perfectly manicured, fidgeting hands. We get a few curious stares from people passing us by, no doubt finding it peculiar to see a girl as small as I am holding hands with an Amazon like Cara in the middle of the sidewalk. A pervy guy lets out a snicker as he waltzes past, and I'm sure he's playing every girl-on-girl porno he's ever watched in his tiny little mind with Cara and me as the main attraction.

Any other day, I would call this stranger out, but I have bigger fish to fry, like getting my best friend to do something she's never done before—*lie.*

"Look at me, Cara," I cajole, rubbing her cold hands affectionately. "Don't stress out on me now. You're not exactly lying to Layla and Alaric, just omitting some facts."

She chews on the corner of her naturally plump lip, still looking like she might puke instead of going through with my plan.

The thing is, I need Cara.

I need her to be my alibi.

Gray might be adamant about not wanting me to help him bring down a pedophile ring, but I'll wear him down. He'll see that I can be an asset sooner or later. It's just a question of time. But for me to actually help, I have to make sure that my sister, and especially my father, are none the wiser about what Gray and I are up to. If Alaric gets wind of my plans, he'd lock me away someplace and chuck the key into the Hudson River.

Hence why I need Cara. She's as wholesome as apple pie. Never one to speak out of turn or get herself involved in anything shady, Cara is the very definition of a good girl, and I need a bit of that wholesome charm of hers to trick Layla and Alaric long enough for me to help out Gray.

"I'm pretty sure omitting and lying are the same thing, Zoey," she retorts anxiously, her soft, silky voice a stark contrast to my rough, quick-spoken one.

It takes Herculean effort for me not to roll my eyes.

"You sound like Gray," I mumble, feeling disheartened.

Her big blue eyes soften as she squeezes my hands. "You like him," she observes, making me pull my hands away from her.

"I like the challenge," I retort on a huff. "You know as well as I do that I don't do feelings. Just sex. And something tells me that sex with Gray will be life altering. So until he gives it up, I'll do everything in my power to get him into my bed. That's it, Cara. Don't go seeing things that aren't there."

Her forehead furrows, and her gaze falls to the pavement for a split second before it locks with mine again. I see something akin to hurt in her eyes. "Don't do that, Zoey. Don't lie to me. Not you, never you."

This time, I'm the one who starts fidgeting. "Fine," I blurt out, throwing my hands in the air. "I like him. He's the most interesting man I've ever met, and I can't stop thinking about him. Happy now?"

The coy smile on her lips seeps into my black heart, warming it from within.

That's Cara for you.

She has this way about her. She makes even the lousiest of people believe that there is some good inside them. I guess that's one of the reasons we've been best friends for so long. She accepts me for who I am and doesn't judge me for it when I've given her plenty of reasons for her to do so.

"Have you told him how you feel?" she asks, bringing me back to the conversation at hand.

"And scare Gray off? Not likely," I scoff. "He's skittish enough. That's why I need you to do me this solid, Cara. All I need is a little time. Please."

I know it's the please that gets her in the end.

Cara has always had difficulty saying the word no, especially to the people she loves.

"Okay, I'll do it," she finally agrees, looking more confident in her ability to pull this off.

"Thank you, babe! I'll owe you big time," I gush.

"I just want to see you happy, Zoey. That's a reward all in itself," she replies tenderheartedly. I still have no idea how a shark of a politician can be this soft, caring person's father.

I plant a fake smile on my face so my best friend doesn't see how her words just pierced right through my heart and left a big hole in the middle. Happiness isn't in the cards for me. I don't think it ever will be. Happiness is letting your guard down, and once you do, it can easily be ripped away from you.

I'll settle for adrenaline.

For the rush.

That's as close as I'll ever let happiness get to me.

These are the thoughts that play around in my head as Cara and I walk up the stairs to my childhood home. After one ring, my sister opens the door with little Sophie on her hip.

"Zoey! Cara! What a lovely surprise," she says excitedly. "You girls should have called to tell me you were dropping by, and I would have made something special for dinner."

"Auntie," Sophie shrieks, stretching her arms out for me to grab her.

"Hey, little munchkin," I coo, taking her off her mother's hip and onto mine. I rub the tip of my nose with hers and kiss her forehead before I gaze over at my sister. "Is Alaric home?"

"He's in the living room playing with Gage," she answers cheerfully, but I can hear the suspicion in her tone. "He'll be so thrilled to see you since he missed Sunday dinner. Come in, come in."

Not wanting to explain why Cara and I are here yet, I tilt my head to my best friend for her to follow me inside. Layla shows us to the living room, and just as she reported, we see my father on his hands and knees, playing Legos with my nephew.

I can't help the smile that bursts forth from the sight before me.

To everyone who comes into contact with him, my dad is the epitome of mean, brooding alpha, but seeing him with his family shows just how untrue that definition is. He's one big teddy bear when it comes to my sister and his kids. A softy if I ever saw one.

He was like that with me as well for the longest time—until I grew breasts and had boys sniffing around me, that is.

That's when my father started laying down the law, and he hasn't let up once.

He's still so wrapped up in building a fort for Gage that he doesn't realize he has company.

"Look who's come to pay us a visit," my sister announces, bringing his attention to us.

The twinkle in his eye and the wide smile he gives me has me racked with guilt, but I push it away and offer him a smile of my own.

"Hey, Dad," I call, genuinely happy to see him.

"Don't 'hey, Dad,' me, kiddo. Where's my hug?" he teases, getting up from his knees and strutting toward me.

I place Sophie on the floor so he can wrap his huge arms around me, making me feel even tinier than I already am, but I don't mind it so much. Sometimes his hugs are the only things that soothe my wayward heart.

"Sorry I wasn't here for family dinner the other day. Missed you, kid."

"Missed you too, Dad," I reply, meaning every word.

Even though Alaric's overprotectiveness can sometimes be stifling, it doesn't make me love him any less. To me, my dad will always be our guardian angel, the man who saved my sister from certain death and then, later on, saved me from the grim reaper's cold hands too. Sure, he manipulated Layla into marrying him beforehand, but I guess love makes you do some crazy shit.

Not that I would know.

You're about to lie to your entire family just so you can help Gray. Sounds like pretty crazy love shit to me.

I bite my inner cheek, pushing that thought as far away from my head as possible, not wanting to give it room to grow—especially with my dad still hugging me.

I pull away from his embrace and walk over to Gage to give him a kiss. He doesn't register my existence, though, since he's too preoccupied with keeping his Legos away from his twin. There is a twinge of sadness that instantly claws into my heart, remembering how his namesake used to keep his toys away from me too—not that my brother had many to keep from me.

The last memory I have of him creeps up on me. He didn't want me to use a plastic bag my mom got him for his birthday as my own personal barf bag. My melancholic expression must give me away, because before I know it, Layla is ushering us to the kitchen, leaving little Sophie and Gage to play by themselves.

"Do you girls want a drink?" she asks, opening the refrigerator door.

"Water will be fine," Cara says sweetly.

"Beer if you have one," I answer.

"Not happening," my father interjects. "Turn twenty-one first, then you can have a beer under my roof."

"You do know I've drunk beer before, don't you?" I tease, nudging my shoulder with his.

"If I didn't see it, it never happened," he deadpans.

"Good to know," I mutter under my breath. "Water is fine."

Layla hands both Cara and me a bottle of water as we sit on stools at the kitchen island. When I see my best friend start playing nervously with the cap, I realize I don't have much time before she flakes on me.

"So this isn't a social call," I start, to which my father instantly chuckles.

"Didn't think it was. You have mischief written all over your face."

Shit.

I didn't think I was that easy to read.

"Go on then. What have you done now?" he prompts before pulling Layla to sit on his lap.

The man can't go two seconds without putting his hands on my sister. It's sweet, even if it is a little nauseating at times. I mean, for all intents and purposes, he is my dad, and just imagining him and my sister getting it on is all sorts of gross, but I'm sure all kids feel that way about their parents.

"I haven't done anything." I huff. "But thanks for the vote of confidence."

"You haven't done anything *yet*. Emphasis on the yet. So spill it," Alaric states knowingly.

"Whatever." I roll my eyes at him. "As I was saying before I was so rudely interrupted, you know how spring break is next week—"

"Yes, and we agreed you were going to spend it with us," he chimes in.

"Can I please get two sentences in before you interrupt me again?" I huff in irritation.

He opens his mouth to protest, but luckily Layla comes to my rescue and covers his lips with hers to shut him up. Once she's certain her husband is good and subdued, she breaks the kiss.

"Be good, husband," she teases him and then whispers something in his ear that has his eyes smoldering.

Like I said, it would be cute if their PDA wasn't so gross.

"Fine. Lay it on me, kid."

"Thank you," I reply. "So as I was saying, I know I promised I'd come home for spring break next week, but Cara invited me to spend it with her at the Hamptons. Her family is going to spend it there, and you guys know how boresome they are. Cara needs me there with her for moral support. It's only a couple of weeks. I'll call you every day if that makes it easier for you."

My dad ponders my request before he sets his gaze on my best friend.

"Is this true?" he asks outright, needing to hear it from the horse's mouth.

"It would be nice to have Zoey with me. My parents are having a party this weekend, and I don't do parties so well. If Zoey is with me, then it might be more bearable to attend."

Technically, it's not a lie.

She would prefer if I was with her up at the Hamptons, and maybe me not going makes me the shittiest best friend ever. I'll make it up to her somehow.

"I don't see why Zoey can't go," Layla chimes in, giving her two cents.

Alaric isn't as easy to convince though. "I don't know," he mumbles, eyeing me and Cara with suspicion.

"What kind of trouble can the girls get into at the Hamptons?" Layla adds.

"If you're asking me that, then you don't know your sister. Zoey can get into a lot of trouble."

"But I'm not going to," I lie. "Come on, Dad. It's only two weeks. Cara needs me. It's not like I've never been there before."

"For a weekend, fine. Two weeks is a long time," he argues worriedly.

"She said she'd call every day, and if she does get into trouble, she's just a car ride away. Let her go, husband. Let her be there for her friend," my sister says, running her fingers lovingly across his stubbled chin.

I remain silent, watching his hard demeanor chip away under my sister's loving gaze. When he finally relents and nods, I do cartwheels inside my head.

"Fine," he concedes but points a menacing finger at me. "But you FaceTime us every day, and if I so much as catch a whiff of a boy there with you, then I'm driving up to Cara's mansion and bringing your ass back home. Got it?"

"No boys. Got it," I reply.

"You women are going to be the death of me," he mumbles, sounding defeated.

Layla claps, satisfied that she was able to get her husband in line, and jumps out of his lap. "Now that that's settled, how about you go check up on our babies while the girls and I make something for dinner."

Alaric reluctantly gets up from his seat and does as he's told, removing himself from the kitchen in search of the twins who are playing in the living room. Layla never takes her eyes off him as he leaves, but the minute she's sure he's not within hearing distance, she turns around to face Cara and me, her easy-going expression nowhere on her face.

"I don't know what you girls are up to, and something tells me that it's best I don't," she explains strictly, "but you have to promise me that whatever you're up to, you'll be safe. If you can't promise me that, then I'll strut right back into that room and tell Alaric that you're not going anywhere. Am I making myself clear?"

"Crystal," I reply.

"Good. So you'll be safe? You're not going to go skydiving or drag racing or some nonsense like that?" she demands. Sometimes I forget how protective she is since Alaric is worse.

"Nope. Nothing remotely that dangerous. Right, Cara?" I demand.

My best friend just nods, because what else can she say? It's not like I gave her an itinerary of my plans for the next two weeks.

"Cara, I love you, but you have a terrible poker face." My sister sighs, her shoulders slumping.

"I'm sorry," Cara murmurs.

"Don't be. You were able to convince my husband that my sister won't be doing God knows what for the next couple of weeks, so that's enough. And as for you, Zoey," she continues, pinning me with her sternest stare. "If you get into any trouble, of any kind, I want you to call me ASAP. Is that understood?"

I nod.

"Good." She walks over to me and places her hands on my shoulders. "Whatever you're up to that caused you to lie to me and Alaric, I hope it's worth it."

"He is," I say, the truth spilling from my lips before I have time to catch it.

"He?" She arches her brow.

I press my lips together, not wanting to say anything else since my big mouth did a pretty good job of giving me away already.

"And by he, are we talking about someone with devastating silver eyes who Alaric not so affectionately calls Ghost?" my sister asks.

My eyes widen in shock, and my throat instantly dries at my sister's perceptiveness.

How does she know?

Gray was only at the house once, and then my father ordered him to stay away if he knew what was good for him. How the hell did my sister immediately think of him of all people?

"You think I don't know what it means when a woman looks at a man the way you looked at Gray when he was here?" She giggles, finding my sudden speechlessness funny. She cups my chin in her hand and smiles tenderly. "Ah, sweet girl. The one time I looked at a man the way you looked at Gray, I married him."

"That's not what this is," I reply, struggling to defend myself.

"Are you sure?"

"I don't know what it is," I answer truthfully. "But I need time to find out."

"Well, you've got it. Two weeks, to be precise. I suggest you get to it then."

I intend to.

S taring at the clock in my kitchen, I count down the seconds until it strikes midnight. Pissed, I rise from my chair, grab the extra plate of food off the table, and scrape its contents in the bin, all the while hating myself for instinctively making more dinner tonight in the hopes that Zoey would drop by and be hungry. I tell myself it's a good thing that she didn't, especially with how we left things the last time she was here.

I fucked her good and hard with my knife, praying that it would scare her enough not to want anything to do with me, but instead she came like a goddamn Fourth of July firework show, lighting up my gray life with so much color I thought I would go blind.

The girl is trouble with a capital T, and even more so now that she got the ludicrous idea that she could help me with my plans into that thick head of hers.

Shit.

Out of all the stuff in my house, why did she have to find that particular folder?

I blame either my rotten luck or my bad fucking karma for being responsible for that fiasco. Thankfully, I could tell that Zoey didn't have the foggiest recollection of the group home mentioned in the files.

I would be able to tell if she had. It was just another job for her. In her mind, she probably thinks this is a contract, one I will be paid handsomely for performing. Little does she know, I'm doing this pro bono, since I'm the interested party wanting to see all those monsters lying in a ditch somewhere. That was my stipulation to the agency when they recruited me. I'd happily kill whatever motherfucker they told me to, and in exchange, I would use their resources to seek vengeance for what that house did to me. The minute the agency gave me the green light and ensured that they would turn a blind eye to my thirst for revenge, I willingly signed whatever was left of my soul over to them.

My plans were as good as gold until she came back into my life. Now everything is all screwed up.

Feeling uncharacteristically sorry for myself, I turn off the lights and head to my bedroom, officially calling it a night. When I'm walking down the hall, I hear a soft knock on my front door. I turn around and head over to it in a hurry, knowing exactly who I'll find on my doorstep.

Excitement pounds through me even as I tell myself it's annoyance.

When I open the door and see her there, something inside me settles. The way Zoey's mischievous smile splits her face in half has me fisting my hands just so I don't reach out and grab her, hoist her over my shoulder, and drag her into my bedroom.

"It's late," I state evenly, not daring to say what's really on my mind.

"Aren't you going to invite me in?" She wiggles her brows suggestively.

"No," I retort, my nails now drawing blood from my palms.

"Too bad." She shrugs. "You look like you need a good fuck to unwind, and as luck would have it, I think I'd be perfect to make that happen."

I have no doubt about that. If she fucked me the same way she fucked my dagger's handle, I'd be a lucky man.

"Go home," I growl, grabbing the door to slam it in her face before I break down and fuck her right here on my doorstep where the world could see.

"Not so fast," she replies, placing her hands on my door to keep it open. "We need to talk."

"There's nothing for us to talk about," I spit, taking my anger out on her. How dare she just waltz into my life and my house like she owns it?

Like she owns me?

"Oh, but there is," she coos, running a finger down my torso, making my skin underneath my shirt burn with desire.

"I don't talk with little girls."

"You only fuck them with your knife, huh?" she taunts brazenly. The sound of my teeth grinding is so loud that the little devil has the audacity to giggle at me. "Oh, don't get your panties in a twist, Gray. We have plenty of time for that later. I just came over to give you the good news."

"Good news?" My forehead crinkles distrustfully. "What kind of good news?"

"The kind where I have an alibi for the next couple of weeks to do whatever I want. My dad thinks I'll be up at the Hamptons for spring break, which leaves us with exactly two weeks to get the job done. And by job, I mean me infiltrating that group home and bringing down all those fucking sickos who get their rocks off with little kids."

I push the door back so hard it hits the wall as I take one large step toward her, erasing the gap between us. Her only option is to crane her neck back if she wants to look me in the face.

"You must be hard of hearing. I told you that I don't need your help," I growl, showing her all my teeth.

"And I say you do," she retorts with total conviction, not the least bit afraid, but she should be. If she knew all the sick, twisted things I wanted to do to her, she would run screaming... or would she? "I'm the best chance you have. You want in, and to do that, you need someone on the inside to help you. Who better to do that than a new foster kid in need of a home?"

I grip her chin so forcefully, I'm sure she'll have my fingerprints permanently carved into her skin by morning.

"No one will believe you're a kid."

"Oh? Then why do you keep reminding me that I'm just a little girl every chance you get?" she fires back, eyes twinkling with excitement.

I let go of her chin and take a huge step back.

"It's not you I'm reminding," I grumble, running my fingers through my hair in exasperation.

Instead of taking my confession to heart and leaving me be, she preens like she just won the Powerball.

"Is that where you've been? At your sister's?" I ask, trying to move the conversation to safer territory.

"You tell me. You're the one who put a tracking app on my phone."

I don't say anything in return, because the truth of the matter is that I have been trying not to seek her out all day, and that included not knowing her whereabouts.

"Whatever." Zoey shrugs when she sees that I'm not going to say anything else. "I'll be here first thing in the morning to get to work."

I stand rooted to my spot as she takes two small steps in my direction, goes to her tiptoes, and plants a chaste kiss on my lips. It takes everything in me not to wrap my arms around her waist and kiss her like she deserves to be kissed.

"I'll be here bright and early. Hope you're ready for me," she threatens before turning on her heel and skipping down the steps like she doesn't have a care in the world.

My eyes never leave her as she gets into her car and says something to someone who is sitting in the passenger seat. I lower to look inside and realize that she came with a friend tonight. A raven-haired girl is anxiously biting her nails at whatever Zoey just said to her. I stand rooted to my spot as I watch both girls drive off, hopefully back to their respective dorm rooms.

"Hope you're ready for me," she said.

I don't think there is a man alive who is, let alone me.

Even when she was just a kid, my heart was never ready for her, but then she coaxed out a protective streak in me I never assumed I could have. And now? Now she brings out the ravenous animal in me, desperate to sink its fangs into her porcelain skin and mark her as mine forever.

Fuck.

I slam the door and head to my bedroom, knowing that for the next few hours, all I'll do is beat my cock into submission with fantasies of the brat who is slowly making me lose all sanity.

Not that I had much of it in the first place.

I'm still in bed the next morning when Zoey knocks on my door. I let her pound on it for a good five minutes, praying that she will just get the hint and not come back, but when she doesn't and starts kicking my door, I get up, knowing that if I don't answer it, she'll knock it down one hard kick at a time.

Relentless.

That's what Zoey Holmes is.

Fucking relentless.

I'd consider it to be one of her better qualities if it didn't grate on my nerves so much. It's plain to see that when Zoey wants something, she would go to the ends of the Earth to get it, and it's just my luck that I am at the top of her wish list.

I'm about to tell her to get lost and truly scare her away this time, but all logic evaporates from my mind the minute I open the door.

"What the fuck did you do?" My mouth is agape as I stare at the girl who has clawed her way into the depths of my tattered soul without permission.

"You like?" She flips her now short hair and waltzes right by me, making herself at home.

I'm still too stunned to give her a reply.

All I do is stare at the hack job she did on her long, beautiful blonde hair, the plaid shirt she's wearing that looks like it was found in a dumpster with how many dirty stains and holes it has, the too large, worn-out jeans, and scruffy sneakers.

All I do is stare, because sitting on my couch is a very familiar version of Zoey that must have manifested from my memories of her— a ghetto kid through and through.

"I did good, huh?" she announces, sounding far too pleased with herself for my liking.

"Good isn't the word I'd use," I finally say, sitting opposite of this haunting mirage.

Her triumphant smile dwindles into a concerned frown. "Hey," she murmurs, getting up from her seat and kneeling before me, placing her tiny hands on my knees. "Are you okay? You look like you just saw a ghost."

Yeah, and I'm still looking at it.

I clasp her face in my palms, tilting her head back so she can look at me.

My Zoey is still there.

In her green eyes, I see the woman I've been fantasizing about for over a year now.

But seeing her dressed like this, like the little girl I tried so hard to protect back in the day, almost makes me feel as if I'm right back in that house, facing my worst nightmares all over again. The two versions of Zoey have somehow collided in my head, and I'm not sure how I feel about that.

This is so fucked up.

"Hey, hey," she says, scrambling up to sit on my lap. "It's me. It's just me."

"Little doe," I choke out, pressing my temple to hers and holding her a bit too tightly.

Zoey doesn't protest, letting me hold her close just so I can smell her scent long enough to remind me that I'm not that scared little boy anymore. No one can hurt me like that again, and I'm not powerless to protect her against the monsters that roam the Earth. I'm a grown man whose kill count is so high that there was no use in keeping count anymore.

I also remind myself that she's safe, but now she wants to go back into the lion's den.

For me.

"I can't let you do this," I finally utter, my voice shaking.

Ever so gently, she pulls my chin up and kisses me softly, lovingly, earnestly—everything we're not.

"Look at me, Gray," she orders, and like a fool who can't deny her, I do just that. "I'll be fine. You'll be there with me all the way. Nothing will happen to me. I promise. I can handle myself."

I start to shake my head, but she keeps me from moving an inch.

"Answer me this," she murmurs patiently. "Will you let anyone hurt me?"

"I'd kill every last motherfucker who tried," I sneer on a loud growl.

"Then that's good enough for me. It should be good enough for you too. This isn't about us, Gray. This is about saving innocent kids who can't defend themselves. If we don't do something about this now, then we will regret it forever. After I read that file, there was no way I would let you do this on your own. I need to do this too. For those kids."

"I'm not doing this for them," I mutter, but it ends like a question.

"Then who are you doing it for? And don't tell me it's because of the money, or I'm going to lose a lot of respect for you," she presses softly.

I'm doing it for us. For you and me.

For the two kids we were and the ones we could have become if it wasn't for that place.

"Gray?"

Instead of answering her, I push her off my lap and get up.

"Where are you going?" she calls from behind me.

"I need a drink."

"It's eight in the morning," she accuses, never leaving my side.

"Still need one."

Thankfully, she doesn't say anything else when I grab the whiskey bottle from my kitchen counter and take a good long drink of it. She lets me take a few more swigs in silence before opening that beautiful mouth of hers.

"Can you tell me why you're acting this way? It's so unlike you."

"And you're such an expert on me? Is that what you're saying?" I scoff between gulps.

"I know enough. I know all I need to."

"You know nothing, Zoey," I snarl.

She giggles in response.

"What's so funny?" I bark out, feeling the effect of the alcohol on an empty stomach seep through my veins.

"Nothing. You just sounded like you were an extra on *Game of Thrones* for a second there." She chuckles as she hops up on the counter and swings her legs back and forth.

"What's that?"

"You don't know what *Game of Thrones* is?" she replies, shocked.

"Should I?"

"It was only one of the best TV shows in history a few years back until they fucked up the ending," she exclaims, holding her hand to her heart like she's genuinely concerned.

"I must have missed it when I was keeping this country safe from terrorists," I snarl.

"Right." She kicks the air at her feet. "Dad told me you had been deployed in Afghanistan before you took a job with the agency."

"Amongst other places. Never thought I'd ever say this, but your father talks too much."

Zoey laughs. "Alaric is the last person I'd ever think someone would call a gossip. And besides, he didn't tell me you were in the Army; he told my sister. I just couldn't help but eavesdrop when he did."

"Wrong place, wrong time, huh?"

"More like right place, right time." She beams, breaking through my barriers with her light.

"What the fuck am I going to do with you?" I shake my head.

"Whatever you like," she teases. "I think I've made that obvious to you by now."

"Too obvious," I growl, stepping up next to her and placing my hands on her slender hips. "Your father would put a bullet through my brain if he knew you were here, but he'd torture the fuck out of me if he knew I was actually considering putting you in harm's way. Here lies the rub, little doe. I'd fucking let him. If anything happens to you, I'll never forgive myself."

Zoey places her palms on my chest and bats those gorgeous emerald eyes at me.

"But you won't let anything bad happen to me, so that's a moot point. Trust me. I've got this."

I think long and hard on her proposal to be my eyes on the inside. It would make things a whole lot easier having an inside man or, in her case, an inside brat.

"Do you always get your way?" I ask once I've made up my mind.

"Always." She giggles.

"Fuck my life," I mumble before pulling away from our embrace to pick up my phone. "Step back for me, little doe. I need to take a picture of you."

"Is it for your spank bank or just something to remember me by?"

"Enough of that. If you want to be in the game, you need to be thinking with your head and not your…"

"Hooha?" she finishes, pointing to her greedy cunt to bring the point home. All it takes is another growl to have her laughing her head off. "Okay, I get it. I get it. No more playing around. But only if you promise me one thing."

"What's that?" I mumble.

"That one night you'll ask me over here so we can just Netflix and chill."

"I have no idea what that means," I reply, feeling confused.

"Oh, my sweet wolf, there is so much I still have to teach you." She smirks with a twinkle in her eyes.

Trying not to think of all the things *I* could teach her, I step back and take a picture, immediately forwarding it to Hale. Not two seconds pass before he starts blowing up my phone.

"Good. You're up," I snarl, turning my back on Zoey and that cocky smile of hers before they both get fucked.

"Who says I've been to bed yet?" Hale replies with amusement. "But my bedtime is beside the point right now. I'm more interested in knowing what the hell I'm looking at," he adds, referring to the picture I just sent him. "Any reason why you sent me a pic of Alaric's kid in hand-me-downs?"

"I need you to work your magic and make up a background for her that is bullet proof if anyone goes sniffing."

The line goes silent for an excruciatingly long pause.

"You still with me?" I ask after I've had enough of his silent treatment.

"I'm still thinking," he retorts, no longer sounding like his aloof self.

"Well, think faster. If you're not up for the job, then I'll find someone who is," I warn, meaning it.

He chuckles. "Good luck finding anyone who is willing to go against Alaric and put his baby girl in danger. You know he'll have your balls if he finds out what you plan to do, right?"

Alaric will have my balls one way or the other. There's no changing that. Sooner or later, I'll break and give Zoey what she wants, which means I'm a dead man no matter what I do next.

"Clock is ticking, Hale. Are you in or out?"

"I'm in, motherfucker. It's your funeral, not mine." He sounds nothing but gleeful about that.

Sometimes it's easy to forget that Hale is one fucked-up, scary bastard since he usually acts normal, but occasionally he slips up and gives his true bloodthirsty nature away.

"We all have to go one day," I reply, not caring if Hale would actually enjoy seeing Alaric and me duke it out. "Just have it done by the end of the day." With that order, I hang up and turn to face the cause of my impending demise.

Either Alaric will kill me or her fucking smile will.

I'm fucked either way.

CHAPTER 12

Gray

H ale comes through within an hour, driving over to my place, ready to get this show on the road, the cocky bastard, making it impossible for me to put this off any longer. Not that I want to. Not after a buyer came by the home late last night and set off my cameras.

Thankfully, I managed to sneak them in last week when I disguised myself as a repair man with the sole purpose of planting them. However, the group home's electrical system is so old that I worry my little devices might croak at any given time, which means I have to work faster.

Not that seeing all the skinny, dirty, empty-eyed kids wasn't incentive enough to get the job done ASAP. Seeing all those blank expressions made me so angry, I wanted to go on a killing spree right there and then. I look just like they do, and I remember perfectly well what happened to cause the emptiness in my gaze—the exact same horrid things that are most likely happening to them on a daily basis.

I cup Zoey's face, uncaring that Hale is lounging in a car that is definitely not his since it's a beat-up old Honda, and force her eyes to mine. "Listen to me, and listen to me good, little doe," I warn, and for once, she doesn't give me any lip. Good. I need her to listen, to understand. There's this anxiety, this fear in me that is so strong, I actually have to swallow it back to stop myself from throwing her over my shoulder and locking her in my house where no darkness will ever touch her again.

But it already has, and I can't protect her from that anymore.

"Keep quiet and keep your head down. Don't draw attention to yourself, and if you become worried at any point, you get the fuck out of there or signal a camera, which I managed to put in every room."

"Even the bathroom? You sick boy," she teases, but I snarl at the reminder of the one place in the world that was my happy place.

It's clear she doesn't remember. Will going there jog her memory? I hope not, but even if it does, it's too late to back out now.

"I mean it, Zoey, please." It's the growled plea that makes her sigh and lean into my touch.

"It's going to be okay, Gray. I can handle myself. Besides, I've never felt unsafe when you are around. You have my back, and I have yours." She kisses me.

It starts off slow, but I yank her hacked off hair back and take over, kissing her hard and fast, swallowing her moans.

I feel the need to consume her and leave my mark on her so no one else will ever touch what is mine, so I deepen the kiss until the only oxygen that fills her lungs comes from mine.

"Come on, lovebirds, we are losing daylight, and I have things to do in the dark," Hale calls, breaking us apart at a good time since I was debating fucking her right here to remind her to listen to me.

She turns and flips him off, winking back at me. "Your friend is hot but super annoying, you know that?"

"Not my fucking friend," I snap and lean in to bite her lip until she gasps. "Call him hot or look at him again, and his brains will be on my sidewalk in ten seconds flat. Do not make me kill him since he's your ride."

The little giggle she lets out only makes my cock harder than it already is from just one kiss.

"Hey, what can I say? I prefer cold, scary, and emotionally scarred to a pretty face any day." She turns away, whistling as she heads to the front seat of Hale's stolen car. Blowing out a breath, I slam her door for her and lean in, placing my hand on the roof as I focus on Hale.

"I'll follow you there in the van. Keep her safe," I order, letting him see the warning in my eyes. If anything happens to her, I'm blaming him and coming for a pound of flesh in retribution.

"You've got it," he replies, sounding serious for once, and then he grins at Zoey. "You like rock music?"

"Love it." She turns up the nob, and I groan as they start to sing along together to some mainstream rock ballad bullshit.

Never put two crazies in a car. I should know better.

Not wanting to hear the off-key karaoke routine longer than I need to, I head over to my van, pulling my ball cap on and tugging it down to hide my face as I climb behind the wheel. This will be my home for the next couple of weeks since it's where I'll set up surveillance to watch over Zoey, not wanting to be too far from her in case she needs me.

I follow them through the city, having to honk a few times to remind Hale to slow down since he's speeding with the only person in this world I give a fuck about. When we finally get there, I park around the corner, making sure the van is out of sight, and climb into the back before turning on the computer and watching all the monitors come to life.

Thirty cameras cover every inch of the house. There is not one fucking blind spot except for the buyers' rooms, which I couldn't get into without a key. If she goes in there, all bets are off anyway. Leaning back in the chair, I watch as Hale holds the door for her and grabs her ragtag bag we put together to make it real. Whistling, he walks her to the door that opens to hell.

It's a place I wouldn't even voluntarily walk back into, yet this girl is, so bravely, for me.

My heart is in my throat as I track her through corridors and watch Hale hand over her information, pretending to be her social worker, before casually walking back out once he's done delivering my heart into the pits of hell. He gets back in his car and drives off, but my eyes are on her as she's shown to a room with the other older girls. We aged

K.A KNIGHT & IVY FOX

her at seventeen to be safe. Zoey might look young, but anything younger would be a stretch and might raise some alarm bells. This way, they'll think child services is just leaving her here until she ages out, with no real concern of finding Zoey adoptive or foster parents to take her in until she does. It's the type of shit that happens often enough that no one will look into her backstory too much, and if they do, Hale has it covered.

When the back door jerks open, I point my gun reflexively before relaxing when Hale climbs in with a laugh. "Down, dog," he teases. Flipping him off, I look back at the cameras, not even blinking as I watch her sprawl out on the tiny bunk bed and close her eyes. She's not afraid, unlike me.

"You like her," Hale teases. I ignore him, but he carries on. "You more than like her. I've never seen you give a shit about anyone but yourself. But you kissed her, you let her in your house, and now you're watching her like you're debating on dragging her out and blowing the mission—something you never do. Tell me, Ghost, does Al know you're fucking his daughter?"

"Keep running that mouth, pretty boy, and I'll kill you right now," I snarl, still looking at the monitor as she sits up and greets the other kids there. Most of them are angry or withdrawn—I know that feeling. Even if they weren't in that place, being a foster kid is hard enough.

With nobody to care if you eat or if you're okay, planning for your future is lonely and makes you bitter.

"Hey, man, she's going to be okay. Al trained her; you know that. She's probably stronger than most hitters in this world."

"Not strong enough for in there," I mutter.

"What is it about this mission that has you rattled? Is it just her, or is it your past with the place?"

Slowly, I take my eyes off the monitors and meet his gaze, letting him see the cold death there. "I warned you once and I will warn you again, do not ever look into my past. That is my secret to bear, not yours."

Hale holds his hands up, but his eyes are serious as he watches me. "I'm here for you, brother. That's all I'm saying. Whatever that place is

doing to you, work it out before that sweet little thing pays the price."
He climbs from the van and disappears just like he came.

Ignoring his words, I continue to watch Zoey.

I won't sleep or eat, not while she is in there.

Not while she's so far away from me, facing the place that even ghosts are afraid of.

I t's surprisingly boring being undercover.

    I lounge in my room, listening in to the others' conversations. I catch a few names, but I won't be staying here long enough to be friends with any of them, and part of me doesn't really want to get too close because I know what is happening here, what is happening to them, and I can't save them yet.

I close my eyes and pretend to be napping, supposedly exhausted from Hale dragging me here from the streets after I ran away from another foster home. They talk freely around me, not the least bit worried since they think I'm another teenager.

They think I am one of them with my beaten-up bag and dirty clothes, and once, I could have been. If not for Layla... In fact, I wonder if the home child services placed us in before we went to Aunt Lucy's was like this too. I find myself frowning as I try to remember, but then one of the conversations catches my attention, and I zone in.

"She's in the hospital. I guess whoever had her last night got too carried away." I stiffen at that, wondering if they mean what I think they mean. My hands clench into fists as I listen to their hushed whis-

"They always do, especially that new one. He's..." She trails off, her voice laced with fear.

"Evil," another girl finishes.

Motherfucker.

This is personal now. Whoever hurt these girls, whoever scared them so badly that their voices tremble in recollection, needs to pay, and I know just the killer to make it happen. I crack open my eyes and yawn as I sit up, and they stop talking, eyeing me worriedly.

One even stares at me with pity, as if knowing what is in store for me.

There are twelve old metal bunks in here, all occupied with trunks at the bottom and metal lockers along the back wall. The floor is an old, scarred wood that creaks as I swing my legs up and put my booted feet on it. There's one arched window at the end of the row of beds, but it's dirty and not letting in much light. I noticed the door had a lock on the outside, but other than that, that's all there is.

"When do we eat around here?" I grumble as I stretch.

They share a look before the more talkative one, a girl with mousy brown hair but hard eyes, replies, "In an hour, but don't get your hopes up. It's nasty." She cringes, the ring in her lip moving with the movement. The blonde girl who looks like a pixie next to her nods before averting her eyes. The third, a pink-haired rocker girl with dead eyes, watches me, and I arch an eyebrow, making her look away.

"Cool, then I'm gonna go explore." I root through my bag and pull out the fake pack of smokes and lighter, and with a grin, I bounce from the room, ignoring their hushed, hurried whispers. Once I'm out in the creaking corridor, I pull the earpiece from the pack and shove it in, pulling my hair over it and putting the pack in my pocket.

"Are you secretly hoping I'll go to the showers next so you can jerk off while you watch me?" I murmur to Gray, and there's a relieved sort of breath through the mic.

"Focus, don't let them see you talking out loud," he mutters, but there is a reluctant thread of amusement in his tone.

"Yes, boss." I salute a camera as I head to the winding, wooden grand staircase.

There are more dorms down here for the men and younger kids, but there's also a staircase that leads up, and I haven't seen anyone climb it yet, which makes me wonder where it leads. Not wanting to be caught on my first day, I flounce around downstairs, wandering through the industrial-sized kitchen, laundry room, and lounge with one shitty TV and five ratty mismatched sofas and some chairs. That's all there is, other than a downstairs office, which is locked. There is a certain kind of comfort that comes in knowing that Gray is tracking my every move as I case the joint.

"I couldn't get in there last time. It would have raised too much suspicion, but that's where whoever runs this place works."

"And where the information we probably need is," I murmur, pretending to look at a notice board.

"Don't," he snaps.

"Don't what?" I grin.

"Don't do what you are thinking about doing." He groans.

"I have no idea what you are talking about." I turn when I hear voices, watching a big girl barrel toward me. Her eyes are locked on another girl who looks like she's been crying as she drags her by the hair.

Bingo.

Slipping my hand into my pocket, I extract one of the bugs Hale gave me from the packet and fist it in one hand while I step into her path. She slides to a stop, letting the young girl go as she focuses on me.

"Move, newbie. You don't want to make an enemy out of me on your first day."

"Maybe I do, and maybe you should pick on someone your own size." I ignore the crowd gathering and grin at her as she narrows her eyes.

"Zoey, stop now," Gray orders, but I ignore him.

"Unless you're afraid?" I taunt her, needing this to be done quickly before he pulls me out of here for not listening to him like he warned.

With a yell, she throws herself at me, her movements uncoordinated but powerful. I sidestep her clumsy attempt and swing my arm up, hitting her. She tumbles to the ground, shock coating her face, just as two guards rush in, hauling us apart.

"You, upstairs now!" one yells at the girl while the other sneers at me.

"You, get in here." He yanks open the door near me and throws me inside to see the shocked but annoyed face of a tall, skinny man who's sitting behind a desk.

I pretend to fall as I stumble into the office and shove the bug under the desk, ignoring Gray's barked warning in my ear.

"You've only just arrived, miss... Ivy Knight." He sniffs as he looks me over. "And you are already in trouble. We will let you off this once since you are new, but you will be reprimanded if there is any more fighting or unruly behavior. With three strikes, you'll be out of here and put back in the system." His cruel eyes narrow as he leans forward across the shitty desk. "I don't need to remind you how bad that is."

"Sure thing, boss man," I retort as I stand. "Can I go now?"

"Go." He waves me off. "Fucking kids," he mutters under his breath as I stroll from the room, winking at the girl I hit before heading back upstairs.

"You are in so much trouble, brat," Gray snarls.

"Yay. I sure hope your brand of punishment is better than that jerk's," I taunt.

"Oh, believe me, it will be," he growls, the animalistic sound going straight to my clit.

"Then I'll hold you to it."

"Are you done having fun at my expense, brat?"

"I haven't even started having fun with you, wolf." I wink into the camera and lick my lips. "Now, how about that hot shower I was talking about?"

When he growls louder, I giggle as I skip all the way to the bathroom to give him a show he'll never forget.

"This is fucking ridiculous," Hale complains as I press the barrel of my gun deeper into his temple, making sure to leave a mark on the pretty boy's face.

"Just keep your fucking eyes closed, and I won't have to blow your brains out," I warn through gritted teeth, keeping one eye on him and another on the screen showing a naked Zoey in the shower. As she whistles to herself, she purposely bends over, putting on a show.

A show he will never see, or it will be the last thing he does.

"Like I couldn't steal the gun out of your hand before you even pulled the trigger," he scoffs.

"Try it and see," I deadpan, shoving the barrel farther into his skin.

I watch him grind his back molars, considering if he should put his theory to the test or not, but thankfully, he saves me from killing his ass and keeps his eyes shut as ordered.

But Hale is right; this is fucking ridiculous.

I wouldn't need to pull a gun on Hale if Zoey didn't insist on playing with her pretty cunt, knowing full well who her audience was. The little vixen is testing my restraint, hoping I'll bend and break to her will. I should have just fucked her long and hard before she went on this godforsaken mission. Maybe then she'd be satisfied enough not to toy with me.

What am I saying?

This is Zoey.

The girl lives to torment me.

She fucking thrives on it.

I make a note to spank her beautiful ass raw the minute this shit is done so she doesn't pull another stunt like this ever again. If it were only me watching her come on her hands, then I wouldn't mind it so much, but she knew fucking Hale was with me, trying to piece together why this mission is so important to me.

They both have no idea why I need to bring this place down, and I want to keep it that way, but if Zoey keeps pulling these types of stunts, then she'll force my hand, and I'll have no choice but to break in and take her out of that place just so I can have a little peace of mind.

I mean, what if one of the guards came in while she was pleasuring herself?

They'd put her head on the chopping block immediately and offer her to the highest bidder.

She has no clue what kind of danger she's in.

And with the way she's acting—getting into a fight with one of the older girls and then going into a bathroom just so she could fuck herself while muttering my name—she'll be on the guards' radar in no time.

Fuck.

I never should have agreed to this.

What the fuck was I thinking?

"I don't hear the water running anymore, so is your girl done or what?" Hale asks, bringing me out of my thoughts.

I glance over at the monitor and verify that Zoey is now fully dressed, combing what's left of her hair. Slicked back now, the haircut actually favors her, showcasing her long neck and angelic face. Or maybe it's just my lovesick eyes that are fooling me. She looks so fucking innocent like this, but as time goes on, innocent is the last adjective that I should use to describe my girl.

"Fuck, is that a smile on your face?" Hale suddenly asks, bringing my attention back to him.

"Who said you could open your eyes?" I growl.

"Oh, just fucking shoot me. Watching you being pussy-whipped by Al's kid is torture enough. Put me out of my misery already," he jokes, gripping my gun and shoving it farther into his forehead.

I mumble incoherently under my breath as I pull my gun away from his head. "Go home, Hale. I can take it from here. I've got this," I grumble, hating that he's right. I am pussy-whipped, hard.

"You don't got shit, Ghost," he retorts, leveling me with one of his lethal stares. To drive his point home, he points to the screen where Zoey blows a kiss to the camera before leaving the bathroom to go on her merry way. "That piece of ass has got you all twisted up inside. That's the very definition of not having your shit together—not that you weren't acting cagey and on edge to begin with on this job—so you either admit what the fuck is really going on, or my ass isn't getting out of this van."

My hand itches to grab my gun again, but with the way he's glaring at me, I know he'd love nothing more than a shoot-out, and that shit will draw too much attention and probably blow Zoey's cover. Instead of telling him the full story, I give him a crumb big enough to keep him subdued.

"It's personal." When he just raises his eyebrows, I try again. "This job is personal to me. That's all you have to know."

"No shit it's personal. I got that much. I want to know why," he demands.

I shake my head, not wanting to relive my past and cough it up to Hale, no less.

His shoulders slump in defeat, but his glower never leaves my face. "Answer me this then. Is it personal because she's involved or because you are?"

"Both," I confess. "Satisfied?"

He strokes his chin in thought and then nods. "No, but it'll do for now. I don't like getting involved in jobs where I don't know what is really going on, but for the time being, I'll ease up and leave you to it."

He picks up his jacket and starts heading toward the door, but he stops when his hand is on the handle and looks over his shoulder at me.

"Don't do anything stupid, Ghost. Do what you came here to do and then bounce. Remember that it's not only your life that hangs in the balance. It's Zoey's too. And if Alaric ever finds out that you got her involved in your shit, well… there isn't a corner in this great blue ball in the sky that you can hide from him. You're as good as dead, you feel me?"

I give him a curt nod, biting into my cheek.

"Don't say I never warned you," he scoffs. "Call me when you need to sleep and shit. I'll be here."

My brows furrow as I watch him leave. He almost sounded like he cared, which is bullshit since Hale doesn't care about anyone but himself. Sociopaths aren't known for having a heart. I should know since I met many in this life of mine.

And now Zoey will too.

With my head back on the game at hand, I get comfortable and watch Zoey go downstairs into the common area where a bunch of kids are sprawled on couches either watching TV or just talking amongst themselves. Everything looks normal, or as normal as these types of places are, but as soon as night falls, my skin begins to crawl as I watch the day shift get replaced with familiar faces of my haunted past. My first instinct is to run over there and rescue Zoey, even if I have to drag her out to do it. It takes everything in me to stay rooted to my spot and just leave her there.

Don't do anything stupid, little doe.

Please.

I'm not a religious man. Faith in prayer was swiftly extinguished out of me the first couple of nights I lived in that house of horrors. Yet here I am, praying that my girl won't do something dumb, like put herself in harm's way out of her senseless need to help me. Her father might go to the ends of the Earth to track down anyone who puts Zoey in danger, but I'd go to hell itself to kill anyone who laid a finger on her pretty little head.

The devil would be the least of their problems.

I'd make sure of it.

CHAPTER 15

Zoey

"Take a picture, why don't you? It'll last longer," I taunt, grinning at the girl who is sporting a black eye courtesy of me and the little rendezvous we had in the corridor earlier today.

Her nostrils flare in anger, but she's smart enough not to do anything about it, preferring to finish up her dinner instead of giving me more shit.

Not that I blame her.

The dining room is packed with guards in every corner, keeping a watchful eye on all of us as we eat. All it would take is for them to take off those ugly polo shirts they are wearing and replace them with a prison guard uniform for this to feel like a real prison. Even the food tastes like shit here, much like I imagine prison food does. My stomach churns at the slop on a plate before me. How can anyone live like this? The only thing these kids are guilty of is having the bad luck of not having any parents, yet they are treated like criminals. No wonder most of them become one when they age out of the system.

It's all they know.

My hand grips the plastic knife in my hand, threatening to break it in two, remembering how these poor conditions aren't the only hardships these kids go through in this particular group home.

They suffer much worse.

So much worse.

I'm still in my head when I feel someone place their hand on my shoulder. On instinct, I fly out of my chair and hold the knife up to their chin.

"Easy there," a woman I haven't seen before says, gently moving the tip of my plastic knife away from her throat. Her gentle smile remains intact as she shakes her head to the guards who are rushing to her side.

"Is there a problem here, Maeve?" one of them questions, giving me the evil eye.

"I don't think so. Is there, Ms. Knight?" she asks me.

I shake my head and sit back down, pretending that the whole room didn't just go deathly quiet because of my rash impulse to defend myself.

What was I going to do?

Slit her throat with a plastic knife?

Alaric taught me to defend myself in tight situations, but none of his techniques involved plastic cutlery.

With an audible sigh, the woman pulls back the chair beside me and takes a seat. "I'm sorry I startled you. I just wanted to see how your first day here was going. I know how hard it is to fit into a new place," she offers sincerely.

"Harder still when strangers think it's okay to touch me without my consent," I reply, choosing each word perfectly to see if I can get a rise out of her.

"You're quite right." She continues to smile at me. "I'm a firm believer in respecting people's boundaries. I'm sorry that I crossed yours. It won't happen again."

My forehead crinkles at the sincerity in her voice. Unlike the other guards standing post here, she isn't wearing a uniform, nor does she look pissed to be here. She must read the questions in my eyes, since the next time she opens her mouth is to answer some for me.

"We haven't been officially introduced. My name is Maeve Burgess. I'm one of the guidance counselors on staff." She holds out her hand to me, but I refuse to shake it. Her smile never wavers as she pulls back her hand. "So are you going to tell me how your first day here has been?"

"Eventful, but you probably know that already," I reply, using my fork to play with the mashed potatoes on my plate.

"Yes. I did hear that you made quite the impression on one of the girls here. Not one to make friends, I gather?"

"Don't intend to be here long for that." I shrug.

"I hope that doesn't mean you're already thinking of running away. I read in your report that you have a tendency of running away from good homes," she replies sadly.

"Is this a good home? Feels more like a prison," I retort and point at all the guards.

"Oh, they are harmless. Just here to keep the peace. You'd be surprised how many kids here like to cause trouble just to get attention. You're not going to cause any trouble, are you, Ms. Knight?"

"Depends." I shrug sourly.

"On what?" she presses.

"If I get bored or not." I flash her all my teeth, but then my smile falls off my face when she starts laughing.

"You are a firecracker, little one." She laughs.

The way she's being so nice to me is setting my teeth on edge. I can't get a read on her. I'm not sure if she's full of shit or being a hundred percent legit with me. I eye her, taking in anything that will give me any insight on this stranger who is adamant about being my friend all of a sudden. In her late forties, maybe even early fifties, she is well put together. Her strawberry-blonde hair is pulled back into a ponytail, making her hazel eyes stand out. Their hue is just as soft as the expression on her face. Nothing she's wearing really gives too much away. Wearing a simple white shirt and jeans, she looks like your average soccer mom. The only thing that stands out is the watch on her wrist. It's a Cartier, which is something that a social worker or guidance counselor could never afford on their salary.

"Nice watch," I blurt, hoping it will strike a nerve.

"Do you like it?" she coos, twisting her wrist out to me to get a better look. "It was a gift from a boyfriend whose name I can no longer remember."

"Boyfriend? No husband?" I find myself asking.

She shrugs. "Unfortunately, I don't have much time to keep one. These kids are my family, and not many men like to be put in second place," she explains wistfully.

My brows furrow deeper on my forehead, still unable to read this woman. Suddenly, an epiphany hits me, making me ask her another question to see if my suspicions are on the mark.

"Does that mean that you live here with us?"

She lets out another chuckle.

"I'm known for taking my work home, but not to that extent. No, I don't live here. In fact, I shouldn't be here at this hour, since I only work here from nine to five. But I knew we were getting a new girl, and I just wanted to meet you on your first day to welcome you into our home."

Day shift.

She works the day shift.

Fuck.

From what I read in Gray's file, it's only some guards in the night shift that are selling off kids to the highest bidder, which means this poor woman is probably completely unaware of the horrors her so-called kids are exposed to when she clocks out and calls it a night.

Feeling sorry for her, I summon my first genuine smile. "Thanks. I didn't need a welcome wagon, but thanks anyway."

"Sure thing," she retorts, getting up from her seat. "Maybe we can talk again tomorrow. Would you like that?"

"Why not? Not like I'm going anywhere soon."

"We should hope not." She smiles and goes to rest her hand on my shoulder again, only to swiftly pull back. "Boundaries. Can't forget those boundaries." She waves me off before walking out of the room.

I bow my head and stare at my uneaten food.

My job just got a whole lot more messed up.

It would have been simpler to believe that every adult in this place was the devil incarnate, but now that I know that there are actually good people who care and have no inkling of what is really going on here, it makes all of this that much more painful. It means that these kids could have had a shot if there weren't assholes taking advantage of their vulnerability for an easy buck.

Goddamn it.

Pushing my plate away from me, I cross my arms and tilt my head to the same guard who came to Maeve's aid.

"I'm done. Can I go?"

He looks around the room at all the kids who are still eating their dinner and then nods at me. Without a second to lose, I take my leave and go upstairs. It's only when my hand is on the railing that an idea pops into my head. Most of the guards are in the dining room right now, which means the rest of the house is unattended, and it will remain that way maybe for the next ten minutes, so I have to act fast. I rush to the floor where the locked office of whoever runs this perverse circus is and go to my haunches to pick the lock with a bobby pin I shoved in my hair for this very purpose.

"Just what do you think you're doing?" Gray growls in my earpiece.

"You'll see." I smirk.

When the lock gives way, I look at one of the cameras Gray installed in the hall and throw him a mischievous wink as I remove the earpiece from my ear.

"Zoey!" I hear him yell out before I shove the device between my breasts, silencing him for good.

He'll probably kill me for what I'm about to do, but hopefully it will be worth it.

I step inside the dark room and flip the light switch. The minute it turns on, I'm disappointed to see that it looks like just your run-of-the-mill office. There is a desk in the middle of the room, with a computer and a few carefully placed papers. I quickly go and check those out first, but nothing screams pedophile ring.

"There's got to be something in here," I mutter under my breath.

I turn around to the filing cabinet behind me, thinking if I were a kingpin of a criminal enterprise, then I'd probably have my secrets locked away but easy to get to in a pinch. With my bobby pin still in my hand, I try to get one of the filing cabinets open. When I'm hustling to break into the damn thing, something grabs my attention.

There's a small Newton's cradle right in the center of the filing cabinet behind the desk. It's not something that looks too out of place, just some tacky decoration, but its presence still bothers me, and I don't know why. As if under a spell, I raise my hand and flick one of the silver balls, making it hit the other, and it's the sound of them singing in unison that pulls me out of my reality and back into a distant memory I have no recollection of.

"Please. I just need to call my aunt. She'll take us in. She will. She has to," Layla pleads desperately while I stare at the Newton's cradle device on the oak desk.

"We've made every attempt to reach your next of kin, but unfortunately we haven't been successful," a soothing voice explains.

"Then let me try. Please. I know I can get through. I just know I can. Please," Layla insists.

I tune out the rest, focusing on how one silver ball hits the one next to it. The clicking sound is loud in my head, like a bullet piercing through the air until it hits skin. Much like how my father killed my mom and brother. Much like how the avenging angel that was in the car shot my father down.

Clink.

Clink.

Clink.

One bullet.

Two bullets.

Three.

I hold onto the armrest of the chair, digging my nails into the upholstery as the silver balls hit one another.

One body dead.

Two bodies dead.

Three.

But there are five balls. Five bullets. Each one with our names on it.

Mom.

Gage.

Dad.

Layla.

Me.

I swallow dryly at the thought, holding onto the armrest to keep me tethered to the present and not back on that lonely road where most of my family died, but I can't stop replaying the sound of each bullet in my head.

Five balls.

Five bullets shot.

Five bodies slain.

I shake my head, my eyes burning with unshed tears that I refuse to let go of.

I'm alive.

Layla's alive.

He didn't kill us. He didn't.

So why do I feel like death is just biding his time, as if I owe him a debt that only my life can pay?

"Zoey. Zoey!" I hear my sister call out, holding my hand to lift me up from the chair.

I follow her lead, my eyes locking on the ugly bandage on her shoulder, proof that my dear sister danced with the devil and won.

"I'll get us out of this place. I promise," she whispers as she pulls me out of the room. "I promise I'll keep us safe."

I grimace at the hope in her voice.

No one can keep us safe.

Not even our angel.

Not when death has a debt to collect.

A cold shiver runs down my back, bringing me out of that somber memory. It takes me a few seconds to remember where I am and what I'm supposed to be doing here, but the minute I do, I just want to get out of this room as quickly as I can. The need to escape makes it hard for me to breathe, much less concentrate. It's almost as if the grim reaper is smiling down at me, whispering in my ear that he has been waiting for me. Clumsily, I shove the pin into the small lock again, twisting and turning it like a woman possessed. When I hear a familiar click, I rush to open the cabinet drawer, not bothering to look at the names on the files as I take as many as I can hide under my shirt and get the hell out of there.

As I run out of the office and into the corridor, my skin feels like it's being burned alive with how the files scrape against my stomach and chest. I push forward, hurrying my steps to the front door. I can still hear the commotion coming out of the dining area, alerting me that I don't have much time. When I turn the knob to my prison and see Gray jumping over the fence to reach me, I finally take a full breath of air into my lungs.

"That was stupid, little doe, so stupid," he reprimands me, but I don't feel his angry words on me, only his warm embrace. I rest my head against his chest, listening to his heart beat a mile a minute.

He's alive.

Layla's alive.

I'm alive.

I hold onto him tighter, as if he's the only one who can cast my demons away, and when Gray tightens his hold in response, kissing the top of my head affectionately, all the tension in my limbs evaporates. Knowing the clock is ticking, I reluctantly pull away just enough to hand him the stolen files.

"I hope those help."

He takes them from me, but he doesn't spare the files a second look, preferring to stare into my eyes.

"What's wrong, little doe?" he asks softly, lifting my chin with his knuckles.

I turn my head to face the front door of the house, dread instantly starting to seep back into my bones.

"I'm not sure," I reply, unable to vocalize what I just went through.

I'm about to try and explain that a long-lost memory from my past almost crippled me when he flings me around, my chest hitting his, right before his lips fall on mine. His kiss is uncharacteristically soft, his lips molding onto mine in the sweetest of ways. His gentleness makes my breath catch, and it was as if he knew that I needed solace to push the chaos away. My mind instantly goes blank as I give in to the kiss and offer my heart to him on a plate.

It was always his for the taking anyway.

This kiss just proves it.

"What did you do that for?" I ask when he grudgingly breaks the kiss, his hands never leaving my hips.

My lashes bat profusely as I stare up at the face of the man they all call Ghost. He doesn't look like a ghost to me now. He looks and feels human to the touch, as if life has been restored to him somehow. The silver hue in his eyes twinkles like moondust, but when the shade of gray darkens as he keeps staring at me, I see something in them that I never thought I'd ever see—*fear*.

"Don't lose yourself in there," he warns. "Remember you don't belong to them."

"No?" I swallow.

He shakes his head. "You belong to me."

CHAPTER 16

Zoey

I hate weakness, detest it actually.

Yet here I am, unable to sleep in this unfamiliar bed with all the unfamiliar sounds surrounding me. The other girls are snoring while the wind hits the shitty windows with a bang, making me jump every time. There is all this noise where I'm only used to silence, and it's pissing me off as I twist and turn in the bed, trying to get comfortable.

I know I need to sleep to keep my wits about me.

It's easy to blame the noises, but I know the truth. Today's events have unnerved me, and I can't even explain why. What was that in that office? Could those really have been memories?

They can't be.

Huffing, I give up and head to the bathroom where I splash water on my face and stare at my puffy, tired eyes.

"You should be asleep, little doe," the growl says in my ear. I didn't want to take the earpiece out in case it was found or lost, and now his lazy growl makes me shiver as I stare at myself in the mirror, wishing he were here.

Gray makes everything better, even when he doesn't realize it. He distracts me from my issues, worries, and fears.

He makes me feel strong, sure, and able to take on anything, and right now, I feel anything but.

"I can't sleep," I whine, knowing I sound like a petulant child. "I never could in unfamiliar beds. It takes me weeks to get used to them," I admit softly.

He sighs down the mic. "Go back to bed, little doe, now."

Flipping him off, I purposely take my time, making sure to dry my face, relieve myself, and wash my hands before dragging my feet as I head back to the shadowed bedroom. Slumping in the lumpy bed, I'm just about to force my eyes to close when a shadow detaches from the wall and stops above me. My eyes narrow as I reach for a weapon, anything, before a hand covers my mouth and he leans down.

A familiar voice purrs, "It's me, little doe, scoot over. I'll hold you until you sleep."

I shoot him a wide-eyed look, trying to convey my worry about them finding him. His familiar scent wraps around me, settling me like nothing else as his soft lips meet my ear once more, making me shiver in need.

"I won't get caught. Now move before I drag you out of here and back to my own bed so we can both sleep."

Unwilling to argue further, I flip onto my side and scoot to the edge of the bunk. The mattress sinks behind me as my shadow curls around my back, wrapping his arms around my waist and tugging me back until we are plastered together. His lips go to my ear once more. "Sleep, little doe," he orders.

"Goodnight, Gray." I yawn and snuggle in closer. I feel his lips brush over my temple as he holds me tighter.

"Goodnight, Zoey."

Within seconds, I fall asleep to his even breathing, his soft touch, and his slow, steady heartbeat.

When I wake up, Gray is gone and the sun is streaming through the room. I'm disappointed before I remember why he can't be here.

Stretching, I head to the bathroom, showering and dressing just as the alarms go off, waking everyone else up. Happy to miss the crowds, I head downstairs in search of food, ignoring the looks thrown my way.

"Well, good morning, rockstar," a familiar, jarring voice greets in my ear, making me snigger. I move to the window to disguise my lips moving. "Don't you look dashing today."

"Morning, Hale. Where's Gray?" I murmur.

There's a fake gasp. "Am I not good enough? And here I thought we had a connection, though I must admit I prefer my women... sweeter," he purrs and then sighs dramatically. "I relieved him so he could piss, eat, and sleep. He'll be back soon. Until then, it's you and me, kid, so behave. I like my brains inside my head, thank you, and I'm much too pretty to die so violently."

"Much too vain too," I joke.

"Touché, so what's on the agenda this morning? Killing them all, burning down the house, or just taking over the world?" he teases.

"Breakfast." I yawn, turning when the others troop downstairs in a rowdy group.

"That's good too," he replies. "I have a delicious sausage, cheese, and egg bagel."

"Bastard," I hiss as I get in line to be served what looks like sloppy oatmeal.

"It's so good." He groans, his mouth full of food. I know what he's doing, he's distracting me and keeping me with him, and it works. I'm in a good mood despite the situation and place, and I don't feel as alone.

I don't think it would be possible to be in a bad mood with Hale in my ear anyway. He intrigues me. He has this all-consuming aura about him. It's similar to Gray's, but something tells me Hale's darkness hides underneath pretty smiles, whereas Gray wears his like a shield.

After breakfast, a lot of kids either go to work or just leave the house. I have no desire to do either, so instead, I explore. I know the layout already, but it can't hurt to know the exits, and you never know what I might find in this twisted scavenger hunt of mine. Hale talks incessantly, and I reply as much as I can.

I reach a bathroom upstairs. It looks the same as the others... the exact same...

I don't know why I rush inside, but I do, and once there, I almost rock back on my ass. Memories cloud my brain, ones I have to grasp like smoke, but they are memories, nonetheless.

Of a boy... standing before me, protecting me.

Holding me.

Comforting me.

It's just flashes, but I know they are real.

The boy runs to me, wiping away my tears and looking deep into my eyes.

It's Gray. I would know those serious, hard eyes anywhere.

Why is Gray here?

And why is this my memory?

Something about Gray always felt familiar and safe, and I never knew why I was drawn to him.

Is it possible I knew him?

If so, why hasn't he said anything?

"Why is this place important to Gray?" I find myself asking, cutting off Hale's story about the time he had to fight a bear.

There's silence for a moment, heavy and loaded. "I don't know, kid, but I've never seen him like this. Whatever that place is to him, it has him angrier than I've ever seen and more fucked up. Gray is not someone I would ever want to cross. That anger... I've only seen it once, when we were overseas and he was captured, and trust me when I tell you, it got many people killed."

Leaning back into the wall, I stare at the spot where I can still see the young Gray, and I find myself asking questions I know I shouldn't. "Tell me about him then, before... everything."

"Well, that could take a while," he jokes. "But Gray was pretty much always the same, fewer scars but always as serious and angry. He was a twisted-up kid when I met him in basic. He carried a lot of weight and a lot of scars, if you know what I mean. Anyway, it got better, I guess, when he had a purpose. He was good at fighting, but then he was captured, and it was just dumb luck that I was there when he was and got my ass captured too. Somehow, we got split up. They thought they had killed me, but as you can see, I'm very much fucking alive. But that's my own story to tell. Gray? Our people left him behind, thought he was dead too. He wasn't either, though, and when he finally managed to escape and kill his kidnappers... Well, let's just say that he was never the same again. I don't know what happened to him there, and I don't think anyone ever will, but it wasn't good."

I inhale, and I hear him sigh sadly. "They called him Ghost after that because he was supposed to be dead. As serendipitous as it sounds, I reconnected with him when I found him working for the same agency that hired me, using that same set of skills that helped him survive in the desert. Talk about a small fucking world. You see, Zoey, men like us are good for one thing and one thing only—killing. We live for it. We exist in that darkness so others don't have to, and Gray? He's the darkest motherfucker out there."

"I wonder if that's why he won't let anyone close," I murmur, my eyes going back to the spot where the kid with Gray's eyes held me.

"It's okay, little doe, I'm here."

The voice floats through my mind like a comforting embrace, but not from Gray now... from then. It makes me forget everything Hale is saying as I focus on it.

I reach for the memories until Hale's sharp, commanding voice interrupts me.

"Uh-oh, it looks like our time is up, kid. You might want to head downstairs."

I hurry to do as he says, and when I get there, I screech to a stop, because standing in the foyer is Gray—but not like I've ever seen him before.

He's in a suit, a waistcoat, tie, and jacket. Even his shoes are polished and his hair is perfectly styled. He looks incredible but nothing like the man I... care for. The only thing that settles my worry is his eyes, which blaze with fury, but you wouldn't notice until you knew to look for it. For a moment, his eyes land on me before he turns away to greet the same pencil dick whose office I was thrown into the first day I got here. Then he walks away with him, leaving me gawking after him.

"I hope you know what you are doing, Gray," Hale mutters.

"So do I," I reply.

CHAPTER 17

Zoey

I don't see Gray again. I try, but he either spends his time in the office or sneaks out when I don't notice. Instead, I pretend to watch TV, even as I let my mind wander.

With nothing else to focus on, it goes back to those memories.

First, the one in the office, then the one in the bathroom.

It's clear they are real, but how can that be? Did Layla and I come here after Mom's death? Was this the group home we had been placed in before we went to Aunt Lucy's? If so, was Gray here with me? It would explain a lot, but that means he also knew me before I remembered he even existed.

I'm so confused, my past and present colliding, until I feel like my head might explode as I try to figure it out, and the one person I need to ask isn't here.

Sighing, I give up and head to bed, deciding to nap to get rid of the headache. The familiar pain makes me wince as I drag my feet, and for a moment, I panic that the tumor is back before I breathe through it.

It's just stress, that's all, Zoey. You know the doctor said it's all gone.

Get your shit together, girl.

Escaping my worries and confusion, I collapse onto the bed, and before I can even wonder if I will fall asleep without Gray, the darkness takes me under.

———————

I'm shaken awake.

I jerk around, searching for the source, expecting Gray to be lying at my side, but standing above me in the blackened room is a guard smirking down at me. I blink to focus. The room is dark, and girls are sleeping next to me. Did I nap all day?

That means I missed meals, Maeve, and Gray.

Shit, shit, shit.

"Time to earn your keep," the guard sneers as he grabs me and hauls me up, dragging me from the room.

I don't know what he means, but I can guess, so I start to fight his hold before I relax, knowing Gray is watching. If something is wrong, he would come for me. "I need to pee," I snarl, and the guard groans before dragging me to the bathroom and tossing me into a stall.

"Thirty seconds, or I'll come in after you." His arms go across the open door as he grins at me, his brown eyes filled with lust. "And trust me, you don't want that, little girl."

No, I don't. I pee quickly when he shuts the door, not risking calling to Gray through the earpiece. I wash my hands, only for the bathroom door to fling wide open, and then the guard yanks me down the corridor before I'm even done. The guard's rough, bruising touch makes my heart slam in fear.

I'm led up the stairs I was curious about, the hallway so narrow it feels like the walls are caving in. The rooms have cell doors on them, and a bad feeling starts to build in my stomach, crawling up my throat and making it hard to swallow my dread. I want to scream and fight. I could take this one guard and get out; that much is true.

But then the mission would be blown.

Gray will kill them all, and everything we have done will be for nothing.

Instead, I pretend to sag in fear, trusting Gray like I've never trusted anyone before in my life.

I'm led to the last door, which the guard opens before tossing me inside. I stumble but manage to stay on my feet as it slams behind the guard with a bang loud enough to jar me.

"On the bed," he orders, and I hesitate, not wanting to put myself in a situation I can't get out of, but I have no choice as he comes toward me. I know he will force me to if I don't, and I want to keep his hands off me long enough for Gray to come to my rescue, so I climb onto the king-sized bed. Once there, he grabs me and I scream, struggle, and fight, but I don't put all my strength in it, confused about what's happening.

His deft, sure hands slam my wrists above my head and quickly wrap black rope around them, which is chained to the wooden head-board. Moving down my body, he captures my kicking feet and does the same to them, leaving me tied up and splayed as he climbs from the bed. The guard looks me over and licks his lips as I shiver in disgust.

His hand strokes down my body as I twist, trying to get away. "I'd stay and play, but your buyer will be here soon, and he won't like it if I spoil the goods before he gets a taste. Next time." He winks before turning away, leaving me here. The door slams behind him once more, making me curse through gritted teeth.

Motherfucker!

"Gray!" I almost scream into the mic. "Tell me you see this. Tell me you have a plan."

But there is no answer.

Trust him, trust him, trust him, I chant to myself.

Gray would never put me in danger, I know that, so instead I focus on testing the bindings. They are tight, but if I wanted to, I could get out easily enough. I mean, it would hurt like a motherfucker, but it's not impossible. That gives me a small amount of relief as I look around the room and wait for my so-called buyer.

Apart from the huge bed I'm tied up on, there is a window covered in bars, letting in the moonlight, and lit candles around the room, giving the space a soft glow to hide the stained, tattered walls. The floor has the same creaky hardwood as the rest of the place, and other than the bed, there is no furniture.

It's a room for sex.

All our worries about this place are true. They are selling kids, and me?

I've been sold.

Before I can start truly panicking, the door opens and shuts again. I crane my head, almost sobbing when I see Gray. He's in the same ridiculous suit, but it's him.

Locking the door, he turns to me, his eyes gleaming with lust and anger before he rushes to my side, cupping my face. "I'm here, little doe. Sorry I couldn't answer you. They would have become suspicious if I tried. I've been waiting all day for you to be 'prepared' so I could spend some time with you. I couldn't leave you alone anymore, and I thought we could talk this way."

"So you bought me, huh?" I joke, but even I can hear the fear in my voice.

"For the night." He smirks. "Are you okay? Did they touch you?"

I shake my head, and only then does he relax. "We have a few uninterrupted hours. I thought we could take this time to discuss a plan. I don't want you here a moment longer than you need to be."

"A plan. Right. That's good." Yet as I stare into his stormy eyes, the last thing I feel like doing is talking, especially with his talented hand stroking my neck possessively.

Leaning up as far as my bindings will allow, I grin seductively. "You didn't kiss me hello."

His brow furrows as he searches my gaze before he leans in and kisses me softly. I don't let him escape though, kissing him harder before pulling back. "You know, you did buy me, so why not make the most of it?"

"Zoey," he warns, trying to pull away, so I bite his lip, making him groan. "Don't."

"Why?" I lean back, grinning at the frustration in his gaze and the pure hunger flashing in those gray depths. "You know you want to." I blink innocently at him. "Oh please, Gray. Look, I'm all tied up and in urgent need of rescuing."

"Stop it," he snaps, nostrils flaring.

I drop the innocent act as I arch my chest, drawing his gaze there. "I'm tired of talking, and I'm tired of you watching me like you want to eat me whole, so do it already. Fuck me, Gray, like we both know you want to."

"Zoey," he reprimands on a growl, his body almost vibrating with the tension he's holding back.

"Stop fighting this. I know that some deep, fucked-up part of you wants this as much as I do. You know as well as I do that a little part of you knew that buying me for the night would lead to this. Don't even try to deny it. You want this. You want me. Don't you, Gray?" I rub my thighs together, moaning at the friction it causes. "Want to fuck me when I can't fight back? Can't push you off? You want to control me, own me."

"You've always been mine, Zoey. I didn't need to buy you to know that," he retorts.

"Then prove it." I grin, daring him. I need him to ground me, need him in this place since I'm so lost when he's not around.

I've never craved another like I crave him, nor have I ever needed someone so badly my pussy is slick despite our surroundings.

His eyes rove over my body before clashing with mine. "You want me to fuck you, little doe? You want me to fuck you like some random whore I bought?"

"Fuck yes."

Lust spreads across his features as he watches me, and when he jerks to his feet, I almost flinch. He rips off his jacket and tears off his shirt, exposing his tan, scared, ripped chest.

Licking my lips, I watch him undo his slacks, reach in, and rearrange himself before he climbs onto the bed. He straddles my waist and places his hands next to my head as he leans in, running his lips over my cheek to my ear.

"You are so wet, I can almost smell your cunt, little doe," he growls. "You love it, don't you? You love the idea of being tied up for me, mine to do whatever I want?"

"Why don't you find out?" I challenge, my voice breathless with my own need.

Most girls would balk and demand to be released, but damn if I don't love this fucked-up little game we are playing. Gray doesn't scare me, but what does is how much I need him.

His talented fingers remove my pants, leaving me in nothing but a tiny thong. Reaching into his pants, he pulls out a knife and cuts my shirt away, leaving me bare. Holding my gaze, he bends down and rips my panties away with his teeth.

"So wet," he purrs and licks my panties before shoving them in his pocket.

"Dirty bastard." I lift my hips, spreading my legs wider, even though they are tied, and exposing my dripping pussy to him.

"Fuck, you really want this. You are goddamn dripping, baby." He sounds shocked as he leans in and drags his nose along my folds, making me groan as inhales me. "You smell fucking delicious."

"I bet I feel even better," I tease, my voice breaking when his fingers dance teasingly across my pussy. His eyes come back to mine as his eyebrow arches.

"Is that so? I guess I should see." Two fingers slam inside my unprepared cunt, making me scream at the invasion. I'm wet, but fuck if they don't stretch me. Snarling, he kneels between my legs as he thrusts into my pussy.

His hand covers my mouth as he leans into me, silencing me even as his other hand continues fucking me. "Is this what you want, little doe? To pretend I'm some sick pervert who bought you?"

Moaning, I lift my hips to ride his hand as he grunts.

"Some sick bastard who saw you and had to have you? Who found you tied up so sweetly for him, begging to be fucked?"

My cunt clenches around his fingers in answer, and he snarls, adding a third finger and stretching me to the point of delicious agony. "That's what I am, after all, Zoey. I saw that young little girl in her father's backyard, and I had to have her even then. I was a sick bastard,

I knew it, but it didn't stop me from touching myself to the thought of you and this young cunt stretched around my cock. And here you are, nearly coming already with just my fingers inside you."

I mumble behind his hand, but he tightens his grip until it hurts, his eyes taking up my whole world as he works my cunt. He forces pleasure from me even as it hurts so good, I know I'll crave it for the rest of my life.

"Tell me why I walked in here and saw you tied up and couldn't stop myself. Tell me why, despite how fucked up this is, all I could think about was ripping off your clothes and taking this soaked little pussy, letting your screams ring off these walls as I fuck you in every single hole you have until you can't walk."

Nipping his hand, I narrow my gaze, and he finally pulls his hand away from my mouth. "Fucking do it," I beg, even as his hand twists, stroking that spot inside of me that has an orgasm slamming through me. My clit throbs, needing attention, and my tits bounce with my heavy breathing.

He hasn't touched another part of me, yet I fracture for him.

He swallows my scream, fucking me through my release. Those thick digits fight my clamping cunt as he swallows my pleasure, and when I relax, he sits up and watches his fingers fucking my cunt, the wet sound so loud it turns me on further.

"Please!" I almost scream, desperate for his cock, his mouth, for him to touch me all over.

"They don't get to hear your pleasure," he snarls possessively, covering my mouth, but he soon discovers that just won't do since he wants both of his hands free to touch me. Snarling, he grabs his ruined shirt and shoves it in my mouth, making me bite down on it. "You want my cock, then you keep that in your mouth."

Even as it pisses me off, I do as I'm told, and I watch as he pulls his fingers from my cunt and licks them clean, sucking every drop of me from them.

Groaning, he closes his eyes for the briefest of seconds before opening them again. His gaze is completely on fire, like bolts of lightning shooting right through them.

"You are going to wish you never asked me to fuck you, little doe, because you jokingly called me a wolf, but you were right. I'll eat you whole, take every inch of you, and scare you, making you wish that you never walked into the wolf's den so willingly. I won't stop, not even when you beg for me to, not now."

I can't respond, but I know he sees the challenge in my eyes, because there is nothing he could do to me that would scare me. The only time I feel alive is when I'm pushing boundaries, and I want to push them with him.

I want him to make me feel alive and bring me back from death. I want him to pull me from the grave.

Grabbing me, he flips me over and pushes my face into the bed, the ropes above me twisting to the point of pain, but the discomfort fades into pleasure as his hands grip my ass and yank it into the air. My legs are stretched wide for him, and my pussy is on display.

My body is his, just like my soul and heart.

I give myself over willingly. After all, he's right. From the day I laid eyes on him, he owned me, and my ghost is finally here to collect.

His mouth drags along my ass, and his tongue darts around my hole, making me bite into his shirt. "Later, I'm going to fuck this. Every hole you have will be dripping with my cum, and when we get out of here, I'll lock you in my fucking room for weeks until I've had my fill of your body," he threatens, but I push back, wanting more.

His taunting mouth dances across my pussy and strokes my throbbing clit. His hands cut into my hips, yanking me back and holding me still for his attack. His lips drag over me again and again, until I shiver with the force of my need.

Pleasure rolls through me so hard my toes almost clench, his seductive teasing nearly painful, and he knows it. He wants me to suffer for making him want me, for making him break.

I'll bend, though, so he doesn't have to, because it gets me what I want.

Him.

His teeth nip my clit, making me groan as I rub my tits against the bed, the friction against my nipples making me cry out around his shirt. His wet fingers circle my hole teasingly as he licks and sucks my clit.

Moaning his name around the shirt, I grip the rope to hold on.

"Delicious." He groans against my skin, his mouth skating down before he thrusts his tongue inside me, making my eyes slam shut as I rock my hips back.

His fingers push in alongside, stretching me before he goes back to lashing my clit in a steady, slow pace that has me building toward another release. My cream drips from me, and my drool soaks into his shirt as I gasp and moan around it.

Every nerve in my body lights up and focuses on his cruel grip and pleasurable tongue.

The mix drives me mad as I twist and grind. "Come now, little doe, come on my tongue for me." His teeth lock on my clit at the same time his fingers curl inside me.

What choice do I have?

I explode into a million pieces, seeing stars as he licks me through it. His fingers thrust in and out as he laps up my release. The pleasure grips me until it's too much.

And then it's over, and I flop onto my front, his mouth still leisurely cleaning my cunt.

I'm still recovering, panting and drooling around his shirt, when he flips me back again, the sudden rush of blood to my arms almost making me cry. I blink away the tears in my eyes as I get my first look at my avenging angel.

My ghost.

His eyes are brighter than I've ever seen them, his face is stark with hunger, and his lips and chin are coated in my cream as he crawls up my body, kissing me around his shirt as he looks into my eyes.

"I fucking hate how much I want you," he admits. "I hate how fucking weak you make me. How wild." He rolls from the bed, and I watch with wide eyes as he kicks off his slacks, his peachy ass flexing as he turns, stroking on his huge cock as he watches me. "Is this what you want?" he asks.

I nod jerkily, my pussy clenching at the sight of him.

How could I ever want anything else?

"The night I saw you at the party, I went home and fucked my hand so many times I had blisters. I imagined you in every single way I could, and when it wasn't enough, I found your Instagram and came all over my phone to your teasing pictures."

Fuck.

Crawling onto the bed, he grabs my hips as he settles between my tied legs. His cock drags along my pussy as he coats himself in my cum. "I'm so twisted, little doe, but you want me anyway. I still can't believe it, and you'll regret it, but I couldn't stop even if I tried. You are mine." He slams into me, impaling me on his cock, the angle making him slide so deep it hurts.

It feels so good, and it aches so badly, I'm incapable of anything but screaming around his shirt. He rips it from my mouth and tosses it away, pressing his lips to mine. The kiss is all crashing teeth and tongue as he pulls out and slams back inside me, groaning into my mouth.

"You shouldn't feel this good, so fucking tight and wet, so hot for me. You shouldn't feel like your cunt was made to take my cock. You shouldn't feel like I can't stop, like I'm powerless." He grunts into my lips as he hammers into me, his huge length dragging along those nerves that have me jerking and moaning. "You feel too good, and I hate it. I hate that I'm yours, but I am."

"I'm yours too," I whine into his mouth as he reaches down and rips off the ropes on my feet so I can wrap my legs around him, digging my heels into his ass as he hammers into me. "Yours," I cry out as he leans back, watching his length slamming into me, stretching my cunt.

"But are you, little doe?" he snarls, gripping my throat and squeezing. He can have it all as long as he doesn't stop.

"Yes," I rasp, but it's just a breath. His eyes narrow, glancing to the bed before he picks up his knife. He continues to fuck me as he runs the blade between my breasts, flicking my nipples until I clench around him, and then he presses the point just above my cunt.

"Beg me to," he demands, squeezing my throat to the point of pain, but I embrace the darkness. I let go of all I know, everything but Gray and the freedom he offers.

He gives into my needs I didn't know I had.

"Beg me to scar you, little doe, beg me to carve my name into your skin."

I clench around him. The idea of him carving himself into my skin should horrify me, but it makes me so wild I can barely see. I want that; I want his name in my skin. I want him to see it every time he looks at me.

Right here and right now, I am wholly his.

"Beg me," he snarls, stilling inside me.

"Please, Gray," I plead desperately. "Please mark me, fuck, carve anything you want into me. I want to wear your name. I want you to see it every time you look at me. I'm yours."

His eyes close as he slams me down so hard on his cock it hurts, and then he stills and presses the knife into my skin. He watches me, as if waiting for me to back out, but I don't.

I tilt my head and meet his eyes as the knife cuts into my skin. He glances down as he starts carving the G and then stills, waiting for me to reject him.

But I'm willing to do whatever it takes to have him.

"Finish it," I beg. Snarling, he finishes the G and starts on the R, but the sharp pain mixed with his huge cock has me winding my hips.

"Stay still or it will be messed up."

"I can't." I've always loved pain mixed with sex, and he has to pin me down as he continues to carve into my skin.

I feel the blood dripping down me, the pain obliterating everything else as he bathes me in his fire.

With his eyes on me, he lifts the knife, checks out his work, and brings it to his mouth before licking the sharp edge, cutting his tongue as he tastes my blood.

"Fuck!" My head drops back, but he forces me to look at the knife as he goes back to my skin just above my mound.

As he carves the last letter and bottoms out in me, I come so hard I pass out.

The pain fades into exploding pleasure until I submit to the welcoming darkness that is always reaching for me.

I should have known my ghost would drag me back to the living, though, and when I come to, he's hammering into me, watching me wake up with his cock in me. He stares at the carving as he pounds into me, and it seems to drive him wild.

Snarling, he pulls from my cunt, pumps his cock, and squirts his release all over my cunt and his carving.

I slump then, feeling his release, my blood, and sweat on my body, and I've never been so happy in my entire life. Grunting, he licks the carving and his cum. "Fuck, little doe, you shouldn't have let me do that."

"I don't regret it. I'll have it tattooed on my face if you want," I tease, and despite the self-hatred I see filling his eyes, he chuckles and kisses above his name.

He reaches up and releases my hands. They flop back, and he massages them until I sit up and look down. There, in smooth lines above my cunt, is his name, and the sight of it sends a pulse of pleasure through me.

If he's fucked up for liking it, then so am I, but fair is fair.

Wrapping my legs around his waist, I roll him so he's under me. He lets me, clearly expecting me to attack him, so when I grab the knife and hold it above his chest, he merely folds his hands under his head, daring me to kill him.

"Do it," he demands.

"I'm not going to kill you, Gray," I murmur as I lean down and kiss him. "I'm just going to carve my name into you so we'll match, and every time you look at your chest, you'll see me. I want you to know that you belong to me as much as I belong to you, my ghost."

He jerks beneath me, but when I straddle his torso, he doesn't protest, even as I grind my dripping cunt along his abs. "What, nothing to say?"

"I'll happily wear your name, little doe. I've always been yours, no one else's. Cover my entire body in it if it will make you happy," he says without reservation.

Why is the idea of this dangerous, huge man willing to scar his entire body to make me happy so fucking cute?

Pressing the tip over his heart, I arch my brow, and he leans up into the blade, piercing his skin. I watch the blood drip down his chest, and he groans. "Go ahead, little doe, ruin me. Do whatever you want to me."

Licking my lips, I start to carve. The Z is easy, and the O is harder, but I start to get the hang of it during the E as he grunts below me. I feel his hard cock grinding into my ass.

"Shit." Groaning, he lifts me and slams me down on his cock, making me fall forward. "Don't let me stop you," he orders, fucking me shallowly as I try to finish carving.

"Behave," I demand, even as I moan. Grinning like a naughty kid, he settles back as I finish the E and start on the Y. When I'm done and eyeing my puffy, bloody name, he stops behaving.

He forces me to ride him, and I happily help. My hand lands on the carving, and the pain makes him roar and hammer up into me, both of us chasing our own release.

"I can't—fuck, Zoey, I can't take it. I can't stay away. I need you so badly, baby. You are the only fucking person in this world I care about. Do you know how scary that is? What I'd be willing to do for you?"

I ride him faster, the pain of my stretched, cut up skin only adding to the pleasure. His hands cover my breasts, squeezing hard before he tweaks and rolls my nipples. The pleasure arcs straight to my abused clit. "I'd kill anyone who even looks at you wrong. I don't need money; I don't need a job or shelter or anything. All I need is you, and now you're mine. I'll never let you go. I'll always be there in the shadows, right behind you."

I lean down, grinding my clit and my carving into his skin as I feed him my breasts. He licks and bites them as our blood smears across each other, binding us in this promise.

"Good," I respond, biting my lip. "Because I need you there. I need you always."

I kiss him desperately, using my lips to tell him everything I'm too scared to—everything I never knew I could feel before him.

Together, we find our releases, swallowing each other's cries of pleasure as his cum fills me and I lose myself in ecstasy.

Breaking apart, we share a dirty smile before I collapse on him and he holds me tight. "Shh, little doe, I'm here, rest."

I do. I sleep, and when I wake up, he's inside me once more. His hard cock shallowly thrusts into me from behind, his arm around my waist, and I come before I'm even fully awake.

"There you are. I couldn't resist." He groans as I roll onto my chest, and then he climbs behind me, jerking me to my knees again as I moan, unable to move.

"Hold on, little doe. I'm going to ride you quick and hard," he warns before he eases his cock into my still fluttering cunt. We both moan, his thrusts slow and easy as we rock together. I grip the bedding as he speeds up until he's hammering into me once more.

Reaching forward, he grabs the rope and wraps it around my neck, tightening it as he holds the other end. The pain and sudden breathlessness make me clench around him as he controls me with it. Yanking my head back painfully, he cuts off my breath as he pummels into me.

"Look at you. Look at how fucking perfect you are," he snaps. "I meant what I said, little doe; you're mine now. Every inch of you." As if to prove it, his other hand skates down my back and over my ass cheeks.

His finger presses against my hole, and I push back, taking it inside me as he adds another. He stretches my asshole as he fucks me, filling me completely. The feeling of being so full, so stretched, is what sends me over the edge.

I gasp as I come, milking his cock until he hammers into me before stilling above me, his release splashing inside me.

Both of us try to rein in our breathing as he unwraps the rope and kisses my neck gently. Gathering me into his arms, he just holds me for a while, but we both know our time is running out and our bubble will pop.

We'll have to go back to playing our parts.

Neither of us are in a hurry to move, but a fist raps on the door. "Ten minutes or five grand extra," the sharp voice calls, and all my good feelings disappear.

"I'm sorry, little doe. Next time I fuck you, it will be in my bed," he promises as he kisses me.

He helps me clean up and dress. We have to leave his shirt off and just button up his jacket, leaving his tantalizing chest on display. I lick at it, making him grin as he cups my cheek and kisses me softly.

"That wasn't just talk, baby. I'm yours and you are mine. Not even Alaric can stand in our way now. But know this, little doe, I protect what is mine, and I always come back for it."

"Then it's a good thing I'm yours," I vow as I kiss him.

"I have to go, little doe." He seems like he would prefer to do anything else rather than leave my side. He cups my face as he searches my gaze. "You will be safe, I promise."

"I know." I do. He will always protect me. I want to ask about my memories, but now doesn't seem like the right time. Instead, I lean in and kiss him. He kisses me back, deepening it and taking control of my mouth until I'm moaning.

Ripping himself away from me, he glares. "If I kiss you again, I'll have to kill them all and take you away from here so I can fuck you for the next week straight. So behave, little doe, and trust me to watch over you."

Turning away, he heads to the door, placing his hand on the doorknob as he looks back at me.

For a moment, I remember a time when a little boy with his eyes did the same thing to me in this place.

Gray... It was him always watching over me.

I know it in my very soul.

"See you soon, little doe," he promises, and then he's gone, leaving me staring after him.

My heart is in tatters, but one thing is certain—Gray has always been a part of my life.

Maybe the guardian angel wasn't just Alaric after all...

Maybe it was the boy with the stormy eyes too.

CHAPTER 18

Zoey

"I need you to do something for me," Gray murmurs through my earpiece, his low voice sending a delicious shiver down my spine.

"Anything," I reply, sounding a little too breathless for my liking.

This man has fucked me up good with his secrets, lies, and dirty, seductive games in the bedroom. Even the color of his eyes is my undoing.

And last night, I let him brand me, and I branded him.

I'm so fucked.

"What do I have to do?" I add a little more sternly, hoping he didn't catch my slip up.

"I need you to get back into that office," he replies a moment later, his voice softer than before.

My forehead crinkles at his request. "You need me to steal more files for you?"

"No," he answers evenly. "I need you to find me something else. A place like this needs to keep its clientele anonymous, but that doesn't mean they don't know exactly who pays the large fee for their nightly visits. It won't be on the computer since it's too easy for someone to hack into. It'll be somewhere else. Somewhere no one will think to look."

I snort, feeling amused since Gray probably had Hale try to hack his way into every computer inside this house first before he ever let me step one foot in the door.

"There must be some file or notebook hidden away with that information, and I need you to find it for me," he finishes.

"Why didn't you say anything when I went in there the first time?" I chastise.

"I would have if you hadn't taken out the earpiece I gave you."

My teasing smile drops from my face at the fuck up I unknowingly made. "Oops." I wince.

"Yeah. Oops."

"Don't get angry at me now," I joke. "I'm sure I paid in full for my mistake last night."

The low growl that sings through my earpiece makes me a total hot mess. The man could just say my name now, and I'd probably come from his voice alone.

This shit is so unfair.

I'm starting to really catch feelings, while he refuses to truly trust me.

I know he's lying to me. Lying about his time in this house. Lying about how we met here when I was just a kid. Lying that he's known me all along and has probably kept tabs on me throughout my life.

I would bet my bottom dollar that's exactly what Gray has done. He and my dad might not be BFFs at the moment, but they sure have the same obsessive stalker vibe down to a T. They are more similar than they realize, that's for goddamn sure. Maybe it's true what they say after all—all girls end up falling in love with a version of their father.

Fuck my life.

Then again, all I have are these hazy memories that come to me every now and then that raise my suspicions that Gray isn't giving me the whole story. If I want answers, real answers, there is only one person who can give them to me, and that's my sister. Even though

Layla was in the group home with me at the time, she had spent most of it on the phone negotiating with Aunt Lucy to take us in and the rest sleeping off her pain medication. I'm sure she'll remember the name of the group home. If not, then she'll at least know where I could find our social worker who was in charge of our case. She'll have it on our records for sure, and then I'll be able to know for a fact that I was placed in Mercy Village Group Home. Then, and only then, will I be able to confront Gray. I'd like to see him wiggle out of that clusterfuck of a conversation.

"It looks safe now. Go," he orders, completely bypassing my last remark.

"All work and no play makes for a dull life, Gray. Didn't anyone tell you that before?"

"No more games, Zoey. Go now," he instructs more forcefully.

"You're no fun." I pretend to pout, just so he doesn't read what is actually running rampant in my mind.

I'm about to head to the office again when I suddenly hear my name being called out from behind me. I turn around and find Maeve walking toward me, all smiles as per usual. I flash her a grin of my own. It isn't as bright as the one she's sporting, but it's a smile, none-theless.

"Just the girl I wanted to see. Come help me, will you?" she asks, waving her hand for me to follow her out the door.

"Where are we going?" I ask, surprised that she's taking me outside the house.

"I have to go on a few errands, and I thought you might like to tag along."

"Lose her," Gray orders in my ear.

"What type of errand?" I retort instead of doing as Gray commanded.

If we are going to have any real relationship in the future, he's got to let me do my own thing and not boss me around twenty-four seven. I already have a dad. I don't need another one.

"Only one way to find out." Maeve giggles, juggling her car keys in my face.

I laugh at her carefree nature and walk beside her, crossing the street to her parked car.

"These your wheels? Nice." I whistle at the shiny black Escalade. "Let me guess, it was another gift from that ex of yours."

"I wish." She laughs. "Nope. Just a loner from a friend."

"Really? Must be nice having rich friends." I snort, ignoring Gray's angry growl in my ear.

"Can't complain either way. Now, are you coming in or what?" she asks, tapping the roof of the car before sliding into the front seat.

With my hand on the car door handle, I turn to the end of the street and see a parked van blinking its headlights at me.

"Don't do it. Make an excuse and get back in the house. Now!" Gray orders, his voice deadly.

"What did I just say about all work and no play, my wolf?" I tease, sticking out my tongue before entering the car.

On reflex, I cover my ear with my hand when the loud sound of Gray throwing his mic down to the ground threatens to burst my eardrum. As Maeve starts driving down the street, I quickly glance at the rearview mirror and verify that we're being tailed by Gray's van.

"What's so funny?" Maeve asks when she hears me giggling.

"Oh nothing. I'm just glad to be out of that house. That's all."

"Still having a hard time settling in, huh?" she questions sadly.

"You can say something like that." I huff.

"I figured. The first week is pretty rough for the new kids. But don't worry, you'll feel right at home in no time," she explains, sounding hopeful.

Yeah, right.

Little does she know that her colleagues, and probably her boss too, are letting sick fucks abuse those defenseless kids while she isn't looking. It's fucking sickening. The way that guard prepared me last night for my supposed buyer is still making my flesh crawl. He took pleasure in humiliating me, tying me up, and leaving me completely helpless against my would-be attacker. Not only did he enjoy knowing that I was going to be taken against my will, but I'll never forget how his eyes gleamed with lust and he basically drooled with envy that he wasn't the one to do it. I pretend to cough into my fist just so I don't heave all over Maeve's friend's nice car.

"Hey? You okay over there?" she asks in concern, patting my knee comfortingly. "You're not getting sick on me, are you?"

"No. It's just a frog in my throat. It'll pass," I lie, trying to bury the memories of last night down to the darkest corner in my head.

Well, not all the memories.

The time I spent in Gray's arms as he fucked the very life out of me will be something I want to remember until my dying day.

"Ah, good. Looks like you're regaining some color in your cheeks. I was getting worried you got that flu that's been going around lately, especially since Tim told me you spent most of yesterday sleeping."

"Tim?" I parrot back in confusion.

"The other guidance counselor who works nights. You've met him before. He's the one who broke up the fight you had with Britney on your first day here."

"Oh, right. The stiff. Yeah, I remember him," I reply on autopilot, penciling his name down for future reference. "Nope. I'm as healthy as a horse."

"Glad to hear it," she says, steering the wheel of the car to turn right into a busy street.

"So, are you going to tell me where we're going?" I ask, feeling antsy with Gray following us.

"I will, but first how does lunch sound?"

My stomach instantly makes itself known with its loud growling. "It all depends. It's not going to be the same slop you guys give us back in the home, is it?"

"I was thinking burgers." She laughs.

"Definite improvement." I giggle along. "But seriously, is there any way you guys can feed us real food? It's atrocious what we eat on a daily basis."

"Oh, I know. Believe me, if there was a way that we could get better food, we would. I hate to say it, but government funds can only stretch so far. If we rely purely on the government's share that is given to us, then we wouldn't even have the slop you're complaining about now. Luckily, we do have some Good Samaritans who give to the cause. You'd be surprised how much we lean on other people's charity to get by. It wouldn't have to be that way if our country put our kids' lives first. Better education. Better health services. Better counseling. All of it could be so easy if someone on the top of the totem pole would just give a crap. Instead, they focus on spending billions on wars and guns across the globe instead of protecting our children right in their front yard."

I lean against my seat, hearing the anger in her voice. She really does care for those kids. Passionately so. Suddenly, the urge to tell her that the kids she's so fond of aren't safe under her roof starts burning through my vocal cords, almost as if keeping myself silent is physically painful for me to accomplish.

But I can't put her in danger.

Once we know exactly every name of every person who is involved in the sick fuckery that is going on in that house and get rid of them for good, those kids are going to need a familiar face to lean on. Someone they trust to confide in and heal from the trauma they have suffered. If I tell Maeve now, then she'll just end up blowing a gasket and putting Gray's whole mission in jeopardy. We've come too far to have it all be ripped to smithereens.

"Those kids are lucky to have you," I finally say when I see that she's composed herself.

"I'm the lucky one. Those kids are my life. I'd be lost without them."

Her heart-filled words stab a dagger in my heart.

She'll be absolutely inconsolable when she finds out what has taken place right under her very nose. I'm surprised no kid has ever come forth and told her as much, but then again, fear and intimidation work miracles to keep victims of abuse quiet. It's a tale as old as time, one I learned really fast when I was just knee high. My father, Roy, made sure to rule our home with an iron fist. There aren't many memories I have of that time, but I do remember hiding in closets and under my bed when he had too much to drink or even when his favorite sports team lost a match. Both my mom and Layla took most of the brunt of his fury, but even then, I knew it was only a question of time before he started wailing on Gage and me.

"Hey, are you still with me?" she asks with concern when I go quiet for longer than I'm used to.

"Yeah. Just hungry, I guess."

"Well, good thing we're here then," she replies whimsically, pointing at a McDonalds across from where she's parking the car. "It's not fancy, but it'll get the job done."

"I'd kill for some fries and a milkshake." I salivate, wiping the drool off my chin.

"Then let's do this," she proclaims with utter glee, looking younger than her years as she jumps out of the car.

I rush to follow her, but then I stop on the sidewalk when I feel steel silver eyes weighing me down.

"Do you have anything to say to me?" I ask, locking my gaze with his through the van's windshield.

To my disappointment, he doesn't answer me with that low, gravelly voice of his. All he does is curtly shake his head in response.

"Then I guess I'm having lunch." I cross the street and follow Maeve to grab a nice juicy burger, trying my best to forget the broody alpha-hole in his van.

Three hours later, with my belly full of junk food and all of Maeve's errands done, we park back on the somber street that holds the infernal group home.

"Not glad to be back so soon, I see," Maeve states insightfully.

"I don't think anyone ever gets used to this place."

"Just give it time. It grows on you," she retorts with a smile.

So does fungi if you let it, Maeve, but I wouldn't want that shit anywhere around me.

I keep my witty comeback to myself and walk to the trunk of her car to pull out all the bags filled with books and toys that had been donated to us by the sisters of Mercy Convent. I couldn't help but laugh at the name when we got to the convent during our errands, since it sounded awfully like one of those old rock bands Hale likes so much.

As if he knows I'm thinking of another man who isn't him, Gray finally breaks his vow of silence and speaks to me for the first time in hours.

"Help her out and get to work. We lost enough time as it is."

"Oh, don't get your panties into a bunch. You'll be covered with wrinkles, worrywart, if you keep going on this way," I whisper.

I'm waiting for Gray to return my sass with his all too familiar growl, but it's Maeve who responds as well.

"You're right. I should really chill and not worry too much. I'm sure the kids will love these gifts."

I offer her a fake smile, because it dawns on me that she must have said something while I was trying to push Gray's buttons.

"They'll love it," I agree.

"I hope so. These kids are all about iPads and iPhones and whatnot, even if it means they have to steal on the street to get the fancy gadgets. What are books compared to that?" she says holding up a copy of *The Lion, the Witch and the Wardrobe*.

I take it out of her hands and fondle the old cover.

"Don't be too quick to discard books. I have a friend that lives and dies for them. She's the kind of girl who has no idea what the new show on Netflix is, but she could recite the last book she's read word for word."

"Sounds like you miss her. Maybe you should invite her here one day. Just because you're in a home, it doesn't mean you can't have friends. It might be nice seeing a familiar face. Might even help you feel more at home here."

I offer her another fake ass smile, because like hell would I ever let Cara anywhere near this place. It would swallow her whole with a flick of a finger. I'd be the shittiest best friend in history to let any harm come to Cara. Even though she hates it, I'd rather have her tucked away in that ivory tower of hers in the middle of Manhattan than ever risk her coming down to this house of nightmares.

Not wanting to touch the subject of bringing Cara here again, I grab a few bags and hurry inside. Thankfully the minute I do, a bunch of the younger kids circle around me, eager to see what I've brought.

"No need for chaos, little ones," Maeve mutters behind me. "Help

Ivy and me take these bags into the living room so you can all pick what you like best."

The kids cheer in jubilation, making the pit of my stomach hurt for them. They have so little, get so little, that receiving a broken toy or worn book feels like Christmas to them.

"Ivy, do you mind getting the rest from my trunk and locking the car once you're done?" Maeve asks, throwing her car keys to me before I have time to respond.

"Sure thing," I shout over the loud ruckus.

I head outside again, only to find a very pissed off hitman leaning against Maeve's car.

"What?" I ask a little too scornfully.

"You know what. We're here to do a job and you're losing focus."

"No, I'm not," I reply, pulling the remaining bags from the trunk before slamming it shut. "I'm just taking a breather while making a few kids forget that they have such shitty lives. Can your thick head comprehend that at all? Do you have any empathy for these kids in the slightest, or is it all about the money for you?"

He grabs my arm so forcefully, the bag I'm holding drops to the ground.

"You think I'm getting paid for this?" he snarls, nostrils flaring.

"Aren't you?" I cock a brow.

"No. No, I'm not. What I'm doing here, what we're doing here, is all because of those kids. You think a toy or a book will keep away the devils that torment them at night? They won't. Now either you're here to help me save every last one of them, save them from the hell they have either already suffered at the hands of the people working there or eventually will, or you're just another delusional fool in my way."

I avert my eyes from his since the disappointment in them makes me want to curl into a ball and cry.

He's right.

Toys, books, and better food are nothing but Band-Aids for them.

They need real safety.

I lean down and grab the bag I dropped and push Gray aside with my shoulder.

"Where are you going?" he yells behind me.

"To do what I came for."

Once I'm back inside, I hand off the bags to one of the bigger kids who is waiting for me in the hall and place Maeve's car keys in her open purse, which she absentmindedly left on the entryway table.

Knowing that most of the kids, and probably now a few guards, are in the living room, I walk in the direction of the closed office. I pull the bobby pin out of my hair and get to work. Gray wisely remains silent in my ear, knowing he's not one of my favorite people right now. Once I hear the lock click open, I slide inside the room, turning on the light switch so I can see my surroundings better. That's when I realize that there aren't any windows in the room to speak of. It immediately strikes me as odd since the room is large enough to warrant one. With my hand pressed up against the wall, I walk slowly around the room, inspecting every inch of it, and then I feel it—the place where a window once belonged.

It was sealed brick by brick, ensuring no one could look inside nor get inside through it. It also means that there is only one way to escape. If someone went to all this trouble to get rid of a window, maybe they also went to the trouble of building some sort of hiding place. Just as I think it, I feel a rough edge on the wall where most of it had been smooth. My hands follow the miniscule indent, and as my fingers glide through it, I immediately know what else was bricked off from the room—a fireplace.

"Tricky, tricky, tricky," I mutter under my breath as I go to my haunches, letting my fingers find their way across the fabricated wall.

I slam my hand over my mouth to keep my excited squeal in when I finally find a narrow sliver just big enough for my nails to open the wall.

"Bingo," I cheer when the fake brick opens up to reveal a steel box, much like those safe deposit boxes you would find in a bank.

I bet that it's not jewelry or family heirlooms that I'll find inside. Whatever is carefully placed inside it is way more valuable than that. No one would have gone through all this trouble if it wasn't.

I go to retrieve the bobby pin again to use my magic and see if I can pick the lock when Gray stops me.

"Don't bother. Just get out of there. Now."

"But then whoever we're looking for might see that it's been stolen and ditch town before we ever put our hands on them," I hiss.

"That's just a risk we'll have to take. Now leave."

I hesitate, looking at the box and then at the fake wall, thinking it would be better just to take what's inside and leave the box in its hiding place.

"I mean it, Zoey. Now. If you're not outside in the next ten seconds, I'm coming in there to drag you out, and then all this shit would be for nothing."

He means it.

His voice is too on edge for him to just be bluffing. This box represents all the danger I've been in since I set foot in the place, and now that I'm holding it in my hands, it's too much for Gray to bear.

"I'm going. I'm going," I mutter, putting the fake brick back into its place, praying that whoever owns this box doesn't have a nasty habit of retrieving it often from its hiding spot.

With the steel box under my arm, I rush to the door, turning off the light and carefully shutting the door behind me. My heart thumps with every step I take down the hall and then down the stairs to the main floor. I stall when I reach the banister and wait until I'm sure no one is paying any mind to the main entrance, too preoccupied with the gifts Maeve brought everyone in the living room. Once I'm sure the coast is clear, I dive out of there, rushing down the outside steps and through the iron gate where Gray has the van's side door swung open, waiting for me.

"Get in," Hale shouts, stretching his hand to me.

I give him my free hand for him to pull me in. The minute I am safe inside the van, Hale slams the door shut and Gray drives off like a bat out of hell.

"What are you doing?" I yell, grabbing onto anything I can find to keep my balance.

"Getting you as far away from that place as possible. We got what we came for," Gray shouts back.

"You don't know that. We haven't even opened it to find out what's inside this damn thing. It could be stale air for all we know."

"It's not," he retorts with a snarl.

Knowing that I won't win this fight, I sit down on the floor and pull my knees up to my chest and lean my chin on them.

"Your friend can be a real dick when he wants to be," I mutter at Hale.

"Hey, not my problem. He's your boyfriend, not mine." He smirks.

My forehead wrinkles at Hale's comment, wondering how he came up with such a ludicrous idea. Gray and I have this undeniable heat between us that threatens to burn us both to a cinder, but that doesn't mean that Gray is now my boyfriend.

Does it?

Just as the thought seeps into my head, it's my heart that offers a true response.

Gray is so much more than that. He's the man I'm falling in love with. He's the man who carved his name into my flesh just as he branded my heart with it.

I am his now, unequivocally and forever.

And he's mine.

Unequivocally.

And forever.

Live with it, bitch.

CHAPTER 19
Gray

"**Y**our girl is pissed," Hale mumbles in my ear, loving the tension in my living room.

"How can you tell?" I ask sarcastically, since it's evident that she is by the way she's hammering the lock on the steel box she was able to steal from the group home. I'm sure she's picturing my face with each forceful strike.

I could have whatever is in that box in my hands right about now, but I knew Zoey needed to blow off some steam, and usually for her that involves either fucking or breaking shit up.

With Hale here, I thought the latter would be preferable.

"And this is why I prefer my women docile. I could never sleep at night thinking that the woman lying next to me had the power to cut my balls off," Hale adds mockingly.

"Don't fool yourself, Hale. I'm sure there are plenty of women out in the world that fantasize about cutting off your junk," Zoey interjects between hits, making us aware that she could hear every word we just said.

I try to keep my smile in check, but it's hard to pull off when she's acting like a brat.

"Fantasizing and actually having the balls to do it are two different matters," Hale responds, holding his dick in his hands to drive the point home.

"What is it with men and balls?" she proclaims, stopping her hammer in the air to raise her eyebrow mockingly like we are naughty kids. "If I were you, I'd be more scared of some girl messing up that pretty face of yours. In fact, I'd love to see one of them try it."

"Not the money maker," Hale retorts, aghast. "You know what? Your girl is evil. I'm grabbing a beer before she gets any ideas of swinging that hammer on me."

"Good call," Zoey teases, watching Hale leave the room for the kitchen.

When her eyes fall off him and onto mine, her teasing smile disappears from her face.

"You done?" I ask, crossing my arms over my chest.

"Does it look like I'm done?" she sneers at me.

Fuck, I shift and try to ignore my hard-on. That fire inside her makes me crazy, and despite her anger, I'm debating letting her rip at me with her claws if it means getting in that bratty cunt.

"I'm not talking about the box. I'm talking about the temper tantrum you're throwing." On reflex, I step aside when she throws the hammer in her hand at my head.

"You're a real asshole, you know that?" she shouts, her cheeks growing red.

"I've been called worse." I shrug. I should stop baiting her, but fighting with her is too much fun.

"God! You're impossible. Don't you see what you've done?" she yells.

"What have I done?" I question evenly, keeping my expression blank, even though I'm burning up inside, needing to pick her up, drape her body over my lap, and give her the good spanking she needs to snap out of this shit.

"You... You..."

"I what?" I demand.

"You took me out of there with no fucking warning!" she shouts, getting up from her knees and marching toward me like a bull ready to fuck up a china shop. "You took me out, and now everyone will be looking for me," she adds, jamming her finger in my chest.

"They won't," I deadpan.

She scoffs and takes a step back, crossing her arms over her chest to mimic my stance. "They will. At least Maeve will."

Now it's my turn to scoff. "You think anyone cares about a fucking runaway? You think that woman cares? You're just another drop in the bucket. Another casualty of the system. No one fucking cares. No one!" I shout in her face a little too loudly.

I'm waiting for her to explode on me, but the opposite happens, surprising the hell out of me. Zoey bridges the small distance between us, wraps her arms around my waist, and rests her head on my chest.

"There are still good people in the world, my wolf. You don't have to bare your teeth at everyone. Sometimes it's okay to just let people in and help you. You just have to let them."

It's only when she tightens her hold on me that I realize my whole body is trembling with rage. I close my eyes and wrap my arms around her, letting her soothing scent invade my senses.

"Not all people are good, little doe," I whisper when I feel more in control of myself.

"And not all people are bad either," she retorts affectionately, lifting her head to crane it back just so she can look at me.

I run my thumb over her lower lip, my cock instantly hardening with the way she's looking at me like she wants to save me. The thing is, with each passing day Zoey is in my life, I feel like she already is.

"Ah, good. You've kissed and made up. Bravo." Hale claps when he enters the room. "Now since that's over with, how about we see what the fuck is in that box?"

With my eyes still on Zoey, I lean down and kiss the tip of her nose. "I'll get my blowtorch," I reply, pulling away from our embrace to fetch it.

Not twenty minutes later, I successfully open the safe and am rewarded with a little black book inside.

"Is that what I think it is?" Hale mutters, salivating at the find.

"It's a ledger," I explain, flipping through the pages and seeing familiar nicknames right beside the actual names and addresses of the clientele that frequent the group home.

I scroll through the entire book, looking for the general, but stop when I see another old nightmare's name—Master.

"You'll like this. I promise that you'll love it."

The eerie voice comes to me as if the man himself is right here in this room with us, and panic immediately takes over, as if I'm still trapped in that small room.

"Ghost, you okay over there?" Hale asks, sounding almost concerned.

"Take my hand, sweet boy, and look into my eyes. This is going to feel good. I promise you."

"Gray?" I hear Zoey call out, taking the book out of my shaking hands.

"Let me help you with these clothes, sweet boy. They can't protect you now."

"Ghost, you're freaking me out," Hale pleads as I start hyperventilating.

"On the bed now. I promise I'll make this a night to remember."

No!

No!

No!

I feel his hands cup my cheeks ever so lovingly, making me wince away from his touch, but he doesn't relent and forcefully holds my head in his grip. Then, out of nowhere, I feel his lips on mine. I flinch back from his possessive kiss, but his lips never waver from mine.

But something is different.

His kiss doesn't feel like it's a prison of his making anymore.

It suddenly feels like freedom, like someone handed me the keys to my jail cell and gave me permission to fling the door wide open.

Where before there was only sadistic malice in the kiss, there's love in it now, real love, and it's so palpable that I hunger to taste more of it. When the sound of a familiar moan rings through my ears, I open my eyes and find Zoey kissing me. Her fingers run through my hair as she sits on my lap, her body pressed against mine. I shut my eyelids again and just let her warmth burn all those horrid nightmares away. I kiss Zoey like my fucking life depends on it, and frankly, it feels like it does.

It's her.

My saving grace has always been her.

On a subconscious level, I knew she was my salvation from the first moment I met her in that bathroom. I held onto her innocence to keep whatever was left of mine intact. Now, she's breathing life into a ghost long forgotten and discarded. She's giving me a second chance, one where there aren't any monsters biding their time to capture me in the dark.

I'm the one that monsters should fear.

I'm their living, breathing retribution.

And Zoey is my salvation, the one who will pick up the shattered pieces of my soul and put it back together again when all this is over and done with. Her kiss is the only promise that matters. The only promise that I shouldn't fear. The only one that will save me in the end.

When she senses that I'm back to my old self, she pulls away and gently strokes my cheek with her palm. "Never leave me like that again. Never, my wolf. They can't have you. You're mine now."

I press my temple to hers and breathe her in.

"Promise me," she insists.

"I promise, little doe. I'm yours. Always have been. Always will be," I croak, my voice showing how close I had been to the edge.

She instantly relaxes in my embrace, her head nestling on my shoulder. I pry my eyes off her to look at the other person in the room that witnessed my panic attack.

Hale's hands are in fists at his sides, and his expression is thunderous. We stare at each other until he breaks the connection to point a finger at me.

"One day you're going to tell me what the fuck I just witnessed, and that day, Ghost, better be soon."

I offer him a curt nod, since I know he's giving me some leniency in not forcing me to explain in this precise moment. I don't think I would have had the energy anyway.

"Get some fucking rest. You need it. I'll be back bright and early tomorrow for us to go after the fuckers in that book. Got it?"

Another nod.

"Good, and kid…" He points to Zoey. "Take care of him."

"I will." She smiles, hugging me closer.

He lets out a relieved breath and offers her a genuine smile of his own.

"That's my cue. Now go and fuck like bunnies or whatever you two get up to. I'll be back in the morning."

And with that, he leaves.

Zoey and I stay on my couch, neither one of us ready to let go of each other. I'm not sure how much time passes, but by the way the moonbeams stream through my window, having replaced daylight, I know it's been a while.

"Are you hungry? Want me to fix you something to eat?" I ask, combing her short hair with my fingers.

"No, I'm okay."

"Want to take a shower, or maybe even sleep for a bit?"

She shakes her head.

"Then what do you want to do?"

She lifts her head off my shoulder just a tad and grabs the book I had been holding too tightly with my other hand.

"Show me," she commands with steel in her voice.

I don't have to ask her what she means. I know exactly what she's referring to.

By now, and with the little panic attack I had, it's obvious that she's pieced together that I was in the same group home she infiltrated once upon a time.

"Show me," she insists, holding my finger to scroll down the page of numerous names. I stop immediately when we get to the one that causes such loathing and fear in me.

"Master," she mumbles in disgust. "Mr. Thomas Henderson. 24 Maiden Lane."

I swallow dryly and nod.

She takes her eyes off the name to meet my gaze.

"How about we pay Mr. Henderson a visit? I think he warrants one by now, don't you?"

With my heart slamming against my rib cage, I nod.

"Yes. Yes, I do."

"We should have brought the van," Zoey mumbles, her feet on my dashboard. "At least there would be more leg room in the van."

"You look like you're plenty comfortable to me," I tease, rubbing her cheek with the back of my knuckles, needing to touch her to ground myself.

My emotions are all over the place, and I know seeing him again won't be easy. I need her. Maybe that's why I waited so long to do it, even though I told myself it was because I didn't have the skills yet.

"I could be more comfortable," she retorts, pretending to bite my hand off. "Who would have guessed that casing a joint could be so boring?"

"Part of the job," I explain while keeping a watchful eye on the dark home in front of us.

Master—or Thomas Henderson, as he's known to the outside world —wasn't inside his home when I broke in earlier while Zoey stood outside as a lookout. Not knowing when he would be back, I ran a quick reconnaissance of his home to make sure there weren't any weapons or guns hidden away. Luckily, I didn't find any in the two-story house, but what I did find made me sick to my stomach. As I scoured through the well decorated home, I noticed there were small, feminine touches all throughout the house, such as fresh cut flowers in the hall and a hint of vanilla incense in the air, amongst other things. My skin started to crawl when I picked up one of the various framed photographs all strategically placed around the walls, and on every even surface, and I saw the monster's face again after so many years smiling back at me.

With his hand wrapped around his young bride.

Fucker.

The sick fuck is happily married and leading a perfect, white-collar life, while he made every attempt at leaving my life, and other kids like me, in chaotic shambles.

But that wasn't even the worst thing I found in my search.

It was the small room right next to his bedroom that caused real fear to seep through my pores. Unable to move from the door, I just stared at the empty crib, plus the abundance of boxes lying all around the floor next to it, filled to the brim with everything an expectant mother would need to be fully prepared for when her baby finally made its way into this world. Just as I found the strength to leave, a glimpse of a paperback lying on top of the crib pulled me into the room.

My fingers trembled as I picked it up.

On the cover was a picture of a happy baby boy and the title—*So you're having a boy? 1000 names to choose from.*

As if it scorched my hand, I dropped the book back onto the crib and fled the house. That was two hours ago, and now here I am, sitting behind the wheel of my car, listing all the things I'm going to do to that bastard.

He'll never lay one finger on his kid.

Not one finger.

I'll make sure of it.

He'll take his last breath tonight.

Tonight.

I'm not sure how much time passes when I realize that Zoey has been silent longer than she's capable of.

"Something on your mind, little doe?"

She fiddles with the hem of her plaid button-down flannel shirt, her gaze fixed on one of the red and black squares.

"I was just thinking," she replies, a hint of sadness in her tone.

"About?"

"Just that my dad never took me on any of his jobs, you know? I knew from the start how he made a living, but he never wanted me to be involved."

"Did you want him to?" I ask softly.

She shrugs. "I was always a little curious, I guess. It would have been nice if he were more transparent with his job. I know he took my sister on a hit once. It actually made their relationship that much stronger. I guess I was envious."

"Of your sister?" I arch a brow.

"No. Maybe. I don't know. I guess I always felt like Dad wanted to protect me from that part of his life. Like he was scared that I might... like it."

I take in her confession and chew it for a while before answering.

"Your father and I might not see things eye to eye where you're concerned, but I know that every decision he made in the past was to keep you safe. You can't fault a man for that."

"I'm not. I just wish he would let me live my life how I want to live it, even if it means doing something he doesn't approve of." She sighs.

Again, I take her admission and dissect it for all it's worth.

"You want to follow in his footsteps?"

She bites her lower lip, turning her face toward me to look me in the eye. "Would that have been so bad?"

"Killing scumbags as a profession isn't exactly every father's dream for his baby girl."

"That's just the problem. I'm not his baby girl anymore. I'm a woman—a woman who knows her own mind and can make decisions for herself," she mutters.

My gaze trails over her small frame, and my skin starts to heat with her proximity.

"That you are. My woman."

Her teasing smirk surfaces on her pretty little face, making me that more infatuated with her.

"That might be true, but we're going to need to have a serious conversation about boundaries."

"Boundaries?" I chuckle, surprising myself that I'm capable of such a thing considering the circumstances I find myself in. "Fine. Tell me what type of boundaries you have in mind."

"Well, to start with, you can't boss me around just because it's in your nature. It's okay when we fuck, but not okay in the real world. Got it?" She points at me as if she's scolding me.

It's adorable.

"Go on," I say, making myself comfortable in my seat and turning my body to the side to face her.

All my worries and fears disappear like they always do around her as she brings me back to life.

"I'm going to do a lot of shit you won't approve of, and although I'm totally okay with you giving me your thoughts on the matter and even your opinion, that doesn't mean I'm going to do anything differently. I have to live my truth, whether you like it or not."

"Noted. Anything else?" I try to hide my smile by scrubbing at my face.

"Yes. Just one more." She pauses. "No secrets or lies. Ever. If you really want us to work, I want all the good and bad. Don't hold out on me. I can handle it. Whatever it is."

My hackles immediately rise at the underlying threat in her statement.

"And what if I don't comply? What if I think that some things are best left in the dark where they can't hurt you?"

"Then that can only mean one thing," she retorts sadly.

"And what's that?" I ask, already feeling on edge.

"That you don't love me half as much as I love you."

All the air in my lungs leaves me with her answer. My eyes widen, my pulse races, and my heart beats like a frantic drum, all because this girl, this brat who has captivated my heart and soul, just admitted that she loves me like it was as easy as breathing for her.

"You love me?" I hear myself ask in a ragged breath.

"Duh." She rolls her eyes. "Do you think I just let any guy brand his name on my body? If that wasn't your first clue that I'm hopelessly in love with you, then I don't know what is."

"Fuck," I growl, threading my fingers in her short hair and pulling her to me. "Say it again," I demand, knowing I'm being crazy but unable to stop.

It's all I've ever wanted, and she's offering it to me with a calm smile like she didn't just rip my world to shreds and put it back together.

Zoey lowers her eyes to the hard bulge in my pants before raising them to meet mine. She licks her lips seductively and exhales a shallow breath. "I love you. Now what are you going to do about it?"

To anyone else, her words would have sounded like a threat, but to me, it's an open invitation.

I pull at the strands of her hair. Zoey instantly winces at the pain, and her thighs rub together to ease the throbbing in her clit provoked by my assault.

"This is what I'm going to do, little doe," I explain through gritted teeth. "I'm going to fuck you right here in this car and have you shout that you love me until this whole fucking city hears it."

"Do you think that scares me?" she taunts, her chest heaving in anticipation.

"No. I think it makes you wet. Are you wet for me, baby?"

Her tongue swipes over her lower lip as she basically pants for breath. "Yes. So wet. And if you don't touch me in the next five seconds, I don't know what I'll do with myself."

"I've got you, little doe. I'll make it all better," I promise.

"No more talking, my wolf. I need to feel those fangs pierce my flesh. Now."

"Whatever you say," I snarl before tilting her head to the side and biting the slope of her neck, making sure my teeth sink into her skin and leave their mark.

"Argh!" Her chest lifts, drawing my eyes to her pebbled nipples.

I suck in her blood for a split second and then pull away to latch my teeth on one hard nipple through her clothes.

"Oh my god." She moans as her head falls back, and she grabs my hair to keep her tethered.

I release my grip on her hair to slide a hand between her thighs, the heat of her cunt burning me through her jeans.

"Gray," she pleads when I start rubbing her folds, my mouth pulling back from her nipple so I can lavish the other with the same attention.

"Gray... please..."

"Are you begging already? I haven't even started yet." I chuckle.

"Please..." She moans, inching closer to me.

"Louder," I snarl before biting the fullness of her breast. "Beg louder, baby."

Instead of pleading for mercy, the little devil lets go of my hair and grabs my hard cock in her hands.

"Clothes... off... now!" she commands, squeezing my cock to the point where my precum soaks through my boxers.

I lean back in my seat and tilt my head toward the back.

"Move," I order, and it's enough for Zoey to jump into the back seat. I stay impatiently rooted to my spot as she waits for my next command. "If clothes are your problem, then take them off."

Her face beams with excitement as her fingers start removing each piece of clothing on her small frame. After she strips off her shirt, tank top, and black lace bra, she falls to her knees in the middle of the leather seat like a happy puppy waiting for her treat for being such a good girl.

Fuck, this woman is going to fucking end me with that eager smile.

Satisfied that she's good and well primed for me, I get out of the car and open the back door to slide in next to her.

"No more hands for you," I tell her, slipping her belt out of its loops in one fell swoop. "Give me your wrists."

Pliant and obedient, she follows my instruction to perfection, offering me her wrists.

My girl might love to give me shit every second of every day, but in the bedroom, she offers up all of the control, as if knowing I need to hold on to it to keep sane, especially since everything else in my life, specifically my past, had left me so powerless.

I pull her arms behind her back and fasten the belt around her wrists, making sure it doesn't bite too deeply into her skin. My little doe might like a bit of pain mixed with her pleasure, but hurting Zoey in any way that might cross over her permitted limit makes me physically ill.

She yearns to be dominated, and I can give her that, but I'll never hurt her just because I have the power to do so.

Ever so cautiously, I lay Zoey on her back and start taking off her chucks, followed by her socks, and kiss her ankle as I go about it.

"Is this your way of being sweet to me?" She bites her lower lip provocatively.

"We don't do sweet, remember?" I retort, biting into her calf and gaining a little giggle.

"Then show me what we really like," she taunts, planting her bare foot on my chest.

I pick it up and start sucking each of her toes, biting them one by one, until her gaze turns heady.

"Stop fucking around and fuck me already," she mutters breathlessly.

"Is that any way to talk to the man you love?" I counter, but as the words hang in the air between us, their electricity charges me like paddles to a dead heart, and they revive me.

"Say it again," I order, my voice dropping an octave. "Say it."

"I love you," she whispers in earnest. "So much. So fucking much."

That's all it takes to make me pull down her jeans and fling them into the front seat. I bend down just so I can get a whiff of her greedy pussy, the smell intoxicating. She wiggles down as best as she can with her body still on top of her arms and arches her back so her dripping cunt is in my face, my name etched on her skin right above it, show-casing whom it belongs to.

"Eat it." She pants on bated breath.

Mouth watering, I don't even punish her for her command, and instead do exactly what she wants me to. Ripping the edges of her thong, I discard the useless fabric to the floor and take one long lick.

Fuck.

She's the sweetest poison I've ever tasted.

Unable to hold back a second longer, I latch onto her soaked pussy, licking her desire for me with the pad of my tongue.

"Oh, fuck! Fuck! Fuck! Fuck!" she shouts as I lavish her clit with all my focus and attention, sucking it and grazing my teeth over it until she's a writhing mess beneath me. The minute I thrust two fingers into her greedy cunt, flicking them inside her walls, she squirts all over my mouth and digits, and I lick her juices as if they are the only nourishment a man like me needs to survive.

Zoey's still in a post-orgasmic haze when I lift her up and nestle her on my lap. I kiss her long and hard, letting her taste herself on my lips before I give her an inch of space to breathe.

"Get in front of me. On your knees," I order, close to losing it if I'm not inside her in the next second.

She loves me.

The girl I've been in love with since I was a teenager loves me.

Broken, defiled, fucked-up Gray.

I still can't believe it, but I won't fight her on it. If she wants to love me, I'll let her, and I'll spend the rest of our lives trying to be good enough for her.

Her movements are too slow for my liking, still limp and sated from the mind-blowing orgasm that just ripped through her. Unable to wait, I promptly pick her up by her hips and place Zoey exactly where I want her—with her head smack-dab in the middle of the two front seat headrests. I widen my legs and pull down my zipper, releasing my weeping cock from its confinement before I slap her ass cheek to pull her out of her haze.

"Lean back and sit on my cock, little doe," I command while simultaneously taking my own belt out of my pants.

With my hand on her hip, gently guiding her back, she slowly swallows my cock with her tight pussy until I'm right at the hilt. I hiss, my sight leaving me momentarily, before I'm able to do what I have planned. The soft moan she lets out, as if she's finally found her home, doesn't do me any favors either.

"Don't move." I grunt, my back molars grinding so hard it's a miracle they don't break.

I circle my belt around her neck and twist it in my grip, and her bound wrists beat at my chest on reflex.

"Shh, little doe," I whisper into her ear, biting her lobe to keep her subdued. "You're going to ride me like the good girl you are. If not..." I twist the belt around her windpipe as I stare at her reflection through the rearview mirror. Zoey's eyes glaze over with pure lust, and the sight is nearly my undoing.

My girl is just as fucked up as I am.

Maybe that's why we're such a deadly match.

Kerosine and gasoline have nothing on the kind of flammable heat we can create together.

We burn for each other and crave the blistering heat on our skin, combusting in each other's arms is the sweetest death we could ever desire.

"Move, little doe. Show me how much you love me."

With a wicked wink, my little brat starts bouncing up and down on my length, squeezing her thighs just so. With one hand firmly on her leash, I snake my arm around her waist and slowly trail my thumb down her stomach until it finds her throbbing clit. Her eyes roll to the back of her head as I start toying with it in sync with each thrust. Her tongue parts her pretty little mouth open as I lick the base of her neck, toward her shoulder, and up to her earlobe. I bite, suck, and nibble her flawless skin as I start to increase our rhythm, until I'm the one who's fucking her instead of the other way around.

Suddenly, from the corner of my eye, I see a couple walking their dog starting to pass the car window. Zoey's unabashed, loud moans and wails make them look inside to see what's going on. With my belt around her throat, I push the leather back so she has no choice but to make eye contact with her surprised spectators.

"Tell them," I growl between pants. "Tell them who's fucking you right now. Whom you belong to. Whom you love."

"You! Oh God! You!" she shouts through her restraints.

"Not God. Say my name, little doe. Whisper it, yell it, I want you to fucking taste each letter as it rolls out of your mouth. Scream my name," I order.

"Gray!"

My cock keeps pounding into her tight cunt, growing even tighter with each clench of her impending orgasm. I can't help but look down at us, Zoey's juices all over my cock as she keeps bouncing on my lap. When I lift my head, I get another glimpse of her audience. The woman is visibly turned on as she clutches her dog's leash with a forceful grip, her cheeks pink and her eyes completely half-mast. The guy she's with limits himself to just standing beside her, licking his lips while eye fucking my woman, wishing he could take my place.

I don't think; I just react.

I grab my gun from my holster and point it at him while I keep pounding into the love of my life. Not needing more encouragement than the gun aimed at his head, he quickly grabs his partner and little dog and hightails it out of there.

"I guess they didn't like the show we were giving them," Zoey teases between moans.

"Fuck 'em. I'm the only man you need to please. Me and only me," I snarl, pulling the belt around her neck.

She gasps. "Is that so? Don't I have a say on the matter?"

Fear strikes me to a dead stop. "Do you want anyone else but me?" I ask, trying to read her eyes.

As they soften, Zoey picks up the pace, jumping on my cock in the most glorious of ways.

"All I need is you. All I need is you. Just you, Gray. Just you."

I pull her face toward me and crush my lips onto hers, needing to swallow her precious vow to the pits of my blackened, scarred soul. It's with a kiss that my little doe takes flight and reaches into the heavens. Her pussy squeezes around me, coaxing me to follow her into a nirvana I've never touched before.

Not until her.

When we fall back to solid ground, I remove the belt from her neck and untie the one binding her wrists. I softly kiss the red marks they left on her skin before I cup her face.

"Little doe..." I choke, this new emotion leaving me without the right words. She waits patiently for me, rubbing her cheek against my palm while I try to summon up every dream and wish for the future I planned out for us. She's made me believe that I'm deserving of something better, of an actual life. Before Zoey, I was content living each day as a ghost.

Not anymore.

Now I want to live fully with her at my side.

But all those beautiful words that are so easy for others fail me, and in the end, I say the only thing that matters. The one thing she's known all along.

"I love you too, little doe."

They don't seem like they are enough though. What I feel for Zoey surpasses even the greatest love stories. She's the very air in my lungs, the reason I breathe. The reason my heart beats, and the reason I get up every morning and fight my demons every night.

No, love doesn't compare to the magnitude of my feelings for the woman in my arms, but there are none in the human language that come close to describing them, so instead, I'll show her every day.

The coy smile that stretches across her lips has my heart beating out the syllables of her name. She looks so young in my hands. So fragile. So pure. Just like the first day we met. It's the love that binds us that whispers that it's okay to be vulnerable with each other. That we'll always hold our hearts in our hands and take every precaution to keep them safe.

Two fractured souls now whole.

"I love you, Zoey. With my last breath, I will roam this Earth loving you," I vow.

She pulls my palm away from her cheek and plants the sweetest kiss at its center before she looks me in the eye, endless love swimming in her sea of green.

"Good. I'm going to hold you to that." She smiles, but then there is a hesitant gleam in her eyes that unsettles me. More so when she opens her mouth to speak again. "You and I are the real deal, Gray. Don't fuck it up."

I open my mouth to protest, but she silences me by pressing her index finger over my lips.

"No lies. No secrets. That's what it means to love someone."

Does she know?

Have her memories of living in the group home resurfaced?

Does she remember me?

But all my questions are left unanswered when I see a black BMW drive into the Henderson driveway.

"Get dressed, little doe. We've got work to do."

CHAPTER 20

Zoey

We waste no time after we see the lights turn on upstairs. We make our move, hurrying to the house. I know my job, so I get into position as he silently moves around the side after placing a determined kiss on my lips.

I wait for the signal, a slow whistle, and then I frantically knock on the door, keeping my head down and swaying my body as if I'm in pain. "Please help!" I scream, still pounding. A moment later, the door rips open, and a man is framed in the light. He appears confused as he peers down at me before glancing behind me as I practically faint into him. "Thank God."

"What's wrong?" he asks, grabbing my shoulders and tugging me inside, looking me over. Something akin to glee enters his eyes, even as he pretends to be worried. "Are you hurt? Were you attacked?"

I smirk at him as I straighten. "No, but you're about to be." I giggle and step back as Ghost appears, having broken in through the back door while the man was distracted. He steps behind Master and brings the butt of his gun down hard on his head. The man, Master, collapses forward with a groan, slumping to the hardwood floor with an audible thump.

Grinning at a stern-faced Gray, I whistle as I kick the front door shut and engage the lock before propping my hands on my hips. "Where to, boss man?"

"Living room," he answers as he effortlessly throws the man over his shoulder. I quickly scan the corridor, noting the family pictures and decor before finding the living room. It's to the right of the entrance with huge bay windows. I quickly shutter the blinds and draw the curtains before lowering the lights. Gray tosses the man on one of the perfect white sofas facing a fireplace with a huge painting above it. The fact that this man has white sofas is enough to let me know he's a psycho.

Knowing what Gray wants, I hurry to the dining room I glimpsed on the way in and grab a wooden dining chair, which I haul back and place in the middle of the room on the ridiculous matching white rug. Gray grunts in approval and pulls some rope from his bag. I watch as he ties the man's arms and legs to the wooden chair.

I say nothing, seeing how tightly Gray is wound. He is barely holding it together.

It must be hard for him, and I promise myself to make it as easy as possible.

Gray grabs his phone and does something on it before setting it up on the mantel. Swinging my legs where I'm perched on the sofa, I watch the unconscious man with a questioning gaze. He's not what I was expecting. He's plump around the middle, tall, and good-looking with graying hair and wrinkles, but... normal.

But isn't that the point? After all, I know how easily monsters and evil hide behind a cajoling smile. Anger fills me as I see Gray struggling, his eyes darting to the man, wide and unfocused.

Seeing such a strong, capable, and dangerous man weak because of this very human monster makes me furious.

He's on edge, no doubt remembering everything this man did to him, and I've never hated someone as much as I hate this man tied up in his own living room. I might never know the specifics of what he did to Gray, but I have a pretty good guess, and it makes me feel sick.

And incensed.

Filled with rage, I get up and stop before him, slapping him hard.

His head jerks to the side.

"Doe," Gray warns, but I ignore him and slap this walking, talking nightmare again until he groans as his head lifts. His eyes are slitted, and his mouth is turned down.

I need to prove to Gray he's not untouchable or in charge anymore, and that the only control he holds over the man I love is caused by fear.

This man, this monster, deserves to suffer for everything he has done, and Gray needs to be the one to do it.

"Who are you?" he slurs.

"Your worst fucking nightmare, *Master*," I mock.

He jerks, his entire body stiffening. Grabbing his chin, I force his eyes to mine. "That's right. Tonight, you'll pay for your crimes. Tonight, you'll be the prey, and your predator?" I step behind him, keeping his head up as his eyes land on Gray. "Remember him?"

I feel him swallow against my hand. Gray is stiff, and his face is closed down. I don't know if I'm helping or hindering, but he's unsure, so I'll take charge. I'll make this fucker pay for hurting the man I love since clearly no one else ever has. "Do you remember him?" I scream in his ear.

"Yes," he whispers. "Yes, I remember him."

"Good boy," I purr, squeezing his throat in punishment. I keep my eyes on Gray as I lean in, my mouth near his ear once more. "Then you remember what you did to him. Well, that little boy you hurt grew into a dangerous man, a killer, one intent on getting revenge. A ghost in the system, an animal you made. No one will help you, just like no one helped him. Tonight, you're his." With that threat hanging in the air of this fucking pristine white living room that will soon be covered in his blood, I step back. Gray starts to swell with purpose and resolve, curbing his own troubled emotions. This is not about me or about killing for a job.

This is about him facing his demons, his past, and I'll be right alongside him the whole way until he gets his revenge. To prove it, I walk around the man and grip Gray's chin, tugging him down until I can kiss him. He's stiff at first before he relaxes into my touch. Keeping my lips against his, I whisper so Master can't hear, "If it gets to be too much, if it gets too hard, tell me. I'm here, my love. You are not alone. I'll end his miserable life for you. I'll end them all if it will help," I vow, and it's true.

I would kill every fucker who ever hurt the boy with the stormy eyes.

The boy who protected me.

Who continues to protect me.

He might be willing to walk through hell and endure any pain possible to keep me safe, but me? I'm willing to bathe in blood and watch the world burn to save him.

"Little doe," he whispers roughly, pressing his forehead to mine.

"I mean it, my wolf, I'll kill them all. I'd do much, much worse to keep you whole." Gripping his face, I brush my lips across his again. "So do what you need to and come back to me. Always come back to me."

"Forever," he murmurs before he pulls away. I watch the change come over him. I never realized how much he had softened around me, how much his face had relaxed and started to show emotions until he's back to wearing that hard expression on his face. It's devoid of all feelings, blank and empty. The cold eyes of the killer I first met suddenly stare back at me.

My heart pulses for the boy he was and the man he has become because of monsters like these, but it doesn't matter.

I love both versions of him equally.

"You are going to tell me everything you know about the operation at Mercy Village Group Home."

"That's what you want after all these years?" The man laughs, feeling surer of himself now that he's heard Ghost's demands. But then, just as Gray's expression turns lethal, a gleam of triumph enters this devil's eyes. "Or perhaps you just wanted to see me. Is that it, little boy? You missed the way your master touched you? I'll be honest, I prefer them young and innocent. It's a struggle to get hard otherwise, but for you? I'll always make an exception." He grins evilly, revealing the monster underneath.

I see Gray's shoulders tense as he strikes, smacking the man so hard the chair rocks. "Shut the fuck up. I want names, locations, every-thing you know. Now. You do that, and I'll make your death quick. Otherwise, I'm going to spend all night cutting you to tiny little pieces," Gray warns, and the promised threat even makes me fearful.

The man hesitates, but he saw it—the chink in Gray's armor—and he pounces like every predator does.

"I think you missed the way I touched you. Admit it. Why else would you come here with such a feeble request? No, sweet boy. You missed your master, didn't you?" he goads, looking at me next. "Did you know he liked it? Did he tell you how much he craved my touch on his small body?"

"Do not talk to her!" Gray roars. "Not ever!"

"Oh, but that anger," he coos, a sinister shiver running down his spine in delight. "Back then, he had so much of it. I see it's still the same. The only time he wasn't screaming and fighting was when my hand—" Gray smacks him again, screaming as he rains down hell on the man.

I just watch, knowing he needs to let it out. When he steps back, his fists bloody and chest heaving, I know he's close to losing it, but if I let that happen, then I would never get him back.

The man spits blood on his perfect white rug and grunts at Gray. "Do you remember how you cried for me, boy? Begged and pleaded?" Gray stiffens as he talks, and Master chuckles. "You begged so sweetly, even while your body writhed for me, came for me."

Fuck!

Disgust and fury wars inside me until I want to rip the man to pieces myself for what he did to my wolf, but Gray is always my first priority.

Right now, he needs me. I see it in the shaking of his body as he stumbles back, his face etched with horror as his past tries to pull him back into the darkness.

Well, tough shit, it can't. It can't fucking have him.

He's mine.

"Gray, look at me," I demand, forcing his lost eyes to me as I stop before him, blocking his view. "Only me. You are not back there; you are here with me." I grab his bloody hand and press it to my chest over my thumping heart, letting him feel the organ that beats for him. "You promised, so come back to me, my wolf."

"You remember how much you liked it, boy, don't you?" The man chuckles, his voice nasally from his broken nose. "Oh, how you cried after, but during?" I glare over my shoulder at him as Gray jerks, a whimper escaping his lips. The man licks his bloody teeth as he watches Gray, playing on my love's past nightmares and the horrors he inflicted on him. He's taking him right back to that traumatized child that no one helped.

Fuck this.

"Oh, but you—" Before he can say another word, I grab Gray's knife and turn, punching him square in the face so hard his head snaps back. Using his hair, I drag his gaze back to me.

"One more word, I dare you," I seethe through gritted teeth.

"You little bitch. You have no idea. You could never comprehend. Do you think he has ever touched you like he touched—" I stab the knife into the man's side, twisting it as he screams.

Laughing, I lean in. "Listen to how prettily you scream," I purr, using his words against him. "I warned you. He's mine, and you can't fucking have him, so unless you want me to sit here and carve you to pieces and feed you your own cock, you'll only speak when asked a question, understood?"

He nods slowly as I drag the blade out, making him scream and writhe. "All you bastards are the same, so strong and confident until it comes to taking the pain you so easily dole out, then you're nothing. You're weak. Pathetic." I spit on his face, watching it drip down his cheek. "Nobody protected him then, but I will now. Remember that. If you think my wolf is crazy, then you're in for a rude awakening with me. You haven't seen what I'm willing to do for the people I love."

Arms wrap around me, and then Gray hauls me back and away from the laughing demon bound to his chair. Gray drags me into the hallway where I'm instantly slammed into the wall when we're both out of sight, making the plaster crumble. My legs automatically go around Gray's waist as his lips descend in a furious attack on mine.

I let him hurt me, let him take what he needs.

His hands open my jeans before sliding inside and thrusting two fingers into my unprepared cunt.

I cry into his mouth, biting his lip until I draw blood. It only makes him more determined as his fingers demand my pleasure, thrusting in and out of me so hard it hurts.

It hurts so fucking good.

"Mine, you're mine," he snaps. "Remind me where I am, little doe. Come for me and let me feel it. Let me go back in there with the scent of my girl on me to give me courage."

"I'm yours." I rock into his hand as his thumb ruthlessly attacks my clit, rubbing it until I explode, screaming into his mouth. He draws every drop of pleasure out of me, and only then does he slow, his fingers lingering inside me as he kisses me softly. "I love you, little doe. Now let's finish this together."

"Together." I nod as he slides his hand out and lets me down. He coats his tongue and lips with my cream, dragging it under his nose as if to ward off the stench of the man's evil with my scent alone.

"You good?" I ask, not wanting the devil in the room to smell a hint of weakness right now.

"I'm fine," he replies, and this time, he seems like it. His eyes are clear and hard, and his body is relaxed and in control.

He's fighting his demons, and I helped, and as he steps back in that room, I know Master's control has finally dropped away from him. He has nothing now, he's weak without the control, fear, and shame he exerts over those weaker and younger than him, and Gray will use that.

I sit on the other sofa this time, my legs crossed as I observe, knowing Gray has this. He stops before Master, and I watch the other man's eyes widen in terror as he realizes what I did.

He can't scare him anymore.

He can't make him sick with shame.

Gray is free of his control, and he's learning to live with the memories.

"Names. Each time you deny me, I will inflict another wound. You can't handle the pain, you never could, but me? I can. I've lived my entire life in agony. I know the best wounds that won't kill and where it hurts the most because I've lived it, and tonight, so will you, at least until I tire and kill you."

"Look, I—"

Gray slashes across the man's ankles. He screams in horror and all color drains from his face before he passes out. Gray leaves, and when he returns, he places buckets and bowls of ice water on the floor. Gray waits mere moments before tossing ice-cold water over him, waking him with a splutter, his face sweaty and feet bleeding. "You can live through that, but the pain will start to become unbearable," Gray tells him conversationally. "Names."

The man begins to sob. "I swear, I don't know."

Gray grabs the man's shirt and drags it over his head before pouring water across his face, waterboarding him as he screams and chokes. He stops for a moment and then starts again until the man passes out once more. Releasing his hold, Gray waits for the man to wake up, heading to the kitchen as I watch.

It takes a few minutes for the man to come around, and when he does, his eyes land on me. "Please, please help me," he begs. "I have money—"

"Cool, so do I." I shrug. "And it's much more fun to listen to you scream."

"Oh God," the man cries.

"Not God, but the devil you made," Gray informs him as he steps back into the room with a flaming hot BBQ masher in his hand. With a wink at me, Gray presses it against the man's chest, the smell and sound of sizzling flesh reaching me as he howls and fights to get away from the branding utensil.

He repeats this until Master passes out again. Snarling, Gray tosses the instrument away, his hungry eyes locking on me. "Gray," I warn, but he advances on me.

"Let's pass the time, shall we? Well, until this weak bag of shit wakes up." Before I can protest, he shoves open my thighs and pushes me back. He cuts away the crotch of my jeans, and his lips seal on my cunt.

I scream. I can't help it, especially when his tongue thrusts inside me before he rubs my clit. Instead of fighting it, I reach down and grip his hair, riding his face as his fingers slip inside my wet pussy and start to stroke in tandem with his tongue.

He leaves no part of me untouched, untasted, and the urgent strength of his tongue and fingers has me crying out and arching up to ride his face.

There's a groan, and my eyes flicker to Master as he wakes up, yet I can't stop, and Gray only speeds up. He eats my pussy with such viciousness it almost scares me, even as it makes me gush into his mouth.

Screaming his name as he nips my clit, I watch Master's eyes blink open, going from me to Gray and back again before filling with terror as he slams them shut.

Grinning, I drop my head back and tug Gray closer, riding his face, and when he sucks my clit, I explode across his tongue and fingers, crying out his name. He licks me through it before sitting back.

My cream covers his face and chin, and his eyes are alight with smug satisfaction. "Back to work I go." He winks and closes my quivering legs. "No one else gets to see," he murmurs, and then he's back on his feet, standing before Master like he didn't just make me come so hard I wouldn't even be able to stand.

"Now, where were we?"

"Please," the man begs. "I'll tell you everything I know."

"I know you will," Gray replies calmly. "The question is, will it be before or after I cut off your balls and make you eat them?"

"You can't—"

Gray doesn't hesitate. He cuts through the man's pants and, with a disgusted sneer on his lips, grabs the man's balls and slices. I watch as he screams, all the while Gray using the hot iron to cauterize the wound, leaving his dick hanging. Gray stands and shoves the man's balls into his mouth.

"Swallow. That's what you used to tell me." Covering the man's mouth, he tips his head back, forcing him to swallow his own balls.

When Gray moves his hand, the man turns his head and throws up everything, including his balls.

Honestly, it's the weirdest thing I've ever seen, but you've got to love a man who keeps his word.

We both wait as he gags and spews everywhere, even down himself as he cries and jerks in pain, pissing his pants in terror. When he stops, his head hanging as he sobs, Gray steps before him once again, ready for the next round of torture.

"Names," he demands, voice brooking no argument.

The man begins to rattle off names and addresses of the few connections he made in the group home before pausing. "That's all I know, I swear. I never knew who ran it."

"How did they find you? How did you pay?" Gray demands.

"I-I don't know." Gray snarls, and the man jerks back. "I swear, I hired a prostitute, a boy before, and watched some videos online, but this man approached me, and he knew everything. He told me he could fulfill my wildest dreams and gave me a card. I paid by cash every time at the house. That's it; that's everything. I swear, I know nothing else."

"Then you are useless to me now," Gray mutters.

Without so much as a twitch, he snaps the man's neck.

His death was too quick in my opinion, but this is Gray's revenge, not mine.

When he turns to me, he seems more at peace, even if he's still angry and haunted.

"Come on, little doe, our work here is done," he tells me as he grabs his phone. "I'll edit this and send his confession to his wife so she knows about the monster she was living with. She'll know we did her a favor and saved her and her unborn child by killing the prick."

"In a moment." Grabbing a knife, I pull back the dead man's head and get to work. When I step back, I admire my handiwork and grin at Gray as he chuckles.

Across his head, I carved 'pedo bitch.' This way the whole world will know who he really was and why he needed to die.

"Now we can go." I nod, taking the hand Gray offers me and heading back to the car.

We leave the body and pain behind with each step we take forward.

I fall asleep on Gray's couch while he works to compile lists and information on the names revealed. He grows more and more stressed when he can't find someone called General.

I'm no use to him at this stage, and I will only serve as a distraction, so I decide to get out of the house and meet up with Cara for breakfast and spend some quality time with my bestie, especially since we lied and said we would be together all week. Plus, I think she's feeling a bit neglected since I've become consumed with all things Gray, and I never want her to feel like that. I love my girl.

After breakfast, I wander for a bit before heading to my dorm and getting changed into my normal clothes. After all, it's Sunday, which means it's time for a family dinner, and after being MIA all week, I have no choice but to go, otherwise Alaric will track my ass down and lock me away forever.

Outside of their house, I blow out a breath before letting myself in. It's only been a week, yet it feels like a lifetime ago since I was last here. Everything has changed, and my entire world has shifted to not only include Gray, but my past.

That's something I need to discuss with Layla, but I don't know how. She never brought it up, so my guess is either she doesn't know what happened there or she wants to forget.

Inside, I find Layla cooking, or trying to. Alaric is attempting to pull her away, and as I lean into the doorframe, I smile as he twirls her around the room. A bright smile splits her lips before she laughs, so happy and carefree. I swallow, not wanting to taint their perfect life with the mess in my head.

I hate keeping things from her, and there's so much I want to tell her, to ask her, but how can I ruin it today when she looks so happy? When she spots me, an even wider grin splits her face, and she smacks Alaric away as she hurries to me. Layla wraps me up in her arms, and for a moment, everything is right with the world.

"Zoey! You're early! I thought you'd be up in the Hamptons for another week. Why haven't you called? Oh my god! You cut your hair. It looks so cute on you. I missed you so much," she rambles, embracing me tighter as I suck in her calming scent.

"I missed you too."

Pulling away, she smiles as she looks me over. "Something seems different about you, and I don't mean the new punk rock hairdo." She cocks her head. "Are you okay?"

Forcing a smile, I nod. "I'm good." To distract her, I look over at Alaric with a teasing smirk. "What? No hug?"

Huffing, he wraps us both up in his huge arms, making us laugh while his eyes stay rooted on mine. The fine hair on the back of my neck stands on end as his scrutinizing gaze takes stock of me, noticing everything I'm trying damn hard to keep hidden. With a small grin still plastered on my lips, I look away from his gaze, praying that I haven't given anything away. Completely oblivious, Layla breaks free from our embrace and hurries to the pot that's boiling over. Unfortunately for me, this gives my dad the perfect opportunity to step closer to me and get answers to whatever questions he has in his mind.

"Tell me, kid," he demands.

"Nothing." I lean up and kiss his cheek. "Now, where's my favorite niece and nephew?"

"Sophie is at a sleepover next door, and Gage is at his gramps for the night." He huffs, clearly hating the latter more. "Pops insisted on a boys' day. I just hope he's not showing him how to shoot or something."

"He better not be!" Layla calls out, making us both laugh.

"Missed you, kid, now come on. Let's get the table ready and eat."

I follow after him, knowing he's watching me carefully and spotting too much. After all, I feel raw.

Raw from that home.

Raw from Gray.

Raw from the man we killed.

Do I look different?

I feel different, and that's when I realize the outfit I'm wearing isn't a normal flowery dress. Instead, I'm in tight black jeans, boots, and a crop top.

My outfit is somewhere between my usual and the costume I wear for their sakes.

It dawns on me that all it took was one week with Gray for my two worlds to start to blend together, and the sensation feels like I'm adrift at sea, unsure of which safe port I should be swimming toward.

I'm cutting my meat, listening to a story Layla is telling us about Gage, when the front door opens and slams shut. We all jump, turning to look. Alaric is on his feet in an instant, standing before the table with a gun behind his back.

Footsteps draw closer, but I can't see around Alaric as the person stops at the doorway to the dining room. Alaric doesn't relax, however, and if anything, he tenses more, his finger going to the trigger.

I crane my neck around, and my mouth drops open when I see Gray leaning casually in the doorway, grinning at us all like he was not only invited but welcome.

My heart flips like crazy, and I can't stop the smile that blooms. He throws me a knowing, heated look before stepping into the room, completely unbothered about a bristling Alaric.

"Sorry I'm late." Gray winks at me. "What's for dinner?"

"You have five seconds to get the fuck out," Alaric demands, his voice ice cold.

Gray, completely unaffected, leans around him to wave at Layla, making me bite my lip to stop my giggle.

"Four," Alaric warns, stepping to the left to block his view. "And if you ever come to my family house again, I will not hesitate to kill you."

Shit, this could get bad fast. I'm about to stand when Layla's hand covers mine on the table. I shoot her a confused look, and she smiles softly at me. She searches my gaze, and I don't know what she sees there, but she nods as if she found an answer to something and clears her throat.

Layla looks at me before smiling. "Alaric, didn't I mention I invited Gray? How silly of me. It must have slipped my mind. Please, come and take a seat."

She's lying to her husband for me.

She's giving me her approval of him, and when she leans in as the two glare at each other, I almost giggle. "Any man willing to risk Alaric's wrath by showing up to his house just to see his girl? Well, he's good in my eyes, sweet sister."

I blink in shock and turn to see Gray slide past Alaric and sit opposite me, his feet instantly wrapping around mine under the table as his eyes run over me as if he didn't just see me a few hours ago.

I feel the same, though, and I can't pull my eyes from him even as Alaric sits angrily, like a storm cloud hovers above him. Despite the clear hatred coming his way, Gray serves himself, thanks Layla, and starts to eat.

"Layla," Alaric warns under his breath as he glowers in disgruntlement at his uninvited guest.

"Oh hush and eat, husband. The food is getting cold as it is," Layla snaps, giving him no options. He puts his gun on the table, keeping his eyes on Gray the entire time.

If only my father could see what Gray was doing under the table, his foot running up and down my leg as he eats. His gaze shows he's hungry for more than what's on his plate.

It's possessive and cold.

Mine.

The silence stretches between us, and I shoot Alaric a look, but he's too busy watching Gray. "So how was everyone's week?" I almost squeak.

"Long and hard." Gray grins. My mouth drops open, and he grins wider. "Though there were definitely some good times. I got to try out a new car; it was delicious."

Oh, fucking hell.

"I see, how... nice." Layla looks at me and smiles. "How was yours with Cara, Zoey? Did you have a good time in the Hamptons?"

"It was good," I manage to get out. "I always have fun with Cara. We just chilled and relaxed poolside. Not much worth talking about."

Liar.

Gray's eyes shoot to me with a knowing smirk, yet I see a hint of hurt in his eyes before he covers it, making me feel even guiltier than I already am. I'm lying to Layla and Alaric, and now I'm acting like I'm ashamed of the man I love by lying about us spending this past week together—the same man who admitted I'm his everything and who, despite everything, is willing to show up knowing it might get him killed just to be next to me.

I'm about to call myself out on my lies when Alaric shoots to his feet. "Stop it." He points at Gray.

"Stop what?" Gray asks, leaning back and eyeing him.

Layla tries to cool their tempers. "Boys."

"Stop looking at her. I told you what would happen," Alaric snarls.

"Why would I do that? She's beautiful."

Oh fucking hell, Gray has a death wish.

As if to prove my point, Alaric leaps at him. Sighing, I drop my fork and get to my feet.

"Zoey, let them work it out," Layla orders, but she's clutching at her neck as Alaric takes Gray down. Gray lets him, not even defending himself as Alaric grabs his throat and smashes his head into the floor.

"You do not come near her. You do not look at her. You leave my family alone!" he roars.

"I can't do that," Gray replies, not blocking the blow Alaric lands on his face. His eyes go to me, resigned but uncaring as Alaric punches and smashes his head into the floor.

"Alaric, stop!" Layla screams at her husband.

It's not my sister's loud outburst that shakes something awake inside me. Something glazes over Gray's eyes, and that makes me snap to attention.

I never want to upset Alaric, but I won't let him hurt the man I love either, not even to protect me.

Rounding the table, I lay my hand on Alaric's shoulder. He instantly freezes, his head swinging up to meet my gaze. "Stop it," I demand, my voice commanding. "You hurt him one more time, I'll walk out, and you'll never see me again."

"Zoey." He gapes and gets to his feet, reaching for me, but I step back. His crestfallen expression makes me swallow, and I look at Gray.

"Are you okay?"

"Never better, little doe, don't worry." He wipes his nose and climbs to his feet. Alaric looks between us, his eyes narrowing, so I step closer, drawing his attention from Gray before he starts attacking him again.

"I am not a child anymore, Dad." I hold up my hand when he goes to speak. "Please listen to me. I know you want to protect me from the world, but you can't protect me from everything. You need to let me live and give me space to make my own mistakes and choices. I love you, and I'm forever grateful for you loving my sister and taking me as your kid, but I'm grown now, even if you refuse to see it."

"You're still my kid," he warns.

"I know, and you are my father in every single way that matters. When I was younger, I needed you. I needed you so badly. Your protection, your guidance, and your love. I still need all of that, Dad, but now you'll have to offer me all those gifts in different ways, because if you insist on keeping this tight leash on me, then sooner or later you are going to push me away." He jerks like I struck him.

"Because that's what's happening, Dad. I keep secrets because I know you'll judge me, because you'll lock me up and throw away the key."

"Because I love you," he snarls.

"I know. But love shouldn't come with rules and strict stipulations. You should love me for who I am, every part of me, even if you don't like them. I never loved you less for who and what you are." He staggers back. "That's all I'm asking from you. If you can't do that, then maybe I should leave."

"Zoey!" Layla gasps, her eyes filled with tears.

"I'm not a little girl anymore, Layla, and we both know we've been through too much to think I was even when I was younger. You saved me, both of you, and you gave me a good life, but now I need to live it as I choose to. I spent so long facing death; I need life."

"And him?" Alaric snarls, not hearing me and instead focusing on Gray. "This is all because of him, isn't it?"

"No." I sigh. "It's not. He's a good man. If you gave him a chance, you'd see that. It's only your overprotectiveness of me that refuses to give him one. If you did, you'd see that you and Gray are more alike than you think. It's probably the reason why I—" I cut off right there.

Gray's eyes widen when I say that.

"Get out," he demands of Gray, and he knows not to push his luck.

With one more lingering look at me, he thanks Layla and walks away. I watch him go before meeting Alaric's eyes.

"I don't know what's going on with you, Zoey." My full name makes something inside me crack. It wasn't about me choosing Gray over him, but finally telling him everything I wished I had. "You're changing right before me. I knew every time you lied to me, and it hurt. It hurt Layla too."

"I never wanted that," I tell him, tears filling my own eyes. "I never want to hurt either of you, but I'm so tired of splitting my life just to pretend to be the person you want me to be. Why can't who I am be enough? Why can't you get to know me now as an adult and stop looking at me like a child?"

The look in his eyes is clear. He's not angry, he's disappointed in me, and that's worse.

K.A KNIGHT & IVY FOX

"Go home, Zoey. We will talk when I am calmer. Anything I say now will only hurt us both."

"Al—" I start, but he turns and walks away, slamming a door deeper in the house. I look at Layla, desperate for her to understand. "I didn't want this to happen."

"I know." She smiles softly, walking around the table and cupping my cheek like she did when I was a kid. "Sometimes people have to be pushed to see the truth, and sometimes life is hard and it hurts, but that doesn't mean you stop loving the people you care about. He'll get over it. He just needs time to lick his wounds and realize his baby girl is not a baby anymore."

"And you?" I whisper, searching her gaze.

"I will always love you, and I will always be in your corner. You are an incredible person, Zoey, and I cannot wait to meet the part of you that is willing to stand up for a man like Gray. It's like you said. If Alaric wasn't consumed by his own fear and hatred, he would see he's just like him, and so are you. Stubborn, wild, intelligent, and brave." I swallow back the pain, and she wipes away my tears. "It's why you butt heads. Now go after your man. Anyone willing to risk your father's wrath is a man I can see you loving through thick and thin. You have never been one to shy away from a challenge, my sweet Zoey, and I don't think you should start now."

"I love him," I admit.

"I know, and he loves you. He wouldn't have come here tonight if he didn't," she says with a grin. "All I ever wanted was for you to be happy and safe, but I'm starting to realize the life I wanted for you might have been the life I wanted for me since I never got to live it, and that I shouldn't expect you to follow my own dreams and path. You'll make your own, you always have, and I'll be right behind you, Zoey, cheering you on all the way." She kisses my head and goes after her brooding, hurt husband.

Sure, I did the right thing.

No one has ever stood up for Gray, and if I hadn't, I would be no better than those who hurt him. I'll always stand up for him, even if it breaks my own heart.

Even if that means I lose my father too.

Turning, I go after Gray, hoping Alaric will find it in his heart to understand.

I hope I haven't lost the only father I've ever known, but I'm finally being me.

Every flawed, reckless, incredible part of me.

U sing the hem of my shirt, I wipe the splattered blood off my face, glowering at the pile of gutted flesh bound to his bedpost. Although I worked him over good, I'm still unsatisfied. This piece of trash wasn't able to give me any more intel than Master had.

"Useless. Fucking useless."

This is my third kill tonight, and I'm left with the same unanswered questions as when I started.

Disgruntled, I spit on the dead man's corpse before stepping away from the bed and sitting on the single chair in the corner of his room. With my knife still clutched in my hand, I run my fingers frustratedly through my hair, uncaring that his blood will undoubtedly mat my strands.

Fuck.

I just need a second to get my shit together, but it's no use. No matter how much time passes, my world insists on being one chaotic fuck up. Between my lifelong mission and Zoey, I'm not sure which one is causing the massive migraine I have right now.

It's all my goddamn fault. I shouldn't have gone to her house like that. It was stupid and impulsive—two qualities I thought were lost on me—but when it comes to my little doe, shit, all logic and restraint go out the window.

I may want to make excuses for my behavior, but deep down I know full well why I had been so gung-ho in showing up at Alaric's last night. I wanted to him to know that Zoey was mine now, and that he, or any other motherfucker out there, could never take her away from me. I want to blame my possessiveness as the culprit for my unexpected visit, but it was my insecurity that led me to her family's front door, fearing that somehow her father would say something that would make her love me less.

It was an idiotic move, yet I did it anyway.

Now, while I'm assured that Zoey won't leave me if her father tells her to, in the end, she's the one who's left hurting. She tried not to show how bruised she was after the fucking fiasco that took place with her father, holding her head high when she left his house and came with me back to mine, but I saw it in her perfect green eyes. It hurt her to confront her father that way, to step out of the shadows and show him her truth—that she had been death's mistress long before I ever came into her life. I tried to ease her suffering by loving her the whole night through and most of today, in the spare room, of course, a distraction she desperately needed to make sense of what she did, but when I offered for her to come with me on my *errands* this evening, she refused, explaining that she needed some alone time to think.

Think.

Like thinking will make her loss more bearable.

It might hurt her now, but she knows that the painful conversation she had with her father couldn't have been avoided. Sooner or later, Zoey would have needed to step into her power, and Alaric would have been forced to dryly swallow his fears and worries and let his eldest daughter live her life as she wanted.

But still… It didn't have to be the shit show it was, and I only have myself to blame for how everything went down.

It's not like I didn't know how protective Alaric is of my little doe. Long before he ever introduced me to his family last year, I knew Zoey had her adoptive father wrapped around her tiny little finger. Right from the get-go, when Alaric had started training me to fill his spot at the agency, he would sometimes try to make small talk with me—as small a talk as a man like him is capable of anyway—and every time he did it, all roads would lead back to the two women he treasured most in his life, his wife and eldest daughter. Sure, he would coo and chuckle over something his twins had done, but anytime Layla's or Zoey's names would pop up, there was a tinge of admiration in his tone, almost as if they could do no wrong in his eyes. To him, both women had the strength of steel that many hitmen would foam at the mouth to have just a sliver of. They were his pride and joy, and now, in his mind, I corrupted one of them.

And worse still, I ripped that pride and awe of Zoey's father away from her.

Pissed, I spring up to my feet, jump on the bed, and start stabbing the corpse's face over and over again until he's fucking unrecognizable. It's only when my phone starts blowing up that I stop. Thinking it could be Zoey, I leap off the bed and rush to my discarded leather jacket to pull my phone out. When I verify that it's Hale calling and not my little doe, I drop the bloody knife on the shag carpeting and sit back down on the small chair.

"What?" I blurt out, aggravated.

"Well, hello to you too, asshole. One of those nights, I take it?" He chuckles.

"I'm busy. What do you want?" I spit.

"By busy, I assume you're eliminating one name at a time from that ledger your girl found at the home."

"Hmm." I grunt and nod, even though he can't see me.

"How many have you crossed out so far?" he asks, sounding intrigued.

"Four."

"Four? What are you doing? Napping between kills?" he jokes. "I would have thought you'd be halfway done by how enthusiastic you were to get started."

"Shit came up," I reply stoically.

Hale's right though.

If I wasn't so consumed with Zoey, I might have already had twenty of these pedo fuckers in the grave by now. What he doesn't know, though, is that it's not about the kill. It's about making them suffer until they give me what I want, and what I want are two things— the name of the person who is the head of this revolting ring and General's whereabouts. The little black book Zoey retrieved for me only had the client list, except for one name—the monster who still visits my nightmares every night. The only intel I've been able to glean from the clients who frequented the group home have been low-level guards, but the person who is controlling all the strings is still a ghost. Ironic, really, that it will take a ghost to find one, but find him I will, even if it's the last thing I do. There must be a client important enough to merit meeting the boss. All I have to do is cross each name out until I find them.

As for the man named General, that's proving to be a little trickier.

Most of the clientele is ignorant about who else enjoys the group home's services, their anonymity being the very reason they pay top dollar for the privilege of ruining innocent lives. The only hope I have of finding one monster is to find the other first. Whoever is in charge knows who their full client list is, including General, and when I find him, I'll make him tell me exactly where General lives, just before I slit his throat and rid the world of his brand of evil.

There's only one thing that is bothering me about my plan.

If the book I have in my possession was written by this so-called boss, then why didn't he also add General's info to it? Why leave him out? I guess I'll have my answer when I finally meet him face-to-face, but to do that, I have to concentrate. Right now, it's a hard task to accomplish when all my thoughts end up leading me down one road —Zoey.

"Speaking of shit…," Hale starts, sounding less than amused, and his tone pulls me out of my thoughts. "A friend would have given me a heads-up that Alaric would be paying me a visit."

"He went to see you?" I ask, since everyone knows Hale doesn't do drop-ins at his place. In my mind, I have imagined that he lives in some sort of dark cave filled with computer screens as he spies on the world, but I've never been able to verify if my suspicions are right or not since Hale keeps his home address and everything else pertaining to him off the grid. It speaks volumes about Alaric's motivation to track him down.

"Yeah, he did, asshole. Thanks for that. Not only do I have to replace the door because the prick busted it down, but now I've got a good old shiner to match. He messed with my money maker thanks to you," he whines.

"Me? What do I have to do with it?"

"Oh, I don't know. Maybe because the big, brooding beast thought that somehow I knew you were shacking up with his little girl. FYI, you really need to get more friends. Being the only one who actually likes your fucked-up ass is starting to mess with my looks. How the fuck can I be seen in public with this black eye, huh?" he carries on.

Vain fucker.

If I didn't know Hale was even more unhinged than Alaric and I put together, the way he conducts himself would never hint at the depravities that run rampant in his psychotic mind. Hence why I think he's the most dangerous of us all. He looks like your run-of-the-mill, clean-cut, *GQ* cover model, while Alaric and I wear our damage right on the surface. Anyone who comes close to either one of us knows that we aren't to be messed with.

Hale on the other hand…

He'll win you over with his dazzling, pearly white smile while slowly shredding your life apart, piece by piece, destroying everything you hold dear until you weep for death at his hand. He's shrewd and calculating under the guise of a shallow demeanor.

"Did he say anything to you?" I question, wondering just how deep Alaric's resentment regarding Zoey runs. I don't care if he hates my guts or not, he never cared much for me to begin with, but knowing his dislike of me trickles down to his daughter sets my teeth on edge.

"Oh, you know, the usual. He listed all the ways he's going to kill you. Nothing a big papa bear like him wouldn't say." His laugh grates on me.

My tense shoulders ease somewhat.

"So he only talked about me, not Zoey?"

"Are you listening to a word I say?" he goads. "The man is fantasizing about chopping you into tiny little pieces and feeding you to his dog."

"Alaric doesn't have a dog," I retort, rolling my eyes.

"Oh, trust me. He'll get one just for you." Hale laughs.

"Whatever," I mumble.

The line goes quiet for a while, and the hair on my neck rises at Hale's silence.

"What?" I bark when the silence gets to be too much for me.

"You want this girl?" he asks evenly.

"She's already mine," is my firm reply.

"The fuck she is," he retorts with a scoff. "Look, I'm not an expert of *love*," he begins, the word *love* sounding like it tastes bitter on his tongue, "but I do know something about women. They either hate their daddies and want to rebel with fuckers like you, or they love them to the moon and back, which makes you just a pit stop until they find a guy their fathers approve of. Guess where your girl lands?"

I fist the phone in my hand, almost breaking it in two, but I refuse to say anything in return.

"If you want the girl, and I mean really want her, then get right with her pops. She might say she's okay with going against his wishes now, but sooner or later, she'll resent you for not having him in her life. Remember one thing—she loved him first."

"You done?" I snarl.

"You know what? Fuck it. Take my advice. Don't take it. I couldn't give a shit. Just don't come running to me when she kicks your ass to the curb. I have a feeling you're one of those ugly criers, and who wants to see that shit?"

With that parting remark, the fucker hangs up.

Suddenly, the need to find where Hale lives and bash his face in is overwhelming. Knowing that Alaric had the same gut instinct only serves to aggravate me more. With Hale's advice still polluting my mind, I do the one thing I shouldn't—I call Alaric.

"You motherfucker! You have a lot of nerve calling me!" he rants so loudly I have to pull the phone away from my ear or risk becoming deaf. I let him call me all the names in the book. I let him yell and curse me out. My hands ball into fists with each damning thing he says.

"You think you're good for my baby girl? You think you can ever measure up? She deserves better than you! She always has. That's my baby you're fucking with, you worthless piece of trash. My baby girl!"

My molars grind with each insult, but I take them all with a grain of salt. What if Zoey and I have kids? What if we have a daughter and she brings home someone like me? Would I accept him? Or would I give the dirtbag hell until he was worthy of her?

The answer is simple.

I'd cut his balls off.

That realization is the only thing that keeps my tongue in check. It's the only reason why I let Alaric demean me and spew out his poison, knowing it will never touch me.

Not as long as I have Zoey.

It's only when Alaric starts gasping for air, his curses becoming incoherent, that I see my chance to state my case.

"I'll never hurt her," I tell him. "I can promise you that. I'd slit my own throat first before I ever cause her an ounce of pain." Alaric grows so quiet, his shallow breathing is the only thing that tells me he's still on the line. "You don't have to tell me she deserves better because I already know. That doesn't mean I won't do everything in my power to be worthy of her. I know you think I'm this soulless ghost, devoid of feeling and empathy, and to a degree, you're right, but not when it comes to Zoey. Never her. I'll treat her with the utmost respect, protect her, and care for her. She will always be safe in my hands. If anyone even tries to hurt a hair on her head on my watch, I'll willingly go on my hands and knees and let you kill me. You have my word."

"What is the word of a killer, Hart?" he asks, using my last name to detach himself from me.

"You once gave your wife your word that you would do all these things I'm offering your daughter. Are you saying you lied and that your word meant nothing?"

The loud growl that howls through the line would petrify a normal man.

But I'm not just any man.

I'm a ghost.

One that has been brought back to life by my little doe.

"Alaric?" I say when he refuses to engage. "I will not be the reason why my girl loses her father. Here is my olive branch to you. You either man up and accept it or lose her for good. The ball is in your court. Not mine. Do with that what you will."

With that warning hanging in the air between us, I pull a Hale and hang up the phone.

There are only two outcomes that I see.

Either Alaric accepts me and welcomes me into the fold, or he'll kill me.

Either way, I'll never stop loving Zoey, not while I have air in my lungs or when my bones have turned to ash.

Not ever.

CHAPTER 23

Zoey

I stir in the center of the bed, waiting for sleep to arrive, but it never does. Serves me right. If I had accepted his offer to accompany him on his killing spree, we would probably be home by now, tired and satisfied that we eviscerated one more monster in the world.

But my heart was just not in it, not after what happened last night.

Maybe I could have approached things differently and made it so my father could understand where I was coming from. Maybe I could have done something or said something differently for him to accept the path I was on. I know my dad is hung up on me being with Gray, but deep down I know that's not his biggest fear. He's petrified that I will follow in his footsteps, and worst of all, that I'll like it, but this is me. It's who I am. It's who I've always been.

Why can't he see that?

With a loud, audible sigh, I pull the pillow over my head, needing to inhale my lover's scent, hoping it will soothe my chaotic mood. Unfortunately, there isn't even a whiff of Gray in this room since his bedroom remains locked for some reason, and I had to make do with

"Fuck this," I mumble, throwing the pillow across the room before I jump up from the bed and walk over to the bathroom. I turn on the shower, hoping that the hot water will relax my tense limbs and offer me some form of reprieve from my thoughts. The small bathroom fills with steam as I wash away the day—not that it was very productive. All I did was sit around Gray's house and mope like a fucking child. God, I hate this. This is not who I am, and yet carrying my father's disapproval on my shoulders is wearing me down.

He's not the only man in my life who is causing havoc on my nerves though.

The man I love, the man I have committed my heart and soul to, is still lying to me, and I don't know why. I've given him plenty of time to come clean, and he still persists on keeping me in the dark. The worst part of his omission is that I'm almost a hundred percent certain it stems from the same reason my father had a total meltdown yesterday.

Like Alaric, Gray wants to protect me.

When will these men get it into their thick heads that I don't need protection?

I just need them.

Realizing that no matter how long I stay under the spray of water that it will be of little comfort to me, I step out of the shower, grab a towel, and wrap it around my naked frame. I pick up another towel to dry my hair while leaning against the bathroom doorframe. Absent-mindedly, my gaze scans every inch of the minimalist bedroom. There isn't anything personal or even remotely significant lying around. It's bare and immaculately clean, with no real hint of my wolf anywhere. My heart sinks to the pit of my stomach with the epiphany.

Gray has never had a home or a family to call his own.

He has never had an ounce of love to speak of, preferring to keep his surroundings as bare as possible so as not to allow hope to set in— hope that maybe he's deserving of everything that has been denied to him until now. It's a hope that was buried long ago, with men like Master ruling over him in his young life. Gray hasn't come out and said it yet, but I know that this mission is more than just a job for him. The way he froze when confronting Master told me all I needed to know.

That man abused him and stole his innocence. I saw unbridled fear in his eyes—a fear that can only be summoned from years of torture and abuse.

After that reaction, I'm as certain as I'll ever be that my ghost once roamed the halls of the group home I had been spying on for most of the week. The only thing I still don't know is if I was there, too, and if I was, does that mean Gray was there with me?

Having had enough of pondering the questions which I still have no answers for, I walk over to the bedside table and pick up my phone. On the second ring, my beloved sister answers.

"Zoey? What's wrong?" she asks worriedly. "It's five in the morning. Are you okay? Do you need help? I'll come get you."

Shit.

I should have looked at the hour before I called her. Now Layla is in mama bear mode, and it's going to take me a bit to diffuse the bomb I set off with just one call.

"Layla, I'm okay," I say sweetly, keeping my voice even so she knows I mean it. "I'm sorry I'm calling you so late. I didn't mean to worry you."

"You're my baby sister. I'll always worry," she coos, sounding less hectic. "Just give me a second," she adds, and I hear the ruffling of sheets seconds before I hear her locking a door.

"Okay. Now we have some privacy, kiddo. Mind explaining to me why you're calling me at this hour?"

I chew on my bottom lip for a bit, hesitant about bringing up old wounds, but I need the answers anyway.

First things first.

"How is he?" I ask.

"Alaric?" she asks with a sigh. "Licking his wounds, I'm afraid. It's hard for him to learn that his baby girl is all grown up now. Give him time, Zoey. He'll come around. You'll see."

"I'm not so sure," I mumble, feeling defeated.

"One thing about my husband is that although he's stubborn, he's no fool. It might take him a hot minute to see the error of his ways, but he always comes through in the end. He loves you, Zoey. All he wants is what's best for you. At the end of the day, if you're happy, he's happy. Are you happy, Zoey?"

"I'm trying to be," I reply in earnest.

"But something is preventing that," she surmises intuitively. "What's wrong, Zoey? How can I help?"

My hands start sweating so much that I have to grip the phone tighter or risk it falling to the floor. I sit on the edge of the bed and take a deep breath before bringing up old ghosts.

"Layla," I choke out nervously, "do you...Do you remember the time we spent in the group home before we went to Aunt Lucy's?"

The line goes silent for a bit, which only raises my hackles. "What's this about, Zoey?"

"Layla, please. Do you remember or not?" I beg, needing to know.

"I do," she finally says, letting out a long exhale. "Although, I'm ashamed to say not a lot of it. I was still healing from the gunshot wound to my shoulder, so I was heavily medicated throughout our time there. Any time I was lucid enough to stay awake, I was either on the phone or talking to our social worker to get us out of that place. I know I wasn't there for you as much as I should have been. That's on me. You hated it there so much, and I wasn't able to make the time there for you more bearable, too concerned about getting us out. I'm sorry."

I shake my head even though she can't see me. "No, Layla. That's not why I'm calling. I don't want you to feel bad or have any guilt regarding what happened at the home. You did your best, all things considered."

"Did something happen there?" she questions apprehensively.

"Not to me. At least, I don't think so. I can't remember," I answer truthfully. "And it might be all in my head, but I really need the name of the home, Layla. Do you remember it at all?"

"Mercy Village Group Home," she replies without missing a beat, sending a cold shiver down my spine. "That's what it was called. Mercy Village Group Home."

The confirmation brings tears to my eyes, and my whole body trembles.

"Zoey, please tell me what's going on. Why are you bringing this up now after all these years?"

"Are you sure?" I whisper. "Are you a hundred percent sure?"

"Yes. Now please, Zoey. You're frightening me." As the words leave her mouth, I see a shadow under the bedroom door.

"Don't be, big sis. I've got this handled. I love you." I hang up the phone, locking eyes with the man I love who has lied to me from day one.

Gray doesn't say a word as he steps into the room, approaching me like a predator who has set his eyes on his favorite prey.

"Who were you on the phone with?" he growls, ripping the wet towel off me and pushing me down onto the bed.

"My sister," I reply as his eyes scour over every inch of my naked body.

"Pretty late for a phone call, don't you think?" he says, kicking my legs apart and inching himself between them.

"I could say the same thing about you. Pretty late to come home, don't you think?" I parrot as he lifts one of my legs onto his shoulder and starts kissing and nibbling my ankle.

"Work took longer than expected." He smirks, and God, even though I want to claw his eyes out for lying to me, my pussy instantly grows wet with want. I lick my lips as he continues to kiss the inside of my leg, noticing that although his shirt has some blood spatter on it, the rest of him looks freshly showered.

"If you're going to take a shower at your kill's home, maybe you should take a change of clothes with you next time," I goad, scooting my ass closer to the edge of the bed.

"I'll make a note of it," he murmurs before sinking his teeth into my flesh.

My body arches up from the mattress, my eyelids closing of their own accord as he feasts on my sensitive skin. It's only when he flips me around so that I'm on hands and knees that I open my eyes.

"I need you. Now," he growls, slapping my ass cheek.

"Are you asking for my permission?" I taunt, looking over my shoulder just to catch a small glimpse of the lustful expression on his face. "Then here's your permission," I add breathlessly, rubbing my ass on the hard length of his crotch, my juices starting to drip down my thighs.

Another loud slap hits my ass, and I squirm in delight. I hear my wolf pull down his zipper just before I feel his callused hand wrap around my throat, squeezing my windpipe.

"I'm going to ride you long and hard, little doe, and you're going to take it, aren't you?"

I nod, sucking his thumb into my warm mouth as his other hand goes to my center and starts toying with my clit. My eyes roll into the back of my head as his deft fingers play with me until my legs begin to shake. As if he has an instruction manual on how to best coax an orgasm out of me, he stops his ministrations to thrust two of his digits into my cunt.

"You're so fucking wet, baby. I could probably fit my whole fist into this drenched pussy," he threatens, my core leaking on his fingers, taking his words as a challenge it wants to excel at. As if having a link to my depraved thoughts, he adds another finger, followed by another.

"Argh!" I scream when his hand is fully seated inside me, thrusting into me like a man gone mad.

Sweat pours down my forehead, drenching the sheet beneath me as I rock back and forth at a hectic pace, feeling so full that I might cry.

"Jesus, little doe. You're so fucking perfect. So fucking perfect," he growls, releasing his hold on my throat so he can prime my forbidden hole that's been taunting him. Through all my moans and gasps for air, I still hear Gray opening his bedside table, and when he spreads a cool gel all over the rim of my ass and his fingers, my core clenches around his digits.

"I'll have all of you. All of you belongs to me. Say it, little doe," he begs before lightly priming the rim.

"Yes," I pant excitedly. "All of me belongs to you. Now and forever."

"Fuck," he grunts as he positions the crown of his cock to my opening, working himself past my tight ring of muscles. "I can't get enough of you. I don't think I ever will."

"You'll never need to find out. I'm yours," I assure him just as he takes a deep breath and thrusts fully inside me.

"Gray!" I shout at the top of my lungs. The sensation of fullness is so overwhelming, I lose all sense of direction.

My wolf never falters, keeping our tempo intact as he fucks me with his hand and cock until I can't even remember my own name. This is his power. Gray takes me to the brink of madness and gifts me paradise as my reward. For a ghost who roamed the Earth with no real purpose, he's found it in me. He loves me with his body and soul, whispering words of endearment as he possesses every inch of me until I'm not sure where I end and he begins. All the lies and omissions he's keeping from me vanish from the forefront of my mind, and in their place, only the love I feel for him remains.

"Give it to me, little doe. Come for me," he demands while pounding the life out of me.

On cue, my body responds to his order, shattering beautifully apart for him to put the pieces back together once he's done. My soul leaps out of my chest, watching how perfect we look together from above. We are two lost souls who found each other amidst all the darkness and death. As my soul returns, Gray comes inside of me, falling on top of my limp, sated body. He leans close to my ear, his breathing just as erratic as mine.

"I love you," he whispers with such desperate devotion my heart hurts.

"And I love you, my wolf. Always."

With that soul-felt promise, my heavy lids shut, and I let sleep finally take me under.

"Let me go!" I shout at the big mammoth who insists on gripping my arm and keeping me still.

"Shut up, you fucking brat. You're supposed to be in your room."

"But I don't want to go to my room. I want to see Gray. Why can't I see Gray?"

The man's face turns all sorts of ugly as he leans down and grips my chin.

"If you know what's good for you, you'd stop asking so many stupid questions."

Nostrils flaring, I pull away from his grip, but not before I bite down into his palm, breaking the flesh.

"You bitch!" he shouts, slapping me so hard across the face, my body slams into the wall, making me drop to my knees. "You'll pay for that!" he shouts, pointing a menacing finger at me while cradling his bleeding hand.

As he steps closer to me, fury burning in his eyes, I try to get back to my feet so I have a fighting chance to defend myself, but as he marches over to me, I suddenly find myself hunching into a corner, afraid that this stranger might end me here and now.

"Enough," someone calls out in the dark.

We both stare into the dimly lit corridor, unable to see the woman's face.

"I can handle this," the man says with a snarl.

"You have more important things to do. I can take Zoey back to her room," the woman replies.

I swallow dryly, my eyes falling to the floor as the woman approaches.

"Go," she orders him with steel in her voice. "I'll take it from here."

The guard curses something incoherent under his breath but does as he's told. Knowing that this woman has the power to order a beast like him around pulls at my curiosity. Maybe she'll be able to tell me where Gray is. He's never gone a night without coming to our special spot. Not once. But tonight, he never came, and I didn't see him all day either.

I'm worried about my friend.

My protector.

My wolf.

"Don't be scared," the woman coos, and there is this melodic tone to her voice that instantly sets me at ease. "Grab my hand, little one. Let me take you back to your room and your sister. I'm sure she'll be worried if she wakes up in the middle of the night and doesn't see you in your bed. You don't want to worry her, do you?"

With the mention of Layla, I take the nice lady's hand, the sparkling diamond bracelet paired with a gold watch on her wrist catching my attention.

"Do you like it?" she asks when she catches me staring at it longer than I should be.

"It's pretty. Shiny."

"Yes." She chuckles. "That it is. A friend gave it to me. It's good to have friends who know how to treat you well. I shouldn't be wearing such things here, but sometimes we need something pretty to look at, don't we?"

I nod, not really knowing what to say as she leads me down the dark hall back to my room.

"Can I ask you something?" she coos, coaxing a noncommittal shrug from me. "Why were you out of your room so late tonight? Did you have a nightmare?"

I shake my head. "No. I was looking for my friend," I admit.

"I see. Does this friend have a name?"

I nod again. "It's Gray. Like the color of his eyes."

"Very romantic of you." She giggles, making me furrow my brows in confusion.

Instead of asking her what she means by that, I ask her the question that's troubling me.

"Do you know where he is? I haven't seen him all day, and that big gorilla took him away from me last night."

"Is that so?" she says before giving my hand a little squeeze. "Your friend is fine. He just came down with a cold, that's all, but I wouldn't be too worried about him. You have a big day ahead of you tomorrow."

"I do?" I question in surprise.

"Yes." She laughs softly. "Your aunt is coming to pick you and your sister up first thing. You're going home."

"Home..." I roll the word on my tongue, feeling odd about it.

"Most girls would be happy to go home, but you don't seem like you are."

I offer another shrug since I'm unable to put what I'm feeling into words. Aunt Lucy's home isn't my home, this place isn't my home, and my father made sure that I could never go back to the only home I've ever known. I don't think Layla and I have a home anymore.

Layla is my home.

And Gray.

He's my home now too.

I walk the rest of the way in silence, still digesting the news that we'll leave tomorrow. Once we reach the door, the nice lady opens it and ushers me in.

"Best go to bed, Zoey. You have a big day tomorrow."

I'm about to step inside, but something causes me to remain rooted to my spot. "Can I see Gray tomorrow? Before I leave?"

Even though I still can't see her face through the darkness, I catch the way her shoulders tense slightly.

"I'm afraid not. Like I said, he's very sick. I wouldn't want you to catch his cold."

"I don't mind," I insist.

"No," she retorts a little too severely, leaving no room for negotiation.

I slouch in defeat, hating that I won't be able to say goodbye to the only friend I have. Knowing that there isn't anything else that I can do, I lower my head and walk into the room.

"Pity," I hear the lady mutter in discontent behind me just as I step inside. "Such spirit. I would have liked to have seen how far it would have lasted. Oh well. C'est la vie. You can't win them all."

I wake up in a cold sweat, the memory so real I can still taste the acrid air on my tongue. I turn to my side and see Gray blissfully asleep, his arms wrapped around my waist. Frantic and on edge, I look around at my surroundings, making sure I'm here and not back in that group home. When the glint of Gray's jagged blade on the bedside table catches my eye, I reach out and grab it. Pushing the love of my life onto his back, I wake him from his slumber, straddle his midriff, and place the knife under his chin.

"If you want me to fuck you senseless again, all you need to do is ask. No need for weapons here," he mumbles drowsily.

When I push the knife closer to his Adam's apple, he finally becomes fully alert. To his credit, he doesn't move an inch and lets me press the edge deeper into his skin without taking it away from me.

"You love me?" I ask, heart racing.

"Yes," he replies without even a pause.

"I don't believe you."

His face maintains that blank expression of his that I hate, but it's the glimmer of hurt in his silver eyes that tells me he's still with me.

"If you love me, you won't lie to me."

He starts to protest, making the knife's edge cut into his skin. It takes inhuman effort not to wince at the damage I've done, but I'm too far gone now.

"I know, Gray. I know," I whisper on a choked sob.

His silver eyes turn to liquid metal. "And just what, exactly, do you think you know?" he questions.

"Everything and nothing. I know that Layla and I were placed at Mercy Village Group Home when I was younger. I know that while I was there, so were you. I know that you protected me, even when I didn't know what I was being protected from. And I know… I know that they hurt you."

When he tries to turn his head away from me, I drop the knife and cup his face, forcing him to look me in the eye.

"Tell me. No more secrets. No more lies. Tell me," I beg.

"You should leave," he tells me through gritted teeth. "I need you to go. Now."

"No." I shake my head. "You don't get to say that to me. You don't get to order me away just because it's getting too real for you. Guess what? This" —I point to my chest then his— "is as real as it's going to get. We're real. And if you want us to have a fighting chance at all, you'll give me the truth. All of it. I don't care how ugly and heavy it is. I'll willingly carry the load. But you're going to have to meet me halfway and give me your truth, your pain, my wolf. I can take it."

His entire body tenses beneath me, but he doesn't push me away.

Like me, this omission has been eating him up inside, and it is finally time for it to see the light of day. I should have confronted him after we killed Master. I should have questioned him regarding the filth that sick fuck said to him as it happened. But I didn't. Gray was too raw, too on edge, and I feared he might cast me away if I dug too deeply, much like he tried to do now by asking me to leave.

I won't though. Nothing will make me leave his side, especially not after knowing the damage that was caused to him while he lived in that dreadful house. All I want is for him to share his burden with me, to stop protecting me and let me protect him for once.

"They hurt you, didn't they?" I ask on a whispered breath, already knowing the answer. I watch him swallow down the lump in his throat.

"They did much worse than hurt me. They broke me."

Hot tears well up in my eyes at the confirmation as the truth is finally set free. Just as I suspected, this is why he's been so obsessed with that group home and killing off one pedophile at a time. They used him, sold him, *broke him*, and they would have done the same to me given the chance. The only reason I was left untouched was because my lone wolf stepped in the line of fire for me.

He protected me even then.

"Why didn't you want to tell me? Why try to hide this from me?" I sob, letting my tears fall onto his bare chest. "Why not tell me that you knew me from there?"

"What good would it have done? You had forgotten me, and by forgetting me, you also forgot that nightmarish place. I couldn't risk telling you and bringing back all those memories." He runs the pad of his thumb over my cheek, drying up the errant tears. "Don't cry for me, little doe. Knowing I had a hand in making sure you had a beautiful life was enough for me—*is* enough for me."

I shake my head. "I didn't come back for you. I knew in my bones that the fucking place was no good, and yet I left you there. I didn't come back," I cry, my tears streaming down my face.

"You were a child. You had no way of knowing or being able to save me."

I shake my head. "No. I made myself forget because I couldn't live with the fact that I left you there. The only friend I had. The only person who watched over me at night, making sure that those monsters wouldn't hurt me. I'm so sorry. I'm so sorry."

Gray wraps his arms around me, and in one fell swoop, rolls me onto my back. With his body covering mine, he stares into my eyes, his silver moonlight gaze so soft and earnest it's heartbreaking.

"Look at me, little doe," he cajoles with the softest of timbres. "You couldn't save me then, but you did save me in the end. I'm alive because of you. Every day since you left that rathole, I fought to get back to you. I fought the hands of monsters, and then I fought off soldiers of war. I did that with a big fucking smile on my face because I knew that you were living your best life."

He kisses my lips so gently, his kiss feels like a feathered whisper. When I see his own eyes starting to water, I melt away in his embrace.

"For the sake of honesty and transparency, I admit that I had Hale track you down. It's true I knew where you were and how you were doing. I made Hale send me pictures of you just so I could see what an extraordinary woman you were becoming. But nothing… Nothing could have ever measured up to seeing you in the flesh. I already loved you when you were just a rug rat following me around back at the home, but I fell *in* love with you that afternoon when I went to Alaric's party. I'm sorry I kept the past from you, but know this, little doe. You are my present and my future. Nothing and no one will ever change that."

I wrap my arms around his shoulders, tightening my hold on him as our tears fall.

"We'll get them, my wolf. We'll get every last one of them. I promise you."

Just as he lets out a sigh of relief, the blurry image of the woman with the diamond bracelet seeps into the forefront of my mind, as does the last eerie thing she said to me.

You can't win them all, she said.

Just watch me.

CHAPTER 24
Zoey

L eaning down, I kiss him softly. "Ever had makeup sex?" I tease, making him laugh. It's a bitter, desperate sound, but it soothes my soul.

"No, but I'm more than willing to pop that first." He grins, kissing me back.

He positions himself between my legs, stopping to kiss my belly, my breasts, and then my lips again. "I don't want hard and fast. I don't want punishment or hate sex. I want you, Zoey. All of you. I want you to look into my eyes as you come. I want to take my time. I want slow."

Cupping his face, I press my forehead to his as I look into his stormy eyes. "You want to make love." Nervously, he nods and searches my gaze. "It would be a first for me too, Gray, but with you, it's perfect. I need you to remind me that you love me and that everything's okay, that everything will be okay." Dragging my lips along his, I tease him with my words. "Make love to me, my wolf."

"Little doe," he murmurs as our lips come together in a flurry of loving, drugging kisses.

I don't usually like it slow, but with Gray? I love it.

My every nerve is alight, and lust pours through me until I'm so wet it should be embarrassing. He swallows my whimpers as he rolls his hips, dragging his cock through my wet folds.

"Fuck, I love you," he says when he pulls back, pressing his forehead to mine once more.

Those stormy eyes remain locked on mine as he thrusts into me, slowly filling me inch by inch with his length. Wrapping my legs and arms around him, I tug him down and kiss him again, keeping us pressed together. "I love you too. I love every scarred inch of you, Gray. I always have, ever since I was a kid, and I always will."

"Zoey," he groans and closes his eyes before they snap open and lock on mine as he starts to move, our bodies coming together. Each touch is filled with reverence, passion, love, and promises.

It's a turning point for us. This isn't hate sex or an explosion of need.

This is our love in all its twisted, perfect glory.

Just two souls clicking together.

The ancient Greeks believed people were split in two and spent their whole lives looking for their other half. Gray is my other half.

He's my everything.

No more lies, no more secrets.

It's just us and everything we share.

The past, the present, and the future.

My head drops back when he tilts my hips, changing the position so each slide of his cock hits that place inside that has me seeing stars. "I love you, I love you," I chant, knowing he needs to hear it.

It will take a lifetime for him to believe he's worthy of it, but I'll remind him every second of every day.

"Zoey," he grunts, his neck straining and lips parted. We come at the same time, like a connection tethering us together, and our gazes remain locked the entire time until we kiss again.

"I love you so much," he murmurs. "So much that it scares me."

"It doesn't scare me," I tell him as he turns us so we are on our sides, still connected. "Nothing you could ever do would."

Curled in his arms sometime later, I allow my thoughts to wander and lock on a question I've always been curious about.

"Why do they call you Ghost?" I ask, looking into his gray eyes that I love so much.

Eyes that have been a part of my life longer than anyone else knows.

"Because without you, little doe, my world was gray, empty, and devoid of anything good and colorful. I wandered through it half dead long before they killed me. They call me Ghost because I have no soul. You have it, always have and always will."

"Gray," I whisper, searching his eyes. "I—what was your name? It wasn't always Gray or Ghost, right?" I frown.

"No, I had a real name once a long time ago," he murmurs.

"What was it?" I ask, knowing I shouldn't.

Licking his lips, he eyes me nervously. "Austin, my real name was Austin, but I stopped being him a long time ago, Zoey. Austin was kind. Austin was weak. He didn't know pain or how a belt felt against his skin, and he didn't know the perverted touch of someone else he never wanted. Austin had dreams, but Gray? Gray has nightmares. Austin died the moment I was put in that home, and I was born. I chose Gray because of my eyes—empty and soulless, just like me."

"You will always be Gray to me," I say as I kiss him softly. "Austin, Gray, Ghost... my wolf. Names don't matter. All that matters is that you are mine, and I am yours."

"I think I'd rather be called that," he murmurs.

"What's that?" I smile.

"Yours."

My heart beats triple time as I kiss him softly, promising him he will always be mine without words.

Neither of us need them.

"A shooting range?" I ask, my eyes going to him to see him grinning at me.

"We both have some frustrations we have to get out, so what better place than here?" He grabs my hips and hauls me to him, trapping me against the hood of the car. "Plus, I can test your skills, baby."

"Oh, you're on." I smirk, pushing him away.

He laughs and takes my hand, leading me toward the gun shop, but part of me sags. He's right; we both have frustrations.

We are both frustrated with the mission, and I am definitely upset about Alaric. He won't return my calls, and at first, I was angry, but now I'm just sad.

Actually, I am more than sad. I'm hurt—hurt that he can't accept me for who I am and hurt that the man who promised to always love and protect me and my sister is breaking that promise. He expected me to accept him as a killer, but this? This is too much for him.

Well, fuck him.

Gray is right. I need this.

I let him pay and get all set up as I wander out into the shooting range. It's empty, which is a surprise, and when Gray comes out, I realize why. He's rented the whole place.

He carefully lays out a selection of guns and then steps back, grinning at me. "Ladies first."

Narrowing my eyes, I step up and check out my options.

There is everything from automatics to handguns. I select a smaller caliber, knowing I'm more comfortable and in control, and he picks up a shotgun. "Show me what you've got, baby," he purrs. Excitement flashes in his gray eyes, and I know my own mirror his.

Pulling on the earmuffs, I step into the gate and choose the course on the left, avoiding the immobile targets down the row and instead selecting the assault course. Gray goes right, standing feet from me with a wicked grin, and waves me on teasingly.

Bastard.

It's time to show him exactly why he shouldn't mock me.

Focusing on my stance, I let Alaric's lessons come back to me. He told me I was a natural, and unlike Layla who hated guns, I loved them. I adored the power I felt with them.

A sense of calmness comes over me when I flick off the safety before I lift my arms, part my legs, and begin to shoot. I hit the first target dead center, and then I begin to walk, shooting as I go.

I roll under the next target, coming up as I fire, hitting it square between the eyes. I roll, dodge, and duck around them, hearing him firing seconds after I am. I reload as I walk, shooting four in quick succession before I have to roll over the top of a barrel and drop to my knees on the other side, firing at the moving targets as they grow farther away.

Standing, I start to walk again. I glance over to see Gray mirroring me on the other side. His face is easy and relaxed, and he holds the shotgun effortlessly as he decimates the targets.

Snarling, I round the box, ducking and firing at one of his, and he turns, his mouth dropping open. Winking, I turn back to my own, hurrying to the final sector which has five moving targets covering both sides. I pop two easily, and then he's there, firing at the last three in quick succession.

Flicking the safety on, I aim the gun at the ground as I rip off my earmuffs and glare at him, ready to ream him, but he's suddenly hauling me against him and kissing me hard and fast, and when he pulls away, we are both panting.

"That was so fucking hot, little doe. Now come on, let's play with the big guns." I hear respect and admiration in his tone, and when he leads me back to the stationary targets, he hands me some of the bigger guns and watches me take out my anger and pain on the targets, and then he does the same.

Hours later, we are both smiling and relaxed. He was right; we needed this.

That elated, teasing atmosphere soon disappears, however, when we get back into the car to find his phone buzzing. With his eyes on me, he answers, grunting into it before hanging up. "Hang on, little doe."

"Who was it?" I demand.

"A friend with the intel I needed on our next mark. Strap up, baby. We're going hunting."

There are two of them, and they are in a strip club. I perch on Gray's knees, watching the dancer on the pole. She's really fucking good, but Gray? He doesn't look anywhere but at our drunken targets who are throwing their money around.

Spinning to him, I cup his face and turn it to me. "Who are they?" I murmur against his lips.

His hands slide down to my ass, tugging me closer. "Guards," he whispers. "Still are, night guards."

"Do we know who is in charge yet?" I ask.

"Not yet, but we will," he promises.

"Then we'll kill both," I murmur. "I have a plan."

We have been here for hours, and they show no signs of moving, so I stand and tug off my top, leaving me in nothing but my lace bra and denim shorts. Gray snarls, but I just wink and avoid his reaching hands before swaying my hips as I wander over to them. I drape myself across their chairs, and their intoxicated eyes snap to me, widening in lust as they leer.

"Hello, boys. I can tell you like to party, so do I."

"Is that right?" The one on the left laughs, slurring his words slightly, his blond hair catching the light. He would be young and attractive if I didn't know exactly what he did to earn that money.

Licking my glossed lips, I nod and bend farther down, pushing my tits together. "That's right. Maybe we should party together." I wink and stand before turning and wandering away. I know they are watching, and I know the exact moment they stand.

Gray will follow them, and I trust in that as I head to the corridor that leads to the bathrooms and then keep going right to the back door we scouted earlier. Gray is letting me into every factor of our hunts now, and I helped him recon this place.

I also had to spend the last hour listening to them moan that the girls wouldn't accept their money to blow them, hence this plan. I'm tired of waiting. I want them dead, I want to see Gray in action, and then I want to fuck him while we are covered in their blood.

The fire door is propped open, the alarm long since gone, and leads to the back alley. It doesn't escape my notice that the first time I saw Gray in action was in a similar alley. Turning, I press my back to the wet wall opposite the door and wait.

Moments later, both men fill the doorway. "So you want to play, do you?" the one with black hair and evil eyes calls as they step into the alley.

"So badly." I flutter my lashes.

He's the first to reach me. He tries to spin me and press my face to the wall, but I resist, and he snarls, smacking me hard. "Then let's party." He laughs as the blond watches. The guy fumbles with my shorts, and I roll my eyes, sliding the blade from my back pocket as I see Gray appear in the door behind the blond one.

"Let's," I say, and then I slice up.

He screams as he falls back, his chest, neck, and face cut. He looks down at the wound in confusion and shock. "What the fuck?"

Flashing the blade in the light, I grin. "What? I thought you wanted to party?"

"Oh, you're fucking crazy!" He turns to his friend, but Gray is there with his eyes on the black-haired man as he grabs the blond one and slits his throat. Kicking the door shut, Gray cuts off his escape route as he drops the blond to the ground while he chokes on his own blood.

Gray's eyes are hard, angry, and possessive.

"This one is mine," I purr as I step up to the black-haired one. I tap him on the side, and he spins so he can keep us both in view. "You hear that? You're mine."

"Look, I'm sorry, I didn't know she was your girl," he says, his face pale as he glances at his friend and then Gray.

"Hey, asshole!" I yell. "Stop looking at him. I'm the one you should fear right now."

I leap at him, and he stumbles back, so I ride him down to the ground, pressing the knife to his throat as I lean in. "Tell me, do the people you work for let you touch the kids, or do you just watch?"

He stops breathing as he stares up at me. "Oh God," he whispers.

"Nope, sorry, just the devil and his bitch." I laugh as I lift the knife and stab it into his chest, over and over. I let my anger at what they did to Gray and all those kids flow out of me, and I don't even realize I'm screaming.

His eyes are open, unseeing, and I'm still stabbing him.

Arms wrap around me and hoist me into the air, then a hand grabs my wrist cruelly, forcing me to drop the blade before I'm backed into the wall. Fingers circle my throat until I blink and bring Gray into focus.

"He's dead, little doe," he promises.

I still, waiting and watching. For his disgust maybe?

After all, I just brutally killed someone.

I thought it would feel... *more*, more...fucked up, but instead I feel good, like I've rid this world of an evil bastard and I'm happy for it.

"You are fucking magnificent," he growls and slams his lips onto mine. When he pulls back, he presses his forehead to mine. "Never be afraid of how I will react, little doe. I'm yours. Nothing you could do, say, or think would ever scare me away, baby. This thing... us, it's forever."

Tears almost fill my eyes. "How do you always say the right thing?" I murmur.

"Not always, now make your sexy ass useful and help me clean this scene." He winks, pulling away.

We clean up the scene together, leaving nothing but the bodies behind.

A threat, a warning, that we are coming.

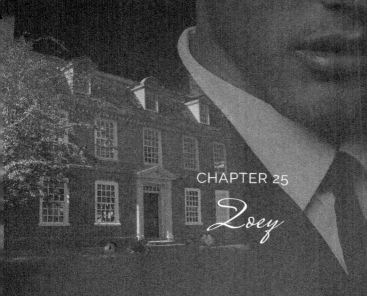

CHAPTER 25
Zoey

I ignore my ringing phone and grin at Cara, watching her lips twist at the sour cocktail I bought her. "Fuck, that's disgusting, Zo!"

"Did Cara fucking Nightingale just swear?" I pretend to be shocked, clutching my chest. She rolls her eyes, even as her cheeks heat. We are in an expensive cocktail bar near where Cara lives since she fears going too far in case her daddy sees her getting up to no good, which he already thinks I am.

He isn't wrong. If he knew what I liked to do for fun and who I was dating, he would keep his baby girl far away from me.

But I need this, need time with Cara. My entire world has been absorbed with Gray and our mission, and sometimes a girl just needs her bestie. "Alaric still isn't talking to me," I admit.

"Oh, Zoey, I'm sorry." She covers my hand on the black table we are sitting at. The booth is tucked into a back corner, away from prying eyes. We keep our distance from the men in suits and the women dressed to the nines, wanting it to just be us. Soft music pumps through the speakers, and the lights are dimmed to create a sultry atmosphere. It's a cool place with a huge bar in the middle of the room that has floor-to-ceiling shelves displaying every liquor imaginable.

I shrug and down my cocktail, grimacing at the sweetness of what she ordered for me—our favorite game. "It is what it is."

"I know, but I also know how much you love him. He's your dad, Zoey. He'll come around," she states, always so sure.

"You think?" I find myself asking, needing some of the happiness and positive energy she carries around with her.

"I know he will. There's nothing Alaric wouldn't do for you." She squeezes my hand and sips her drink again with a gag. "Fuck, seriously, Zoey, what is this shit?"

"It's called a Zombie." I giggle, unable to help it, and she laughs even as she pushes the drink away.

"Of course it is." She sighs and then looks at the table, picking at her nails. My eyes narrow. I've spent this whole night whining about my life, and now that I'm really looking, I realize something is wrong. There are bags under her eyes, which isn't like her—she's meticulous with her sleep and night routines—and her nails are chipped.

Cara is never not perfectly put together. Her father makes sure of that. If there were one loose strand on the top of her hair, I'm sure the man would have a conniption. Anal is the best adjective that I have for her overbearing father, and not the fun type either.

"Enough about me, what's wrong?" I demand.

Her head jerks up. "Nothing, why?"

"Liar." I raise my eyebrow. "I know you better than that, Cara. Talk to me."

"Nothing. Okay, it's just my dad is under a lot of pressure right now, and I guess it's just filtering through. I promise that's all." She smiles, but it doesn't reach her eyes. If there's one thing I know about Cara, it's that she won't talk unless she's good and ready, so I don't push it. "So tell me about Gray." She wiggles her eyebrows.

Laughing, I wave my hand and order us both another round. I lean in, and she copies me, our heads bent together. "He's amazing. I mean *amazing*, Cara, and the things he can do with his tongue—"

The drinks keep flowing, and we laugh louder and louder, talking about everything and anything. There are no worries, just friends in our own little world.

Excusing myself to the bathroom, I leave her reading over the cocktail menu for the next creation she's going to make me drink. As I wind through the tables, a golden watch brushes my hand as a woman in a black dress hurries past me.

For a moment, I still as a memory crowds my mind of a woman in a black dress coming into my room when I was younger, at the home, with a gold watch sparkling on her arm before I blink it away. Turning around, I force my legs to move, and I head downstairs to the bathrooms, the winding metal stairs clanking with my heels. At the bottom, the women's room has a massive line, but I spot a private cubicle, maybe the staff toilet, and quickly pick the lock and sneak inside.

I need to pee too badly to wait.

Turning to the mirror, I rub at the smudged eyeliner under my eye, blinking.

"Lock the door. Shit, this alcohol must be strong." I giggle, and I'm just about to turn to the lock on the door when it suddenly opens and a man slips inside.

I stumble back, blinking as I'm abruptly turned so I'm facing the mirror. Gray towers behind me, so I relax into him with a slightly drunk smile as he arches his brow. "When you said you had plans, I didn't think you meant getting drunk while discussing my cock, baby."

Laughing, I lay my head back as he watches me. "I knew you would stalk me here."

"Hmm, is that why you wore this ridiculous dress I want to tear from your body?" He snarls, tugging at the tight black bodycon material that clings to my every curve. I paired it with the red heels, and I know I look killer.

"Maybe," I flirt, licking my bright red lips as he watches. "What are you going to do about it?"

"Exactly what you want me to do," he retorts, gripping the dress and ripping it up, exposing my naked ass and pussy. "No panties, little doe?"

"Easy access." My hands hit the sink as I push back.

Groaning, Gray slides his hands up my thighs and shoves them open.

"Fuck, I loved watching you tonight and seeing all the men who wished they could get even a glance from you, their greedy fucking eyes watching every move my girl made. You loved it too, knowing I was there and would kill anyone who tried to touch what's mine." He grunts as he cups my wet pussy, grinding his palm into my clit.

I gasp. "Such a stalker."

"You love it," he snaps, biting my neck.

"I do." I groan. "Now fuck me, prove to them I'm yours."

"Oh, I will, baby, and then you'll go back out there with my cum sliding down these pretty thighs for everyone to see," he says as he slides his fingers down my folds and thrusts them inside me. My head hangs as he fucks me with them, but all too quickly, they are gone.

I hear his zipper, and I can't help groaning, knowing what's to come and the pleasure he will give me.

"Gray," I beg, needing him to hurry up.

His hand anchors me, cupping my throat. "Hold on, baby, and be quiet. We don't want to get kicked out before I make this pretty pussy weep for me." He groans as he slams into me, filling me with every inch of his hard cock.

He keeps my head up and my eyes on his in the mirror as he takes me fast and hard. His other hand slides down my torso to play with my clit until I'm gasping and crying out. He releases my neck and covers my mouth, smearing my lipstick, but I don't care. I scream into his hand as he muffles the sounds for me, his lips twisted in a snarl as he hammers into me from behind.

His cock slides across those nerves inside that have me coming within seconds. I scream my release into his hand, and he groans as he fights through my clamping pussy before stilling and filling me with his release.

Gray holds me up when I would have fallen, and we both let our breathing slow before he pulls from my body. He cups my cunt. "Mine," he growls, and then he tugs my dress back down and smacks my ass. "Clean your face, baby."

Huffing, I fix my lipstick and fluff my hair, but I still look freshly fucked and nothing can fix that. Smirking, he goes to slip away, but I grab his hand and stop him. "Meet Cara," I request.

He watches me carefully before nodding.

Grinning, I push up on my tiptoes and kiss him. "Thank you for letting me show you off."

And so, Gray suffers through girls' night. Cara is noticeably scared of Gray at first, but after watching him kiss me softly and fix my dress for me, she falls in love with him too, and surprisingly enough, Gray likes her, even going so far as to talk to her while we both get sloppy drunk.

He holds our bags and watches us dance and drink, and I've never felt safer and more loved in my entire life.

"Alright, I think it's time I got you both home." Gray huffs and, ignoring my protests, throws me over his shoulder before clutching Cara's arm. He steers us from the bar as she tries to escape his clutches and dance.

"When did I become a babysitter to drunk college girls?" he mutters, making us both laugh as he guides us from the bar.

Gray has to help me carry Cara up the back stairs and to bed, and once we are back in the car, he groans and covers his eyes. "Fucking hell, you're going to kill me, little doe. If she had thrown up on me—" He shivers in horror as I laugh, remembering the way we had to stop at least four times on the way home so Cara could upchuck.

She always was a lightweight.

"Oh, you think it's funny?" he warns, dropping his hand.

"I do." I grin and kiss him hard, and when I pull back, he blinks. "What was that for?"

"To say thank you for coming for me, looking after us, and helping my best friend when you didn't have to." His face softens as he cups my cheek, and I lean into it. "I appreciate it. Now let's go home, shall we?"

"Home." He nods and kisses me before holding my hand as we drive back to his place.

I must fall asleep on the drive, because the next thing I know, I'm being settled on an insanely comfy bed. Opening my eyes, I roll onto my back on what feels like satin sheets, and when I look down, I see they are shades of gray.

Of course they are.

The bed is massive, and I realize this is the first time I've been in his master bedroom. Sitting up, I find him undressing before a huge walk-in closet, which is nearly empty.

There's a fireplace to the right, unused with an empty mantel. Apart from that, there are two nightstands with lamps on low, a gray rug that looks hella comfy, and a huge TV, but within seconds, my gaze locks on something else.

Pictures everywhere, on every wall and every surface, of me.

Sliding from the bed, I pad on silent feet to the closest wall. I cover my mouth, and my eyes fill with tears at the collection. He said that Hale had taken pictures of me through the years, but this... I never expected this. I'm alone in most of them, but some have Layla or Cara in them, and they range from when I was really young to a few weeks ago.

His whole room is a shrine to me.

His obsession.

His love.

Turning, I find him watching me carefully, expecting reproach, anger, and disgust.

When I wander toward him, he tenses, but I pull his stiff arms apart and melt into him, meeting his gray eyes. "This should terrify me, but I feel... safe, as if you were protecting me my whole life, and I never knew. I love you, Gray. Nothing will change that."

He's obsessed and crazy, but fuck if I don't love it.

Here's a man who's willing to do anything to keep me safe. Who loves me so much his whole room is a shrine to my life.

If loving that is wrong, I don't want to be right.

"I love you too," he murmurs, relaxing into my embrace.

After kissing me, he orders me to bed and curls up around me. I fall asleep with a smile on my face and my eyes on a picture of me smiling into the camera as if I knew he was taking it.

I wake suddenly, not realizing why at first until I hear a sound—one that must have woken me. It's a mix between a groan and a cry. Flipping over, I find Gray twisted in the sheets next to me, coated in a cold sweat. His eyes are pinched together, and his lips are parted on a whine that makes my soul hurt.

His body jerks as if he's fighting someone off in his sleep.

"Gray?" I whisper, reaching for him.

With a shout, he shoves me away.

Climbing to my knees, I lay my hand on his arm, and he stills. "Shh, baby, I'm here. I'm here, my wolf. It's me, your little doe." I keep talking to him softly as I stroke up his arm and cup his cheek. He twists into my touch as if to escape his demons, and so I slip into his arms, and he sighs.

Slowly, his eyes blink open. "Zoey?" he croaks.

"It's me," I soothe, kissing his chest. "It was just a bad dream."

"A memory," he corrects, shivering in horror as he pulls me closer. "I get them every night, but you make them easier."

"I'm so sorry, Gray. I'm so sorry you had to suffer through what you did and that it still haunts you." Kissing him, I taste the salt of his tears and hate it. "Hopefully ending them will free you a little. If not, I promise to be here every night to fight them off and haunt you so they can't."

His lips curve up as he watches me. "I'd much prefer you haunting me, little doe."

"Good, because you're not getting rid of me." I kiss him once more before laying my head on his chest, listening to his rapidly beating heart. Protectiveness surges within me, as does anger on his behalf.

This poor, scarred man has been through so much, and even in sleep, he cannot escape it.

I wish I could take it away from him, but I know I can't. I'll spend the rest of my life fighting this battle with him and helping him as much as I can, because I love him so much it shouldn't even be possible.

He's so deeply ingrained in my life, in my heart, that I can't live without him. He's the only one who knows the real me and loves me for it, even though I thought he would never admit it.

He still thinks he's a ghost, wandering through life unfeeling, cold, and gray, but when it comes to me, he's anything but.

He can be cruel, angry, frustrating, and infuriating, but never cold.

Not to me.

He saved my life, and years later, I brought him back from the dead.

Our love was always meant to be, and no matter what happens, I'm choosing him.

Time and time again.

"Oh fuck!" Zoey yells loudly with my head between her thighs.

I can barely get air into my lungs with the way she has her thighs tightly locked around me, but who needs oxygen when I have her pussy grinding on my tongue? I'd die a happy man if the last thing I did was eat her out.

For the past few weeks, this is all we've done—fuck like two ravenous rabbits during the day, only stopping long enough to go out at night and slaughter the monsters who have roamed free for far too long. My idea of paradise.

"Please, please," she begs, digging her nails into my scalp while her juices coat my chin as I devour her.

My hands slither beneath her ass cheeks, pulling her up off the bed so I can have my fill.

"Just like that, my wolf. Oh my god!"

I smirk at the way her legs begin to shake around me, her impending orgasm threatening to split her in two. I keep up my tempo, sucking and biting her tiny clit until my little doe soars to the heavens.

"I'm coming! I'm coming!" she shouts.

Just as she detonates, I thrust two fingers inside her, hooking them in a way that has her gasping and gushing all over my face. I lick her clean, my cock so hard it feels like it's about to burst. As her erratic breathing starts to even out, I lean back on my haunches, pulling my little heathen up from the mattress, and wrap her trembling legs around my hips. I grab her chin and force her to look into my eyes, hers still heavy-lidded and soft from the earth-shattering orgasm I just gave her.

"I'm not done with you yet, little doe," I warn, grabbing her ass cheeks in my palms so I can notch the head of my cock against her weeping cunt.

My little doe, now soft and pliant, wraps her arms around my neck, her forehead pressed to mine. "And I'll never be done with you, my wolf. Never," she vows ever so sweetly, cracking my heart open with her loving words.

God, I fucking love this woman.

She sees all the ugly parts of me and still finds it in her heart to love me despite them all—or maybe because of them. Her dark edges fit my ragged ones with ease, and when we collide, we are more than whole: we are imperfectly perfect.

Forehead to forehead, our eyes locked, I slowly thrust into her, my cock going as far as her womb allows. We hiss at the holy connection and stay still for a split second, just relishing in this gift of wonder, but all too soon, my little doe becomes impatient, beginning to slowly lift up and down the length of my cock. I feel her heels dig into my lower back to keep her balance as she fucks me raw. With one hand gripping her waist, I snake the other up her back until it finds the nape of her neck, my fingers wrapping around it. With her hair this short, there is nothing to get in my way. All that exists is flawless, glowing skin exposed for me to brand and mark and make mine. A bead of sweat falls down her neck, and my gaze follows it into the valley of her breasts. I pull back just a tad so I can lick it, my lips settling around her nipple. My teeth graze the bud before I suck it between them, her pussy continuously swallowing my cock. This lovemaking is slow and steady, and yet it feels like she's pulling my soul out of me and caressing it in her embrace, promising to keep it safe from this day on.

"I love you," she whispers, pulling my gaze to her face.

Unshed tears well in her eyes, and her expression is so full of light it takes my breath away.

"Never leave me, little doe. I don't think I'd survive," I say, the words leaving my mouth before I realize what I said.

But it's true.

Now that I have had a taste of her love, life would have no joy for me without it. My life before her was filled with gray clouds and stale air, but now, if I lost her, those bland, lackluster days would have been heaven in comparison.

"Never, my wolf," she promises, and the earnest smile on her lips as a tear escapes its prison makes my heart swell.

"I love you so much. So much," I confess on a loud groan as her pussy clenches around my cock.

Knowing my own release is close, I quicken my thrusts, pounding into her pussy so she can come one more time before I do. Just as my Zoey's eyes begin to roll into the back of her head, I crash my lips onto hers, needing her kiss to push me over the edge. With a kiss, she shatters in my arms as I come inside her slick walls. I wrap my arms tightly around her as she clings to me with the same desperate need as we become one in all ways—heart, body, and soul.

When we catch our breath, we realize that someone is banging on my front door so loudly that it feels like they want to bash the damn thing in.

"Uh-oh," Zoey mutters under her breath, suddenly eager to jump off my cock.

"No," I grunt, keeping her in a vise grip.

"Gray, let me go. You know exactly who is trying to break down your door right now."

"I don't care," I snarl, keeping my hold on her like a petulant child grips their favorite toy when someone tells them playtime is over.

She lets out a little sigh, but my hold on her remains unyielding.

"Look at me, Ghost. He can't take me away, I promise. I'm yours," she vows patiently.

I shake my head before hiding my face in the crook of her neck. She runs her fingers through my hair comfortingly, my cum starting to drip down her thighs. It gives me a sick sense of satisfaction that my cock is still inside her as the other man in her life pounds on my door. She's right though. Only Alaric could be making such a ruckus. Hale's words seep into the forefront of my mind, making me ease up a bit.

"If you want the girl, get right with her father. Remember, she loved him first."

"Fuck," I grunt. "Fine. Get dressed while I open the door for your dad."

"There you go. Progress. I'm so proud of you, my wolf. You're almost acting like a full-fledged adult," she jokes, quickly kissing my lips.

I mumble incoherently, letting my girl jump off my cock in favor of finding something to put on. She plucks my T-shirt off the floor and pulls it over her small frame, the hem hitting just an inch above her knees. The corner of my lips lifts into a smile from seeing her in my clothes, her skin still smelling of me. She might have loved her father first, but I'm the one who has staked my claim on her in every way imaginable.

"Don't just sit there and gawk at me," she reprimands, throwing a pair of boxers on top of the bed. "Put those on before my dad breaks your door."

We hear a loud crash, followed by, "Zoey Johnson, get your ass out here this instant!"

"Too late." I shrug, getting to my feet and putting my boxers on just as I was told.

"What am I going to do with you both?" She rolls her eyes while putting on her panties.

"Let's see what my future father-in-law wants, shall we?" I say, slapping her ass and giving her a little wink.

Zoey's cheeks turn the most beautiful shade of crimson, and her eyes widen as she stares at me, gobsmacked.

"Father-in-law?" she chokes out, no longer in a hurry to meet her father.

"Later, little doe. Let's deal with Alaric first."

She gapes at me, her jaw still on the floor for a full ten seconds, before she snaps out of her shock.

"Zoey! I said now!" Alaric shouts from my living room.

I guess I should be grateful that he had the good sense not to search every room in my house to look for his daughter. With his temper, I'd be a dead man if he caught me in bed with his little girl, that much I know.

"Come on, little doe. Your father is waiting," I tease, and right now, not even Alaric's temper tantrum can ruin my happiness.

She gives me a nod and links her fingers through mine as we both step into the corridor and walk toward the living room. When we finally reach it, we see Alaric didn't come alone.

Layla stands beside him looking just as furious as her husband.

"I'm so sorry, Gray, for my husband's behavior. He's been acting extra Neanderthal lately," she says with a deep frown, crossing her arms over her chest.

"Don't apologize for me, wife. It's these two you should be pissed at. Not me," Alaric growls, giving me his deadly glare.

"Don't tell me how I should feel, husband. Right now, I'm disappointed with all of you," she rebukes sternly.

"At me? What did I do?" Zoey asks in surprise.

Layla's eyes soften as she approaches her sister and places both hands on her shoulders.

"I'm happy that you're happy, Zoey. I really am. But that doesn't mean you should neglect your responsibilities. Alaric and I went over to your dorm this morning, and we found out that you haven't been attending classes since Easter break ended. Now I understand how someone can get consumed in a new relationship, but you shouldn't let it derail you from your future."

My forehead wrinkles. I'm completely taken aback since I, too, thought Zoey was still on a break. Before I'm able to question her about it, she shocks me further.

"I'm not going back to school. I decided to quit."

"The hell you did!" Alaric shouts, stepping closer to her. On reflex, I step in front of Zoey and push her behind me.

"Move away from my daughter if you know what's good for you," he growls in my face.

"No. Let her say her piece."

The room grows so silent we can all hear Alaric's back molars grind.

Before I can stop her, Zoey steps away from me, standing right in the crosshairs of her father's wrath.

"College isn't for me, Dad. It never was. I tried to tell you that from the get-go, but you two were so eager for me to get my degree that I didn't have the heart to tell you."

Layla takes this admission at face value, but she still looks concerned with her sister's decision to quit school.

"We only wanted to give you the best possible chance in life," Layla interjects.

"A college degree won't guarantee that," Zoey retorts.

"No, but without one, your chances of making something out of yourself grow slimmer."

"But that's just the thing, Layla. I don't need one to make something of myself, and I can prove it. For example, aren't you happy with your life?" she demands, my incredible girl holding her ground, refusing to back down.

Fuck, I love her. If Alaric wouldn't kill me, I'd get down on my knees and prove it.

"I am." Layla nods suspiciously. "Very much so."

"I know you are, and you don't have a college degree either. Until a few years ago, you didn't even have a high school diploma."

"That's true, but because of it, we also barely scraped by before Alaric came into our lives. Is that what you want? To live paycheck to paycheck? To live with anxiety, wondering where your next meal will come from or how you will be able to pay rent?" Layla insists, trying to put logic into her stubborn younger sister's head.

"Zoey will want for nothing," I state evenly and mean it.

"Oh yeah, big man? You're going to take care of her?" Alaric blurts out in contempt.

"Yeah, I am."

"Like fuck you are," he growls, and before I'm able to react, his left hook hits me right across the jaw.

I lose my balance for a second, and Alaric takes complete advantage of the situation, throwing another punch into my gut. I should have been more vigilant. We've sparred enough when he was training me for me to know that Alaric doesn't sleep on the job. He makes sure to take advantage of every window he has to eviscerate his prey, and right now, I'm his worst nightmare come to life—the man who is trying to steal his child right out from under him. Every nerve ending in me screams to retaliate and throw him a few punches of my own, but if I hurt him, really hurt him, then Zoey would never forgive me, so I take his abuse one punch at a time while never hitting back.

"Alaric, stop!" Layla screams when he lands a punch brutal enough to lay me out on the floor.

I wipe the blood off my split lip and get back onto my feet, staring the man in the eye.

"I will take care of her, Alaric. You can beat me and make me bleed as much as you want, but I'll never give up. She's mine now. She's my life, my heart. You best get that through your thick head and get on board, because that's how it's going to be from now on."

He tries to catch his breath, still glaring daggers at me, while his hands are balled into fists, ready to swing at me.

"Go ahead. Hit me. It won't change a damn thing," I warn with a snarl.

"God! You two are impossible sometimes!" Zoey suddenly interrupts, stepping between us.

She places an open palm on my heart and stretches her arm to place the other on her father's.

"I love you, my wolf, with my whole heart. I am yours. But I don't need you to take care of me. I'm my own woman," she says, looking me dead in the eye before she turns her attention to her father. "I'm my own woman, Dad. Emphasis on *woman*. I'm not a baby anymore. I can take care of myself and make my own decisions, and if I want to be with Gray and quit school, then that's my decision to make. Not yours."

"I just want what's best for you," Alaric grumbles despondently.

"We both do," Layla agrees.

"I know you do." Zoey sighs, looking at the two people who have been in her corner for most of her life. "And I get that it's scary letting me live my life as I see fit, but you have to trust that you two did an amazing job raising me, because you did, both of you. I would not be the woman I am today without you. Take comfort in that. Please."

Layla steps up to her sister, her eyes watering. "I do trust you. I do. I'm sorry if I made you think that I didn't."

"If that's true, then you will also trust me when I say that school isn't for me. Having some corporate job or a nine-to-five isn't my destiny. It never was."

"Then what is?" Layla asks, genuinely curious.

Zoey looks at me with a mischievous smile and then at a brooding Alaric.

"I'm going to follow in my dad's footsteps. That's what I'm going to do. I was born for it."

CHAPTER 27

Zoey

"Wh at exactly do you mean by that?" my sister asks, still trying to make sense of what I just said.

"Fuck my life," Alaric retorts, running his tattooed fingers through his hair. "She means she wants to work for the agency," he explains, but the proud little glimmer I catch in his eyes lets me know that he's not as opposed to my decision as I would have expected.

My sister's face suddenly pales, and it's her reaction that's more concerning.

"I think I'm going to need to sit down for this," she exclaims on weak knees.

"Let me get you some water, sis," I offer, helping her sit on the sofa. "You two" —I glare at the two most important men in my life— "try not to kill each other while I'm gone, or I'm going to be pissed at both of you. Understood?"

Alaric instantly nods, since he's now too preoccupied with his wife to pay Gray any mind.

"I'll help you in the kitchen," my wolf offers, trailing behind me.

"Instead of water, bring my woman something stronger, will you, Ghost?" my dad says with no malice in his tone.

My tense muscles ease somewhat now that I have my dad's silent support. It's my sister who I'm going to have to win over now.

"Is that really what you want, little doe? We never talked about it," Gray mutters under his breath when we reach the kitchen.

"What's there to talk about?" I shrug and open the refrigerator door. "I can't think of a more worthy cause than to kill every last monster in this world. Can you?"

His head bows before he gives it a shake.

"My feelings exactly." I smile at him as I grab the vodka from his fridge. I place the bottle on his island and cup his cheek. "I'm good at it, aren't I?"

He nods, still unwilling to look me in the eye, causing my hackles to rise.

"What's wrong? Don't you think I'm good enough?"

His shoulders slump a tad before his silver stare meets mine. "You are. Too good. The best raw potential I've ever seen," he mutters like it was dragged from his soul.

"Why does it feel like that's a bad thing for you?" I pout.

"Because maybe Alaric is right. Maybe I am a bad influence on you. This life... It changes you. Once you're on this path, you can never go back."

I cradle his cheeks in both palms as he leans his temple against mine.

"But that's just it. I've been on this path since my daddy killed my mom and brother. Since he tried to kill Layla and me too. I want to do this. No. I need to do this. It's my calling, my wolf. Do you understand that? It always has been."

He lets out a long exhale and then wraps his arms around me. "I understand," he whispers, lifting the huge ass boulder off my shoulders. "I'm with you, little doe. I'll always be with you."

"I know." I grin, kissing the tip of his nose. "If only it was that easy to convince my sister."

"I might be able to help with that," he states evenly, releasing me from his hold to grab the vodka bottle before pouring the clear liquid in a glass. "Follow me."

My forehead wrinkles in confusion, but I follow him willingly.

I'd follow him to the edge of the Earth, so trailing behind him to the living room isn't too hard for me to do. When we reach the room, Alaric's arm is around my hyperventilating sister.

"Here you go, baby. Drink up," Alaric coos at his wife once Gray hands him the glass half filled with vodka.

Layla, however, pushes the glass away, her eyes red with grief.

"Explain, Zoey. Now. I'm losing my mind over here. Just exactly what do you mean you're going to follow in your father's footsteps?" she begs.

I open my mouth to explain, but it's my wolf who decides to take the floor.

"Did you know that during the time you and Zoey stayed at Mercy Village Group Home that I was there too?"

"You were?" she replies, trying to focus her attention on my wolf.

Gray nods, sitting on the coffee table in front of Layla and Alaric, pulling me to sit on his lap. I see my dad's lips twist in disgruntlement at the elaborate show of PDA, but to his credit, he doesn't say or do anything.

"I was," Gray answers, rubbing my back with his hand as if needing to touch me while never breaking eye contact with Layla. "I remember when you and Zoey came to live in the group home. You were so broken, both of you. I didn't need to know the specifics of what happened to you prior to you coming to live at Mercy Village to know that you both suffered one hell of an ordeal, so when I heard that the gunshot wound you had on your shoulder was caused by your step-father, I wasn't surprised," he continues, running his hand up and down my spine comfortingly, as if reminding me that those days are in our rearview mirror now. "Yet there was something about you, Layla," he says. "Something that gave you this silent grace of fortitude. At the time, I couldn't put my finger on what drove you, but I can now."

I swallow dryly as he pulls his gaze away from my sister's face to stare into my eyes.

"It was you, little doe. Your sister would have fought death itself to protect you and keep you out of harm's way, and somehow, even back then, I knew you were going to be my saving grace, just as you were hers. That's why I kept an eye on you from the start and did everything in my power to make sure that horrible place would never touch you. That your sister's sacrifice wouldn't be in vain. I would keep you safe when she couldn't. I'd make sure that they couldn't steal your innocence like they stole mine."

"I love you," I whisper before planting a chaste kiss on his lips.

"I don't understand," Layla interrupts anxiously. "What do you mean about keeping Zoey safe? About maintaining her innocence?"

Gray's silver gaze falls away from mine to look somberly at my sister and her husband. I count my heartbeats as the perverted truth starts to make its way to the surface, defiling the air around us.

"Fuck." Alaric is the first to curse, tightening his hold around my sister's shoulders as she starts shaking like a leaf when the same realization dawns on her.

She stammers incoherently in utter shock. "Are you saying... Do you mean... They didn't... They couldn't have..."

"Yes, they could," Gray deadpans. "And they did."

"Oh my god!" Layla cries out, covering her mouth with both hands.

Alaric holds her close, his blue eyes turning a cold shade of ice. "Did they hurt my girls?" my father demands.

"Never. I made sure of it," Gray retorts.

"You were just a pissant kid yourself. How the fuck did you make sure of it?"

"You know how," my wolf replies without missing a beat, the painful answer piercing my heart.

A deafening silence blankets us as both Alaric and Layla stare at my love in a whole new light. Yes, there is a glimmer of misery and pity in their gazes, but there is something far more tangible in there too —respect and kinship. They are finally seeing my wolf through my eyes. With his confession, he just made a dent in their hearts, a gap that will be filled with nothing but tenderness toward him from now on.

"Then I guess there is only one question I want answered," my father growls furiously, making me grin at his protective reaction. "Who do I have to kill?"

"Actually, that's what my man and I have been working on. Gray and I have been able to obtain a ledger with most of the group home's clientele," I begin, only stopping when I see my sister wince.

Layla has never led a charmed life.

She knows as well as I do that bad men prey on the weak. We're living proof of it. But she's a mother now, and that changes things. Thinking that someone would ever be able to hurt a child in such a horrible way, strip them of their very essence, and then leave them as a shell of their former selves is something she will never condone, and now that she's learned that the man I love bears the scars of sacrificing himself for us, for me, it's going to take her a minute to believe in the world again.

My wolf kisses my forehead and continues for me, sensing I'm unable to.

He tells them everything.

How he was abused at the home, both physically and mentally.

How, to this day, the pedophile ring still exists, leaving more victims in its wake.

He tells them how we have murdered guards and clients alike, crossing each name from the ledger one by one until someone tells us who is running the show. After what feels like hours, my sister starts to regain color in her cheeks, processing Gray's accounts of the past few weeks. Once he's finished, my father looks ready to burn down the place.

My sister, on the other hand, looks more composed.

"I think I'll have a glass of water now," she says, poised.

"Are you sure you don't want something stronger, love?" Alaric questions, still concerned.

"No. Water is fine," she says, kissing his cheek and getting to her feet. "Show me to the kitchen, will you, sis?"

Gray reluctantly lets me get off his lap, but I feel his eyes following my every step.

"I get it now," Layla says when we're out of earshot of our men.

"You do?" I retort expectantly.

"Yes." She smiles. "I always knew there was a darkness in you,

Zoey, and maybe that's why I tried to give you as much of a normal life as I could. Maybe that's why I wanted you to have the college experience and get your degree. I was afraid that if you didn't, you might lose yourself in the shadows, but now I see it so clearly."

"What do you see?" I question nervously.

"That the darkness is what has kept you sane and safe all along. It's where you thrive, where you shine. I thought I was protecting you, but in reality, I was only keeping you from becoming this fierce woman that stands before me now. Maybe I haven't said it enough, but I'm so proud of you, Zoey. So, so proud of you."

Hot tears start to stream down my cheeks at the look of pride on my sister's face.

"If ridding the world of bad men, whose only purpose is to wreak havoc and cause suffering, is where your talents are best served, then I'm all for it. I could not be prouder of you and will support you every step of the way, and so will your father," she promises sincerely.

I launch myself at my sister, wrapping my arms around her while we silently sob in each other's embrace.

"Thank you," I manage to say through my tears.

"Don't thank me. It's our fault you felt you needed to hide this part of you for so long. I'm just glad Gray came into our lives to give us the wake-up call we needed. He really is special, isn't he?"

"So special. He's everything," I confess as I let my big sister wipe the tears off my face.

"I can see that." She offers me a genuine smile, but then her lips thin and her expression turns almost as deadly as my father's. "Now, what are we going to do about finding out who is behind Mercy Village and the horrors that happen in there?"

"I don't know." I shrug, feeling frustrated. "We've been trying to get a name out of these assholes, but no one seems to know who is running the show. They are a ghost."

Layla chews her bottom lip, her gaze still fixed on mine. "Well, if there is anyone here who can capture a ghost, it's you. You've done it once, and you can do it again. Think, Zoey. Think long and hard on who could profit from such a thing?"

It's the word *profit* that causes the bells in my head to ring.

Shit.

Why didn't I think of that before? I was so wrapped up in joining forces with my wolf and killing his demons one by one that I totally forgot the number one rule in any investigation—always follow the money.

A gold watch.

A diamond bracelet.

An expensive Escalade.

Those are all things someone would buy if their bank account was nice and flush.

And I missed it.

"I know that look in your eye," Layla says excitedly. "You've figured it out, haven't you? You know who is behind this, don't you?"

"I think I do." I nod, my nostrils flaring. "And before the day is done, she will rue the day she ever met me."

"I -I think you're right," I murmur as I sit back and blow out a breath. Zoey stops pacing before me, biting her lip, her eyes bright with hope.

Fuck, she's beautiful.

"Yeah?"

I nod, pride shining in my eyes. "I've tracked the purchases to a house. Shall we see?"

"Yes, it's time to end this once and for all." She comes to me, cups my face as she leans in, and presses her forehead to mine, and only then can I breathe. "Are you ready?"

"With you at my side? Always." I look at Alaric. He and Layla refused to leave while I checked out Zoey's hunch. "This is my fight. I'll call you if I need you." I have to offer him that since he looks like he's ready to tear down the entire city.

He nods stiffly, placing his hand on his wife as he looks from Zoey to me. "There's no talking you out of this, Zoey?"

"No. Where he goes, I go. I want to end this; I *need* to. I need them to die."

"She's a better fighter than even I am sometimes," I comment, singing her praises, and Alaric grunts, even as pride for his daughter shines in his eyes.

"Of course she is. I trained her," he replies proudly before blowing out a breath and tugging her into a hug. "I don't like it, but I understand. I love you, Zoey. Always have and always will. You will always be my daughter, and I'm so proud of the person you have become... and I'm sorry for being a stubborn asshole. You'll have to forgive your old man. I just worry, always have and always will, but you're right. This is your life and your choice, and I will support you." Pulling back, he smiles down at her. "I guess this means I should welcome you to the family business?"

She laughs and looks at me. "As long as you welcome Gray into our family too."

"Don't push it," he mutters, but it holds no real heat, and when he looks at me, he nods. "Keep my girl safe, and make the bastards pay."

"I will," I promise, and when we see them out, I turn back to Zoey.

"Wash and dress, little doe. I'll gather our weapons, and then we'll hunt this bitch down."

"Together," she states as she hurries away to do my bidding.

I stand rooted to my spot, watching the love of my life nearly skipping with glee over the hunt we are about to embark on.

How my life has changed.

I always hunted alone, and killing was easy, the only time I felt anything, but it was also a stark reminder of my loneliness. Now I'll never be lonely again. She takes up my world, my soul, and breathes life back into it.

And I am her ghost, her wolf, her fighter.

Together, we are unstoppable.

We will end this, stopping kids from becoming like me, and then will figure out the rest of our lives, but I know one thing—where she goes, I go.

Idling in the car down the street from the gates of the mansion I tracked some purchases to, I hesitate only for a moment. As if reading my thoughts, Zoey reaches over and smacks my chest. "Don't you dare. We go in together."

"I wouldn't dream of denying you, little doe." I grin, even though I had been debating asking her to stay behind. "I'm going to cut the power once we reach the gates. After that, we have to move fast. I count five guards outside, but there could be more inside. You stay low and at my side the entire time."

"You watch my back. I watch yours," she promises as she checks her gun and then winks at me.

Fuck, that's ridiculously hot.

"Later, you are bringing that gun to bed," I growl, making her laugh as she leans in and kisses me.

"That's a promise," she purrs before stilling. "Before we go in there, I have something for you." She pulls a black box out of her bag. "It's silly, but I couldn't resist."

"Nothing you do is silly, my love," I assure her as I take the box and open it.

Something wells deep inside me. I've never had a gift before. Ever.

My heart pounds, and my soul roars in approval. When my eyes find hers, they are on fire with my love and the feeling of possessiveness I have for this incredible woman before me. "Little doe."

"My wolf." She grins. "And that is to remind you, in case you ever forget, of who you are to me. So when it gets rough, I'm always there."

Licking my lips, I tug the thick metal chain out, letting the wolf's head necklace dangle from my grasp before I tug it over my head, feeling it settle against my chest, my heart, where she belongs.

Gripping her neck, I tug her close. "I love it. I love you."

"Good, now let's kick some ass." With that, she slips from the car, forcing me to follow after her.

No more hesitation, no more second-guessing.

It's time to end this.

We crouch low as we run toward the estate. The road ends at the giant black iron gates with a golden M decorating the middle. There's a guard post before it that's empty, since we waited until they started to switch shifts to attack.

It's clear this woman is rich, and knowing the sprawling white mansion beyond is bought with pain and blood makes me want to blow it all up.

When we reach the gate, we crouch there as I check my watch, counting down, and right on schedule, the explosion on the circuit box goes off. The ground shakes underfoot as the gate buzzes, indicating it's dead. Grinning at Zoey, I kick it open, and she hurries in after me. I peek in the guard box to see the cameras are out as shouts go up inside.

The circular driveway is empty, and we slink along the garage to the right, filled with every car imaginable, keeping our backs to the wall of the mansion before ducking under big bay windows. Finally, we reach the huge double doors, and then we kick them open together.

I toss in a flash and tug her back, waiting until it goes off to sweep back in, firing as I go. I take down four, and Zoey takes down two as we move through their masses on the perfectly polished wooden floor of the entryway. I worried my little doe would hesitate, but I should have known better. She holds her gun like a professional, her eyes sharp and ready as she listens to my commands and watches my back.

A huge staircase leads upstairs, with hallways branching off down here.

We should clear it, but I need this to end.

I want this over quickly so no one gets away, so I tug out a grenade and toss it down the corridors where I hear guards gathering like mice. I press Zoey to the wall, and she jerks when it goes off, but there's no more noise after.

I point upstairs, and she nods, pressing her back to mine as I start up them, her gun aimed behind us.

At the top of the stairs, there is a long corridor going both ways. I chose one at random, and after clearing bedrooms, a gym, a cinema room, and a steam room, we turn back to pass the stairs again just as something fires from below. Throwing Zoey to the floor, I take aim over the balcony and fire, spraying the entire entryway, ignoring the sharp pain where a bullet must have grazed my leg. There's a scream, and I watch as two guards go down, their guns held at their sides, but I spot another trying to sneak up the stairs and turn my gun, quickly hitting him before reloading. I'm just changing the clip when a creak makes my head jerk up. There's a guard trying to sneak toward me down the corridor, and I'm a sitting duck.

"Oh no you fucking don't. He's mine," Zoey snarls, and I watch in awe as she hits him right between the eyes.

I can't help but groan. Standing, I yank her to me, kissing her hard and fast. "I don't think there should be any more, baby, but watch my back." I want to drop to my knees and worship her, and show her how much I love her, but we don't have time.

Later, I remind myself. When this is over, I will show her just how much this means to me. How much she means to me.

I head down the corridor. As much as I want to rush, we have to sweep every room until we reach the only one with closed doors.

They have to be hiding there.

Pressing my back to the wall, I lean into Zoey. "Rip open the door for me, little doe, and I'll go in shooting. I'll disable them so we can get answers."

She nods, her expression serious, and I couldn't be prouder. When she counts down on one hand, I almost come in my pants at how hot and capable my love is.

Zoey rips the door open, and I surge in, sweeping the entire room.

It's an office, I realize quickly, but what I see beyond the door has me freezing.

It's a single woman. She doesn't have a weapon, but her eyes are hard.

She was waiting for us. "You don't have to shoot."

"Why is that?" I demand, my gun still trained on her as Zoey slips in behind me.

I don't like it; something feels off.

"Do you see me resisting? No, Gray, this was my trap you walked into, and now we need to talk."

I feel Zoey moving closer behind me and hear her gasp, and my own spine stiffens when I hear my name on the woman's lips.

She knows me.

Fuck.

"I knew you would find me one day. I've been waiting." Her eyes are locked on me, calm despite the threat we pose.

"I've been waiting for this too," I snarl.

Her eyebrow arches. "Oh, that's cute. You thought I meant you. No, I meant her." She glances at Zoey then, pride shining in her gaze.

My head swivels, and my eyes lock on an unsurprised Zoey. "Zoey, you know her?"

The betrayal is thick on my tongue. How could she know the woman behind all this? The woman responsible for my torture and ruining hundreds of innocent lives?

"Maeve," she whispers, her eyes on the woman. "She was there when I was a kid, and when I went back, she was kind to me. She was my counselor."

"Sorry, that's not me anymore." Maeve grins at Zoey. "I truly was one once upon a time. I wanted to help, wanted to do something good in the world, but such selfless acts don't pay the bills. I guess I just liked money more than being altruistic. I've found that it's overrated anyway."

Stepping before Zoey, I glare at the woman. "Where's General?" I don't care if she's a woman, she's as good as dead for her crimes, but I need answers first, and if this truly is a trap, we have limited time.

"To tell you that would be to sign my own death warrant, I'm afraid." She grins, winking at Zoey. "Surely you understand." She wanders across the office and perches on the edge of the desk, totally unafraid. "I'm glad to see you, Zoey."

"Shut up," I snarl and move closer, my gun pointed at her chest, but she completely ignores me.

"I've been waiting for this day for a very long time."

"Why?" Zoey whispers behind me.

"Zoey, don't talk to her!" I yell, not liking the determined glint in this woman's eyes.

"For you, silly, so you could take your place at my side."

"What?" I jerk in shock, truly not sure what to say or do. Maeve was kind, she cared, she brought the kids toys, so why would she do this? I can feel Gray's anger. He's almost shaking from fury, yet she ignores him and leans around him to see me.

Why?

Shock still courses through me. I can't believe she would hurt kids like that. Kids who trusted her and looked up to her. She cared for them. I know she did. I trusted her. I even got in her car, for fuck's sake! She seemed kind and like she wanted to change the world, just like she said, so what the fuck?

Is she that good of an actor, or was I simply blinded by what I wanted to believe, desperately needing some good to come from that place?

"I've been watching you ever since I first met you when you were a child. I saw a spark in you, the same one that is in me. You are a fighter, smart, and pragmatic with the will to win at any cost. You have to be the best, to live dangerously and feel adrenaline just like I do, but I never expected this. You are magnificent, Zoey, everything I knew you could be and more. So strong, sure, and dangerous. You are incredible, unburdened by the laws of our world and stupid morals." She pushes away from the desk, her hands splayed wide. "Think of everything you could do. He's bringing you down, Zoey. He's keeping you locked in a cage when you need to be set free. There is so much potential in you. I see it, and I saw it even when you were a child. Break the shackles he's got you in. Break them."

"Shut up!" Gray snarls.

"You could be the next me. We could rule the world together, never answering to anyone while watching them bow to us, crawling to us for scraps of our power and money. You would never need to worry about your sister again or anyone you care for. You would be untouchable." Her eyes are wide as I drop my gun to my side. "You could have everything you wish for, everything you have always wanted. Name it, and I'll make it happen. You and me, Zoey, we are going to do big things, but first, you have to kill him and end this stupid rebellion. He should have died a very long time ago. There is a reason they call him Ghost, after all."

Gray jerks as I step up to his side, his eyes on her.

"Kill him, that's all I have to do?" I ask her.

"Kill him and join me. We will rule the world together." She holds out her perfectly manicured hand, like she did to me so many years ago.

I glance at Gray, and his gun drops as he turns to me. "Zoey," he whispers, "she's using you."

"And you are not?" Maeve snaps. "Using and draining her life to feed your own? Pathetic. You're unworthy of such a prize."

Swallowing, he searches my gaze before slumping and tossing his gun down, then he grabs mine and lifts it. "She's right. Kill me, Zoey, if this is what you want. I'll never fight you, not ever. I could never harm you. I deserve this. I deserve to die. If it's by your hand, then fine." He closes his eyes for a moment before they lock on me, glossy with unshed tears. "I love you, and if that isn't enough, I understand and I forgive you. I love you, Zoey, no matter what, but you need to decide your future. Not me. Not her. You."

I step back and raise the gun. He stays rooted in place, his hands wide at his sides, waiting for the shot.

He's so sure I'll take it, watching me with peace and love in his gaze.

Acceptance.

He's willing to die for me so I can have the life he thinks I deserve.

"Goodbye," I murmur.

"I love you," he mouths just as I fire.

He jerks as the bullet finds its home.

His eyes widen as he looks down, but my own are locked on Maeve and the blood blooming on her chest.

"Zoey, why?" she gasps as she staggers back.

Dropping the gun, I move toward her, getting in her face. "Gray might think he deserves to die, but he's wrong. He deserves to live and have everything he could ever want. He deserves to live a long, happy life after what you did to him. You're right. I might be smart and strong and successful like you, but I will never *be you*. I could never hurt another just to get power or money. That's where you're wrong about me. I would rather kill myself before I ever became like you." Pressing the gun to her chin, I meet her eyes. "You hurt children, Maeve, those you swore to protect. Gray might be a monster, but you? You're the fucking devil, and now you'll burn with him in hell." I fire before she can respond, knowing a monster like her will never understand.

Blood splatters across me, and when I meet Gray's eyes and hold out my hand, I pray my actions finally give him peace. "It's over. Now let's go home, my wolf."

Taking my hand, he kisses me deeply. "Home is wherever you are, little doe. Never doubted you for a second."

"I know. I saw the truth in your eyes. You would have let me kill you to get close to her."

"Whatever it took," he admits, wiping my face, "for you to live, for her to reach her end... It didn't matter to me. Only you."

"She died too quickly. I'm sorry about that. I'll let you torture me instead." I wink.

"Never torture, baby, never with you."

Kissing him deeply, I let him taste the truth on my lips. "I love you, Gray, and I will always protect you."

"And I you, little doe." He takes my hand, and we step over her body and leave the house behind.

We watch as it goes up in flames, burning away the rot and legacy she imprinted in our city.

We still have names to hunt down, and so long as there are innocent lives out there, there will always be evil to prey on them, but the two ghosts standing in the shadows will stop them.

CHAPTER 30

Gray

With my knees on the cold tile floor, I lean into the tub to collect some water into a plastic cup and rinse the blood out of my love's hair. The crimson gore drips into her bubble bath, polluting the white suds and turning them pink, but my little doe doesn't seem to mind. She lifts one foot to wiggle her toe into the faucet, sighing happily.

"Do you think I should let my hair grow out? Grow it longer?" she asks pensively.

"Long or short, it makes no difference to me. You're beautiful either way," I respond without thought, but it's true. There is nothing in this world more beautiful than Zoey.

"You're becoming a romantic," she teases, turning her head to look at me. "If that's the case, then I'll keep it short. I kind of like not having to worry about it. Plus, it makes life super simple when we go out on missions. Can you imagine the hassle it would be to clean blood out of long blonde hair?" She shakes her head with a wicked grin. "Nah, short it is."

"Whatever you say, little doe." I chuckle under my breath, kissing her temple.

She leans her naked frame against the top, crosses her arms on the porcelain rim, and places her chin on top of them, eyeing me attentively.

"So you're good with me being your partner in crime?" she asks expectantly. "I mean, I told my dad that this is what I want to do with my life, but we haven't exactly talked about it."

"No, we haven't," I retort, squirting some shampoo into my palms and then using it to massage her scalp.

She pouts. "So are you going to weigh in on my decision or just keep me guessing?"

Another smile tugs at my lips as my love waits ever so impatiently for my reply. I think it through carefully. I've never been good at words, and I know these are some of the most important I will ever speak. I want Zoey with me all the time, but I also don't want to take her decisions away from her like everyone else.

"You're your own woman, little doe. You do whatever makes your heart happy. If it's working with me, then I'm all for it. I must admit that working with you these past few weeks has been the most fun I've had in a long time. I know it's weird saying that regarding the circumstances, but it's true nonetheless. In the end, though, it's your decision. Whatever you want, baby, I will support and love you."

Her blue gaze melts as she lets out a pleased sigh. "We do make a good team, don't we?"

"The best." I chuckle, completely content, and then my heart cracks open at the beautiful smile she gifts me. "What?" I ask when she can't stop smiling at me.

"You're different."

"How so?" I question, my forehead wrinkling.

"You smile more now. You didn't do that before," she whispers, her eyes dropping to my lips. I ignore my hard cock. After all, it's always stiff around her.

"That's because I didn't have anything to smile about, but now I do," I admit, nervous she doesn't like the change.

"Yeah?" She grins, fully knowing the reason for my happiness.

"Yeah," I confirm.

"You're going to have to do better than that, my wolf," she retorts, licking her lips as she lifts her hand to play with the wolf pendant hanging against my chest.

I stop what I'm doing and pick up her doe necklace, pulling her to me until our faces are a hairsbreadth away from one another.

"You, Zoey. It's all because of you. All my smiles are yours. I am yours," I vow.

"You better believe it." She giggles, wrapping her wet arms around my neck and kissing me stupid.

My cock instantly hardens further with the way she sucks on my tongue, her soaped, bare breasts rubbing against my chest.

I groan, breaking the kiss. "Let me get you cleaned first, baby, then I can dirty you up as many times as you want."

"Promise?" She flutters her beautiful lashes at me.

My cock twitches in my pants, needing to get her dirty now and not later. Still, I pull back, needing this moment of normalcy after the fucked-up night we had. I knew she would never choose Maeve over me, but I was willing to sacrifice myself if it meant that we would get Maeve in the end. Luckily for me, my love is just as trigger happy as I am, and she put a bullet in the bitch before she had a chance to steal my love away from me.

Zoey follows my instruction and leans back into the tub, her head nestled against the rim while her body is fully submerged under the cherry-colored water. Once I'm satisfied that her hair is clean, I gently pull her under so the water can wash away the shampoo in her hair. When she rises, the little minx sprays me with water, soaking my T-shirt.

"Oops. Guess you're going to have to take that off now. Sorry," she says, not repentant in the least.

I chuckle at her childish antics, reveling in them since I never got this part of life before, and then I pull my T-shirt over my head and throw it in the corner of the bathroom. She bites down on her lower lip, scanning every inch of my chest.

"Now that's more like it," she coos, her melodic voice going straight to my dick like a siren luring me with her song.

"Keep it up, baby. You know I'll just punish you more in the bedroom."

"Promises, promises," she teases.

I let out another chuckle, and the sound doesn't seem so foreign to me as it once did. It feels right, like I was always supposed to be here with her. Call it destiny, fate even, but all roads would have led me to this woman. If I had to suffer hell to taste this bit of paradise, then all those hellish experiences were worth it. I'd suffer that and more if it gave me Zoey in the end. She's my better half, the one I had been missing all along, and now that I've found her, I'll never let her go.

I give her the darkness and safety she needs, and she gives me light and happiness, something I was missing. Before her, there was never laughter or normalcy, but now I look forward to just waking up and seeing her face, eating breakfast together, or watching a film.

And of course, fucking her senseless.

I'm thinking about all the ways I'm going to enjoy my little doe when I feel my phone vibrate persistently in my back pocket.

"Who is it?" Zoey asks curiously as I grab the phone.

"It's Hale," I reply, clicking ignore.

"Why didn't you answer it?"

"Because Hale loves the sound of his voice more than he does anyone else's. I don't have time to waste on him right now. I have more pressing concerns on my mind," I reply, pinching her left nipple.

She squirms under the water, her legs spreading wide of their own accord, inviting me to do my worst. The only thing that stops me is the worried expression on her face.

"What's wrong?" I ask, my brows furrowed.

"Nothing. I was just thinking."

"Apparently not about the same thing I was," I rebuke, dipping my hand under water and sliding it between her thighs.

She locks her legs around my arm, preventing me from reaching her sweet pussy.

"You need to call him back," she states with a no-nonsense tone.

"Why? I'd rather see you come on my fingers."

"Now who's playing dirty?" she accuses with a twinkle in her eye, offering me a small breach to reach her pussy. "But I'm serious. You need to call him back."

"Later," I growl when I push two fingers into her tight core.

She grabs the sides of the tub to keep her balance, her head falling back as I fuck her with my digits while the pad of my thumb fondles her clit.

"I'm going to hate myself for doing this, but you're going to need to call Hale back now."

"Give me one good reason?" I order, hooking my fingers into her dripping cunt and hitting that small spot in her channel that has her seeing stars.

"Fuck," she wails, slapping the tub, her eyes rolling to the back of her head.

"Well?" I tease, inserting another finger, filling her tight pussy just like she likes it. "Cat got your tongue?"

She pants, shifting her ass across the tub to aid my tempo. Water starts dripping to the floor with the way she's fucking herself on my hand, but I couldn't give a shit. Watching her reach her peak is the best spectacle I'll ever have the privilege of seeing in my entire life.

"Gray," she moans, so lost in her ecstasy she doesn't even belong to the real world anymore.

"Are you going to come for me, little doe?"

"Yes, God, yes," she shouts as I fill her up with another finger. "Oh my god! Yes! Just like that!"

All thoughts of me calling Hale are now out the window, and all she can concentrate on is the feeling of my hand. I relentlessly thrust my fingers in and out, crooking them in a way to give her the most pleasure. When I lean in and suck her soapy nipple into my mouth, biting her small bud, she bursts into pieces.

"Fuck!" she shouts at the top of her lungs, ensuring that I become momentarily blinded by her beauty. It takes forever and a day for her to come back to solid ground, her limbs even more relaxed than they could ever be from a mere bubble bath.

"You were saying?" I taunt, sucking my fingers clean of her juices.

With half-mast eyes, she tries to give me a dirty look and fails miserably. I chuckle at the little pout she tries to put on, since we both know she'd rather get off on my fingers than have me stop to call my vain as fuck best friend.

Shit.

Did I just call Hale my best friend?

I must be losing it.

I shake that thought out of my head and grab a nearby towel to wrap her up in. I help her up from the bathtub, but she slaps my hand away, preferring to do it on her own.

"Uh-uh, buddy. You're on my shit list."

"Is that so?" I smirk, keeping an eye on her since her legs still look weak from the orgasm I ripped out of her.

"Yes. I was about to have a real conversation with you, and you completely sidetracked me with those magical fingers of yours."

"You mean these?" I wiggle them in front of her face.

"Stop being so damn cute. All it does is make me want to jump your bones."

"Who's stopping you?" I ask, unbuckling my belt.

"Will you stop?" she protests, placing her hand on my buckle. "I'm serious, Gray. You need to grab your phone and call Hale."

"Not this again," I mumble, turning my back and walking into our bedroom.

Zoey follows me like a thunderstorm, drops of water following her and dripping all over our floor. I sit at the edge of the bed, staring up at her as she positions herself between my legs. My cock is mad that she would rather talk about Hale than have some quality time with it, but when she runs her fingers through my hair, my frustration simmers down.

"You asked me to give you one good reason why I wanted you to call your friend back, and I have one—General."

I hate how his name alone causes old childhood fears to sneak up and claw at my throat. Zoey sees it too, so she sits on my lap and wraps her arms around me to keep me in the present and not trapped in those old, horror-filled memories.

"Maeve said that she couldn't give us his real name since it was as good as signing her death warrant. That's a clue, my wolf. It means he's well connected, a big player in New York. Who better to help us find out who he is than Hale?"

I take her words to heart and think long and hard on the matter.

"If I do this, then I'll have to explain to him why General is so important to me. He's a curious bastard, and he won't just do this for me without wanting to know why."

"Then tell him." She shrugs before cupping my face in her palms. "Never be ashamed of being a survivor, my wolf. They are the ones who should bear that shame, not you. Never you."

I press my temple to hers and breathe in her scent. "Okay," I mumble after a pregnant pause. "I'll do it."

"Thank you," she says sweetly, pressing her lips to mine.

Her kiss alone reminds me that I'm no longer that broken boy who couldn't fight off his predators. I'm her wolf, her protector and true love. They can't hurt me anymore. They can't steal this happiness from me. No one can. My love killed my worst nightmare and bathed in her blood with the brightest smile on her face. Together, we'll fight off all the monsters who are out there, and if, from time to time, that means leaning on our friends for help, then so be it.

I'm done being the lone wolf.

I'm in a pack now, with my little doe right by my side.

On cue, Zoey leaps from my lap and retrieves my phone from the bathroom. She skips back into the room, jumps on the bed, and slides behind me, her bare legs wrapped around my waist and her chin resting on my shoulder. She hands me the phone and then snakes her arms around my chest. With one hand, I keep hers pressed against my heart as I look at the phone screen, seeing that there are three unanswered calls from Hale.

"Huh. I guess that asshole does care for me if he's blowing up my phone like this."

"Why wouldn't he? That's what friends do. They care for each other."

"I wouldn't know. I've never had a friend," I admit.

"Maybe you just didn't know you had one. Don't worry, Ghost.

You have me to point out this kind of stuff now." She snickers, kissing my neck.

"What would I do without you?"

"You'll never have to know," she murmurs. "Speaking of which, when you're done with Hale, you owe my father a phone call."

"I do?" I cock a brow.

She smiles wickedly, making my heart flutter in my chest.

Fuck, I love this woman.

"You do," she replies with a mischievous sparkle in her blue eyes. "If I recall, there was some talk earlier about how he was going to be your father-in-law. For that to happen, you better call him and get his blessing. It's best not to keep me waiting, my wolf. I expect you to be on your knee before the night is done."

"For you, little doe, anything," I promise.

Epilogue

ZOEY

"Hmm," I moan softly as Gray peppers my neck with hungry kisses, his eager cock rubbing against my backside. "You keep doing that, and we'll end up missing our mark."

"The fucker can wait," he growls, sinking his teeth into my flesh, breaking the skin.

I squirm in delight, feeling just as famished as my wolf is. In order to tease his already fragile restraint, I place my palms against the wall and push my ass back to tempt him. I can't help but giggle when I hear him growl his wolfish rumble, followed by the sound of a zipper coming undone.

"Pull your skirt up, little doe. This is going to be hard and fast," he promises.

"Just how I like it," I taunt, throwing him a mischievous smile over my shoulder.

Without hesitation, he captures my lips with his, crushing me with his passionate kiss. I melt into it, quickly pulling my skirt up since I'm desperate for him to consume my pussy in the same way he's devouring my mouth.

"Wolf," I plead when he starts toying with my wet slit with his

"Always so needy," he teases, the lightness in his tone making my heart do cartwheels in my chest.

This is a whole new Gray Hart.

The one I made.

Not those monsters.

Like me, he might still favor the shadows, but now he isn't so immune to walking in the light—not when he has me to hold his hand, and he does.

He has me heart, body, and soul.

My breathing becomes a wanton mess as he keeps sweeping his thumb over my clit, knowing it only serves to drive me mad with need.

"Either fuck me now, Ghost, or you'll have one very pissed fiancée on your hands."

"Fiancée... I love that word." He groans. "But you know what word I'll love even more?"

"What?" I pant, close to losing my mind if he doesn't take me this very second.

"Wife," he snarls.

With that word spilling from his gorgeous lips, he impales me with his cock, making me scream out in pure bliss. He covers my mouth with his hand to keep my wails muffled so they don't give our position away while thrusting mercilessly into my dripping wet pussy. With each deep thrust, he whispers words of praise and love in my ear. Words my wolf only has for me.

"I love you so much, little doe."

"You're so goddamn beautiful."

"Feed that pussy to my cock."

"That's it, baby. Swallow my cock whole."

All his dirty talk, mixed with his words of love, has me reaching for the stars right here in this dirty alleyway, cloaked by a sea of darkness. The only moonlight that shines tonight are the rays of silver beaming from his gaze as he watches me scatter into pieces in his arms. He threads his fingers through mine on the wall, his face hidden in the crook of my neck as he keeps fucking me oh so exquisitely. Ghost coaxes out my orgasm with ease, one vicious pound at a time, and with his name on my tongue, I follow his demand and come.

"So fucking beautiful," he praises, pounding into me once, twice, and then ultimately jumping off the ledge to follow me into nirvana.

I'm right there waiting for him, vowing to catch him anytime he falls, because that's a given in any life.

We'll both fail and fall eventually, but knowing we can pick ourselves up with the support of the one person we love most doesn't make this vicious world feel so scary to me.

When we both come back to planet Earth, Gray spins me around to plant another earth-shattering kiss on me. Afterwards, I melt into his embrace, resting my head on his chest just to hear his heartbeat.

I count each rapid beat until they become as even as my own. My mind travels to the life we have and if there was ever anyone who could have experienced such a consuming love like ours. I start to laugh softly when one such couple comes to mind.

"What?" he asks curiously when he hears my soft chuckles.

"Nothing. I just thought of something." I grin widely.

"You did, did you? Was that before or after you came all over my cock? I know it wasn't during since I doubt you could even remember your own name," he flirts.

I slap his chest and giggle at his attempt at humor. "Stop." I laugh. "I'm serious."

"Okay." He smiles so goddamn sweetly at me that my heart pitter-patters for him, erasing every thought in my head for a second. I'm still lost in my awe of him when he pulls me back to my previous train of thought. "Now I'm curious. Tell me. What did you just think of?" he asks, tugging a loose strand of hair off my face to tuck it behind my ear.

"Promise you won't make fun of me?" I pout.

"Promise," he vows sincerely.

"I was thinking that we're kind of the updated version of Bonnie and Clyde. Only instead of making a living robbing banks, we do it by killing bad guys," I explain a little too excitedly.

"Hmm. You do know that they didn't have the best ending, right?"

"Oh, I don't know about that." I shrug. "They died together doing what they loved most, in their own blaze of glory. There are worse ways to go."

He gently picks up my chin with his knuckle, craning my head back to stare deeply into my eyes.

"I'd rather die an old man in your bed after having lived a full life with you. That's how I want the grim reaper to come to me, with you in my arms," he confesses with a wistful tone.

"If that's what you want, my wolf, then that's how it's going to be, and I'll follow you right after. I'll never leave you. Not even in the afterlife."

His upper lip curls into a smile. "I'm going to hold you to your word. Otherwise, be prepared for me to haunt you, little doe."

"Hmm. My own personal ghost. Why do I like the sound of that too?" I giggle, pressing up to my tiptoes to plant another tender kiss on his lips.

When my feet fall back to the ground, Gray's attention is already on the building across the street. Our mark is finally making his appearance, stepping out of his town car and walking into the structure, completely oblivious that tonight will be his last.

"Looks like it's showtime," Gray teases, grabbing his gun from his holster with one hand while clutching mine with his other. "You ready, Bonnie?"

"With you? Always, Clyde."

Come what may, let the world do its worst.

As long as we're together, I'm ready for it all, because whoever thinks about messing with this deadly match has another thing coming.

Just you watch.

The End

ABOUT THE AUTHORS

Katie and Ivy have known each other since they began their author journey and have become fast friends over the years. Bonding over their love of books and crazy, maddening muses, they have always wanted to work together and finally did.

After deciding to take the plunge, the Deadly Love series was born . . . and matches like these are so deadly that they are bound to set your kindle on fire!

DEADLY LOVE SERIES

Deadly Affair
Deadly Match
Deadly Encounter

A Deadly Sneak Peek

OF DEADLY ENCOUNTER

Want to know what happens when a spoiled princess and a joker with a dark side meet? Turn the page for a sneak peek at the last story in the Deadly Love series!

DEADLY ENCOUNTER
Deadly Love Book Three

Prologue

HALE

I hate parties.

Okay, I love parties, but not ones like this with the city's richest people filling the ballroom.

I can't hide my grimace, so I turn away, fading into the shadows where I watch, listen, and gain intel, trying to find him.

General.

Gray is desperate to find him, and like the upstanding guy I am, I agreed to help. As luck would have it, a whisper on the streets led me here, smack dab in the middle of New York City's elite.

Despite the fact that I'm rocking my usual Armani and a matching half mask like every other rich fuck here, I couldn't feel more out of place.

I'd rather be at home, before my computers, to track my prey down, but sometimes you have to get your hands dirty, and since Gray —and this hurts like a mother to admit—is one of my only friends, here I am, sucking up to the rich and watching women flirt, drink, and talk incessantly about nothing important. It is starting to grate on my nerves, but I am nothing if not a patient man.

I wait and wait for any signs or whispers of *him*—the prick who gets his kicks by inflicting pain on little kids.

To say that it's a boring, mundane evening is putting it lightly. It's fucking boring as hell. These rich fucks would have no idea what a real party is even if it bit them in the ass, but that's neither here nor there. I have a part to play, and in this suit, I fucking play it to perfection.

My mind is still on the task at hand, tracking my prey and mingling with the cream of the crop, when I see her.

She strolls into the ballroom, bringing with her heart-stopping beauty and a breath of fresh air that I immediately suck into my lungs. Her chin is tilted high in quiet defiance, and her baby-blue eyes are hard as she glares at those around her as if she hates being here as well.

I can't stop staring.

I should look away and get back to work, but every part of my being is consumed by the beautiful princess walking through the ballroom like she owns it. She continues on her stroll, completely oblivious to the wanting looks that follow her around. I don't blame them, because right now, I'm just as mesmerized as they are.

Greed, need, and possessiveness flare through me for this erotic stranger.

My eyes drop down her body, and I'm unable to suppress a groan. She's wearing a black silk dress that trails behind her, flashing long, toned, tan legs. Perfect. Red heels flash under the clinging black silk sheath, making her taller, but she easily has to be six feet tall, and for a tall bastard like me, it sends a shot of lust through my system, hardening my cock in my slacks.

The dress itself glitters under the light, clinging onto a tucked-in waist and draping over her impressive chest, which is pushed up and almost tumbling from her dress. I have the insane urge to bite there and leave my mark for all to see.

She turns like she senses my gaze, a waterfall of black, silky hair tumbling over her shoulder as I move closer to get a good look at her face.

Everything else is suddenly forgotten.

The fucking world disappears from my view, until all that exists is her.

Those baby-blue eyes are lined to make them darker, guarded by long lashes shuttering her true feelings from everyone. Her cheekbones are high and glitter with makeup, and her plump lips are painted red, giving me a glimpse of what she would look like if she bled for me.

She's beautiful, so beautiful it actually steals my breath.

She looks like a supermodel or a goddess.

All light, brightness, beauty, and softness.

She is all supple, tan skin and long, unmarred limbs, and I want to ruin her, mark her, and brand her.

I want to see her eyes water with tears while I make her scream and see her on her royal knees as I destroy her and fill those baby blues with agony.

She turns away, stealing her from my view, and a growl erupts from my chest.

Despite the designer suit I wear, there is nothing civilized about me.

Not when it comes to her.

I track my new prey's every move as she's forced to greet and play nice with the rich bastards, but her shoulders are tense, and her eyes are hard with a wish gleaming in them she tries to hide.

She wants to be anywhere else.

It calls to me as I linger in the darkness, watching her.

Stalking her.

When she sweeps from the room and out into the courtyard I scouted earlier, I am helpless to follow. Leaving the shadow for her, I close the doors behind me, trapping her out here with me.

She either doesn't hear it or doesn't care, and fury pounds through me so hard it makes my temples ache. Who is this goddess to be left unprotected? She should be locked away and guarded so that no bastard like me takes what isn't his.

But it won't stop me now, nor would a million bodyguards.

Her back is to me, her hair cascading over one shoulder. Her slender, perfectly manicured hands grip the wooden rope of the swing she is idly swaying on. The moon glows down on her, lighting her up like the goddess she is while I linger in the darkness like the devil I am.

I stare, unable to help it.

I watch her, imagining what she would taste like, what her pain would feel like.

She stiffens, finally sensing me. "Who's there?" she calls, standing stiffly as she looks around. I press my back to the stone wall and wait, leading her into my trap.

She frowns, her black, perfectly plucked eyebrows tugging down as she wanders around the small courtyard, bringing her closer to my hiding spot with each moment, and then she's there, before me.

She squints in the darkness before her eyes widen when she finally sees me, and I smirk as I grab her. I haul her closer and press her against the stone wall, my black suit and hair hiding us from prying eyes as I pin her there.

She's so tall, I barely have to look down, her perfect body pressed to mine as she trembles.

Fear fills her eyes, but she doesn't scream or back down.

She traces my face with her gaze.

"What do you want?" she finally asks, and I almost come from her voice alone.

It's husky, soft, and reminds me of rolling in silk sheets.

"You," I admit without shame, and she jolts. "I watched you float around the ballroom like a princess checking on her loyal court, and I couldn't think of anything but one thing…" I lean in as her eyes widen, her mouth parting on an inhale.

"What's that?" she whispers.

"How you would taste." I slam my lips to hers, stealing her kiss.

It's the last one she will ever have.

Her taste explodes on my tongue, making me grunt like an animal as I grind into her before ripping my mouth away, licking my lips to taste every drop of her sweetness. Her eyes are closed, but they blink open lazily. Her lipstick is smeared, and seeing that imperfection makes a sense of primal satisfaction roar inside me.

"What's your name, princess?" I demand, rolling my hips so she feels my harder than rock dick.

She whimpers and parts her thighs sweetly to give me access, and I take it.

I slam my thigh between hers and grip her hips, dragging her across my leg, watching her eyes blow wide with desire.

I hear someone rattling at the doors to get out, and I know our time is limited.

"Your name," I order in a rough whisper, and like a good little princess, she answers.

"Cara," she replies silkily, leaning into my touch although I don't think she's aware of it.

I lean in like I'm going to kiss her again, and her eyes close, so I smirk in satisfaction. "Until next time, Princess Cara."

Before her eyes open, I'm gone, fading into the night.

I have a new hunt to replace my current one.

Sorry, Gray, but this one is more important.

Cara will be mine, and fuck if she won't wish she never let me taste her or gave me her name.

Because it's mine now, and she will be too.

I stole her kiss, but little does she know that before the night is through, I intend to steal much more.

About K.A Knight

K.A Knight is an international bestselling indie author trying to get all of the stories and characters out of her head, writing the monsters that you love to hate. She loves reading and devours every book she can get her hands on, and she also has a worrying caffeine addiction.

She leads her double life in a sleepy English town, where she spends her days writing like a crazy person.

Read more at K.A Knight's website or join her Facebook Reader Group.
Sign up for exclusive content and my newsletter here
http://eepurl.com/drLLoj

About Ivy Fox

Ivy Fox is a USA Today bestselling author of angst-filled, contemporary romances, some of them with an unconventional #why-choose twist.

Ivy lives a blessed life, surrounded by her two most important men —her husband and son, but she also doesn't mind living with the fictional characters in her head that can't seem to shut up until she writes their story.

Books and romance are her passion.

A strong believer in happy endings and that love will always prevail in the end, both in life and in fiction.

Join her Facebook Reader Group - Ivy's Sassy Foxes or sign up for exclusive content and my newsletter here - https://www. ivyfoxauthor.com/

Also by K A Knight

THEIR CHAMPION SERIES

The Wasteland

The Summit

The Cities

The Nations

Their Champion Coloring Book

Their Champion Boxed Set

The Forgotten

The Lost

The Damned

Their Champion Companion Boxed Set

DAWNBREAKER SERIES

Voyage to Ayama

Dreaming of Ayama

THE LOST COVEN SERIES

Aurora's Coven

Aurora's Betrayal

HER MONSTERS SERIES

Rage

Hate

THE FALLEN GODS SERIES

PrettyPainful

Pretty Bloody

PrettyStormy

Pretty Wild

Pretty Hot

Pretty Faces

Pretty Spelled

Fallen Gods Boxed Set 1

Fallen Gods Boxed Set 1

FORGOTTEN CITY

Monstrous Lies

Monstrous Truths

FORBIDDEN READS *(STANDALONES)*

Daddy's Angel

Stepbrothers' Darling

STANDALONES

Scarlett Limerence

Nadia's Salvation

The Standby

Den of Vipers

Daddy's Angel

Divers Heart

Crown of Stars

AUDIOBOOKS

The Wasteland

The Summit

Rage

Hate

Den of Vipers *(From Podium Audio)*

Gangsters and Guns *(From Podium Audio)*

Daddy's Angel *(From Podium Audio)*

Stepbrother's Darling *(From Podium Audio)*

Blade of Iris *(From Podium Audio)*

Deadly Affair *(From Podium Audio)*

Stolen Trophy *(From Podium Audio)*

CO-AUTHOR PROJECTS - *Erin O'Kane*

HER FREAKS SERIES

Circus Save Me

Taming The Ringmaster

Walking the Tightrope

Boxed Set

STANDALONES

The Hero Complex

Dark Temptations (contains One Night Only and Circus Saves Christmas)

THE WILD BOYS SERIES

The Wild Interview

The Wild Tour

The Wild Finale

The Wild Boys Boxed Set

CO-AUTHOR PROJECTS - *Ivy Fox*

Deadly Love Series

Deadly Affair

Deadly Match

Deadly Encounter

CO-AUTHOR PROJECTS - *Kendra Moreno*

STANDALONES

Stolen Trophy

Fractured Shadows

CO-AUTHOR PROJECTS - *Loxley Savage*

THE FORSAKEN SERIES

Capturing Carmen

Stealing Shiloh

Harboring Harlow

STANDALONES

Gangsters and Guns

OTHER CO-WRITES

Shipwreck Souls *(with Kendra Moreno & Poppy Woods)*

The Horror Emporium *(with Kendra Moreno & Poppy Woods)*

Also by Fry Fox

Restless

Rotten Love Duet

Rotten Girl

Rotten Men

Mafia Wars

Binding Rose

<small>Co-Writes with K.A. Knight</small>
Deadly Love Series

Deadly Affair

Deadly Match

Deadly Encounter

<small>Co-Writes with C.R. Jane</small>
Breathe Me Duet

Breathe Me

Breathe You

Hate & Love Duet

The Boy I Once Hated

Printed in Great Britain
by Amazon

22430938R00165